Muddle Town:
A Self Help Guide for Those Struggling Through the Tribulation

by Christian Lovgren

For
Kelly Mae
Archer Ruby
Quinn Gideon

For more visit:
www.MuddleTown.com
www.ChristianLovgren.com

ISBN 978-0-9850563-0-8

Chapter One

I Fall Down

"I am the image of a frail-old-man, falling to the ground in slow motion. I send dust and ashes to flight." I would mutter this over and over as I resigned myself to live my life in the wet grass with vomit on the jacket that I had owned since the seventh grade. Just then God handed me another onslaught, the world spun, and again I unhinged from reality.

I witnessed the fall of Saddam as I dug my toes into the Iraqi dirt. I knelt in the sands of Israel, once Palestine, once Israel again. I saw Hitler's Germany spread across the globe. I witnessed genocide. Why? Babylon was constructed again and again, torn to rubble and resurrected. Why? I beheld the great behemoth, the dinosaur. The world became a translucent quivering jewel and its creatures regressed to the sea where they gyrated about under a blanket of thick black darkness. All the while I pondered, "Why?"

My eyes sharpened as I beheld the creation of my soul. I inhaled. I exhaled. I cried out and grew ancient among my brethren. But, where was mine architect? He was no where to be found. In his place were four statuesque, winged creatures. They became a fascination in my mind and grew oddly familiar as I watched them crouch at each corner of a golden seat. I observed for one-thousand years and for one-thousand years I called out for answers. But, no one took the seat and no one heeded my call.

As my patience gave way I became increasingly concerned with the subtle gestures of one of the four. I could see what he was thinking. He alone coveted the seat and then smartly concealed his eyes. He alone knelt proud and cocky, tall with shoulders square.

I heard dissent among my brethren. Their voices eerily reverberated, "He is the most beautiful in creation." Others expounded, "He is as enchanting as the moon and glistening like the stars. He is trusted, revered, and placed most high."

I gently spoke as I began to violently shake, "Have I heard this before?"

As my hallucinations faded and I grew nearer to consciousness I saw him draw a map and the last thing that tumbled from my mind into the dream world was his face, full focus. It had turned from stone to a maniacal, sadistic grin and I saw him mouth a single word, *wormwood.*

I wearily scraped my way from the ground and I reminded myself, "We're just crazy, that's all." But, why couldn't I get that damn word out of my head? Wormwood... wormwood.

When I was four-years-old my mother would find me off in strange places thinking about God's life. I don't remember a time that I didn't believe in God. I do however very clearly remember being the weird kid in school, the one that dreamed dreams, the one that preferred the company of adults, and the one that didn't have a choice but to believe in demons, because I saw them. And, they tried to talk to me. But, God taught me how to ignore them and more importantly, he taught me how to fight.

I know how that sounds, but I assure you I'm not a liar. I may be a drunk, an addict, and a ghoul, but a liar I am not. It's just that we don't really have a choice in what we believe. We are all products of what we hear, see, smell, taste, and worst of all feel.

As time went on the word *wormwood* grew louder in my head and I knew I was in trouble. As a child words would get stuck in my head so bad that they would give me crippling headaches. My mother would ask me what the word was and then she would proceed to tell me everything she knew about that word until the headache would subside. My poor mother found herself spending half of her time feeding me an entire thesis on words like *inimitable* and *cholesterol*, so for my tenth birthday she gave me a green, leather bound pocket dictionary with my name stamped neatly in gold in the lower right hand corner of the front cover. The message inside read, "To my little Asher. Take two aspirin and read this every day. Love, Mom. XOXO"

My dictionary said that wormwood was something bitter or grievous. It also said that there was a plant named wormwood whose bitter oils are used in absinthe. But that wasn't it, that wasn't what I was looking for; there was something more to it than that. I slipped my dictionary back into the breast pocket of my seventh grade jacket that had vomit on it and sat down under the buzzing orange streetlight. As I sat there I thought and thought and thought about that word, and as I thought something terrible crept up my spine and took hold. Just like that the same wrenching headache was back and worse than it had been in fourteen years, so I walked to the corner market to buy some aspirin and call my mom.

The phone swung like a pendulum hitting me in the face every odd second. From down on all fours I yelled in the direction of the receiver, "Looks like the market is the latest victim of the times, these hard times. That's alright, these blackouts are getting more frequent and I needed something stronger anyway."

I could hear the concern on the other end of the line. "Where are you, Asher? Where are you, sweetie?"

I heaved and shook the last drops of moisture from my body, the concrete rose to the occasion to meet me half way, and I was out. As the slab embraced my heat my eyes fluttered and fanciful thoughts took hold hard.

"Rise up, now. Rise up! Rise up! Come ye with hardness of heart. Come ye whose will shall be done." A portion of the people cheered with a violence as he speared forth his limestone finger and spilled globs of bile from his lips which soaked his beautiful wings. His architect stood with eyes lowered, heart incised. "We have prevailed," the rebel insisted and a third of the masses excited as Wormwood's finger dropped. His face took a reddish hue and his expression turned to elation of power as the people fell in rank and my view averted to the night sky. A third of the stars in heaven fell at my feet, a third stayed crippled in the cosmos, and the last simply faded.

"Wormwood!" I shouted. "His *name* is Wormwood," I cried at the receiver as it swung over head.

"Does your brother know where you are? Does he know where you are?! Asher, can you hear me?"

My head suddenly propped up and the world repeated thirty fold. Danny knelt next to me, pushed his fake ass cowboy hat back, and with the buzzing receiver in hand he echoed, "Who were you talking to this time, Ash?"

"Mom," I sputtered.

"That's real nice, Ash. Real nice. Mom's still dead you fucking asshole. She's still dead." Danny let go, I felt a sharp, warm split in the back of my head and I distinctly heard sixty cowboy boots click into the horizon like the horse itself. *Clip-clop-clip-clop*. Danny hollered from afar, "Come and get a drink when you're done freaking out." *Clip-clop-clip-clop*.

"I got to admit, a drink sounds pretty good right now," I called out after him.

I gathered my senses and clambered to my feet. My jacket whipped in the thick wind; the trench coat that I had owned since the seventh grade. At some point of course I outgrew the sleeves, so I cut them off and learned to sew. My punk rock friends showed me how to use carpet nylon and a needle to affix band patches and patches that we made with denim and acrylic paint. If you never wash these kinds of patches they acquire a sort of patina, like enamel almost. Those were always my favorites and they covered nearly every inch of me.

The only spots that weren't covered with patches were covered with spikes, or studs, or rings, or lighter tops, or bottle caps. Police loved me. I was easy to spot. My hair was chopped into a lovely indiscernible pattern of hunks, curls, and waves.

The left half was dyed red to represent the fire in my mind and the right half was dyed green to represent my true nature. I am an artist, a musician, an apostle, and a madman.

Around my waist was a girding of chains attached to my belt. They weighed me down and taught me to be silent. My neck and wrists were adorned with spikes and leather and paint. My collar and bracelets were secured with nuts and bolts and if necessary would cut or pierce my wandering brothers in the night. If those didn't do the job my knives would. I was a porcupine and I would not be harmed.

"This is my alley home. These are my slickened streets. This is Muddle, California and this is my inheritance. This industrial complex, these buzzing orange streetlights, the bugs, the waste, the metal and the asphalt are mine. I have grown with you all and I adore you." I called this out to the night. My voice bounced off tin siding, it bounced off giant concrete slabs, and it nestled in my alley home.

To my right at the end of a long corridor of deep-red brick laid my gathering of defective stuffed animals, those that our machines had rejected due to imperfection, piled over the years against the unforgiving walls and pasted with debris. "How you cradle my head, oh you stuffing, you soot soaked stuffing!"

To my left was the factory, the entirety of my childhood and the sweat of my parents. "God only knows what to do with it in these times, these hard times."

People would still come up to me to give their condolences and it was apparent that it was for them, not for me. My parents were beacons in the night. My father: a creator of dreams and creatures. My mother: a lioness and captain of industry. My inheritance: a broken toy factory and the condolences of the community.

"And yes folks, straight ahead this way, right this way. The Eighth Plague, ladies and gentleman," I yelled in disgust and admiration unaware of which thoughts were auditory and which were set to private. Years of my life were spent creating an abomination against man, created for man. When I turned twenty-one-years old Danny and I erected a temple that would attract those looking for anesthesia. We would invite the avant-garde, the strange and outlandish, the artist and performer, and they would come from miles. We became neon sentries in the dark, bleak world and a bane to those that sought control. The sergeant by day would be customer and hound by night and no one would cause a fuss as long as the drinks flowed free and we set them up with the girls upstairs. We were the dirty, sexy secret that Muddle loved to loathe and we loved them right back. We were youth-un-checked.

When Danny and I first set eyes on this complex we were just little kids, untwisted and safe in the arms of Mom and Dad. We spent years in fear as we forced ourselves to investigate every room, hall, and basement of the various dilapidated buildings. We would find the oddest things, like entire storehouses of men's white underwear or boxes upon boxes of unsold Peeps marshmallows. But, the oddest thing we ever found was a mummified transient.

We found him lying behind a stack of broken down crates that he had been using as firewood. He was naked on the bare concrete floor and curled in a fetal position with his mud encrusted clothing folded neatly next to him. There were a few empty cans stacked upright next to a pad of paper, a worn down pencil, and a single picture of whom I assumed were him and his family. On the pad of paper the words "thank you" were written in stubby little letters. I remember when Danny and I found him we didn't scream, we didn't move or speak, we just stopped and stared. Then from out of nowhere Danny revealed a small potato shaped rock and threw it at the man's stomach.

I'll never forget that sound and I am sure that it shapes me to this day. When the rock broke through the man's skin it sounded like a sheet of cardboard ripping and when it ricocheted around his ribcage it made an awful ceramic crackle. The noise forged in me and my imagination filled in all the terrible details. In my mind I could see every fleck of flesh stuck to those ribs, every collapsed vein dried and matted to the underside of his skin, and that is when I started to scream. Needless to say, Danny and I were no longer allowed to tour the complex without an adult and Danny was sequestered to his room with school and the bathroom as his only reprieve. Before he knew it Danny had spent the entire seventh grade in his room. I was only eight-years-old when I saw my first counselor and it quickly became apparent that there was a problem.

From there the problems just multiplied and begat other little problems. Very early on I acquired a propensity for ingesting large amounts of booze. That sweet tender solace. That deafening embrace. The remorse and disgrace. My stomach evacuated. I knew I had a problem; everyone *knew* I had a problem. It's just that I associated so well with that feeling. The sensation of falling in every little movement. The muscles in my forehead overcompensating for my drooping eyelids. My eyes seeing everything at once and questioning nothing. They were only observing. I was faster in that state. I was pure luck and exacting reaction, in that state.

By age eleven I had learned that the madness and atrocities in the world, in my life, could be numbed or somehow rounded with the proper anesthesia. My counselor called this process "self-medication". That term never ceases to amuse me. It's always used in such a negative connotation, as if someone else knew what my body felt like. With enough experimentation I had found my peaks, my valleys, my dead ends, and my nirvanas. I felt more than capable in determining my own dosage.

When I was fifteen-years-old I jumped from a moving train and when I hit the ground I broke my hip, so my doctor prescribed me with a truck load of hydrocodone. He said that it would help with the pain. His exact words were, "It makes the pain feel like it's in the next room." For six months the pain in the next room increased and for six months so did my dosage.

After six months my doctor said my liver was working too hard. "Nothing to be concerned about," he said. "Just working a little too hard."

I asked him, "Doc, if my liver is working too

hard wouldn't it make sense to give me something that doesn't have acetaminophen in it, which is harmful to your liver; isn't it harmful to your liver?"

He cocked his head like a dog, got a right queer look on his face and said, "Yes. Yes, it is."

In a matter of just a few weeks I had managed to nestle down into a rather insidious addiction to oxycodone and for a term this one broke me. I was useless, terrified, and alone in a city that knew me not. I slept under an overpass; how cliché and shabby chic, an overpass. The county had supplied me with everything necessary to destroy my life. Well, you know what they say about good intentions.

Better yet, what do they say about co-dependency? Danny Boy could tell you all about that. That fake ass, suburban cowboy. That loyal and obedient, tried and true good old boy, Danny Boy. My brother, my partner. "I can see the pearl snaps on your four hundred dollar shirt now, Dan!"

I eagerly approached Danny's apartment located on the backside of the bar and I screamed at my capacity, "I love you, Danny. I fucking love you, man!"

Danny ripped the door open as if he'd been angrily waiting. He winged an empty bottle at me which broke over my right shin and he hollered back, "There's that drink I promised you!"

"Oh shit, he's coming in," I shouted while holding my shin just seconds before being tackled.

As my head bounced off the concrete for the second time that night the split on the back of my melon just opened right up and guess what, I was back out. As my eyes closed I heard Danny breathing heavily and in a tone of fear he whimpered, "Oh no, man. Oh, no. Oh God, there's a lot of blood, Ash! Come on, man, get up. Please get up. Are you okay, Asher? Are you o-o-o-o-o?"

I frantically packed my bags with the sensationalistic media blaring on the background television. Clips and phrases formulated and slipped from the lips of the broadcaster, but the message was unclear. I observed my surroundings and the scenery crumbled before my eyes as if merely noticing an item rendered its constitution void. A table became a chair and a newspaper flew away.

As I approached my mahogany dresser I saw family portraits hanging from a lattice of leaky plumbing where the walls should've been. When I opened the top dresser drawer and pulled it away, it dropped with a heavy weight at my side. The handle of the drawer seamlessly became the handle of my luggage and I was ready.

An ornate gleaming door to my left creaked open just enough for me to see an angelic being floating out of a bruised sunset, surrounded by a slew of UFOs pouring mechanically over a dusty violet mountain range. Still caged by the lattice of plumbing I fell to my knees as I witnessed the masses pray and worship. The ground trembled as the being gingerly touched down, a heavy sensation of dread washed over me, and for some reason I sensed that I was too late.

The being spoke, "You may rise. Come ye who

shall come to touch the robe of the ever living God! For I am love and love am I. Come ye who shall come to be healed by the almighty. For I am pure and purity am I."

The being continued as I rose to step in line to meet God himself, but I couldn't get past the plumbing; the door was gone and the room was slowly filling with a quivering blue liquid as it were an invisible cube.

As I struggled to escape I noticed something a little off about this so-called god. The robe that the being spoke of began to melt away, but no one seemed to notice. His gnarled, naked body began to turn green and red as it deformed. He flashed in my mind's eye between a beautiful angel and a creature of unfounded demonic proportions. The creature's eyes locked with mine and its evil eyes began to glow and burn as they spread outward and consumed my vision in a field of golden sulfur. The creature staggered forward like a filthy drunk with its thin lips splitting to reveal a mouth full of knives which smiled wickedly at me. The being let out a great booming, cacophonous noise as if laughter in reverse, and I was fully immersed in the sulfur.

I could feel my passed out body begin to toss and thrash as I dreamed my horrid dream. Suddenly, my nostrils and lungs burned and I violently awoke, drenched in sweat and horrified with Danny shaking nervously at my bedside in the ER. My eyes sharpened as the doctor callously bellowed in a great magnanimous declaration, "See now, worry wart? There he is! No big deal, right?" The doctor slapped me across a fresh row of stitches some five inches long across the back of my head and quickly shuffled away shouting orders to his nursing minions. "Just like a football," my benevolent healer chuckled conveniently just before he fell out of ear shot.

Danny and I immediately locked eyes, his welling with tears, mine bloodshot and heavy. I ripped out my IV, fell into my brother, and I whispered in his ear, "Like a football. A football, he says." And just like always, that was it. No great fall out. No dramatic roller coaster. Just a mean hankering for a double large gin and tonic with extra, extra lime.

Security escorted us out the ER entrance and we embarked on the long walk home in the thick whipping wind, yelling sports analogies and cracking jokes about my cracked head. We finished Danny's flask almost immediately and made a few stops along the way, but we couldn't wait to meet that never ending oasis, The Eighth Plague.

With my arm slung over Danny's shoulder I said way too loudly directly into his left ear, "Man, I can't wait to fill this prescription. I just don't think that gin and tonic is going to be strong enough. But hey, at least I don't still have that word stuck in my head. What was that word again?"

Danny looked deep into my puffy, blackened eyes as we stumbled home with the buzzing orange streetlights over head and said, "I have absolutely no clue what you're talking about, man. But, I love you anyway and I'm glad you're safe."

Chapter Two

My Crippling Headaches

Empty cans, clothing, papers, and other assorted goods seemed to hang in mid air as I ripped through Danny's apartment like a Kansas sized twister. "I can't find it!" I harshly screamed. "Why can't I remember that word, damn it? This is important! Why are you smiling at me like that?"

"Because you're ridiculous, that's why," said Danny so cavalier. "You can't live without your precious little book. It's like a drug to you. That's a problem, Asher. Let me ask you something? How does your head feel right now? You feel okay?"

I rushed to Danny, took hold of his beautiful shirt and whispered, "Hey dip-shit, this time my head hurts because of you. Now stop playing games and give me my book!"

Danny peeled me off. "Calm down, Ash. I'm going to give it back, but first I need you to recognize something. You're becoming obsessed. These headaches of yours are unnecessary. They always have been. You have the power to control your own life and you simply refuse to. Everything you've ever started you let slip right through your fingers and I have to tell you, man, I'm getting really tired of putting a nice little bow on things for you."

"Ooohh, I am so sick of the big-brother-knows-best routine. Did I ever once ask you to do anything for me?" I inquired as my eyes all but popped out of their sockets from the immense pressure that had built in my head. My frontal lobe throbbed and banged against the inside of my skull. "You do nothing but judge me, Dan. You got your shit on lockdown, right? Is that why I had to rescue you? Because, you got your shit on lockdown? Well, how does someone so put together manage to burn down his childhood home, huh? I was fourteen-years-old, Danny. Fucking fourteen-years-old and homeless!"

Danny stood completely still and just stared at me for a while. "Well, no one asked you to leave, Asher. I didn't ask you to leave. You left me," he said mildly and detached as he threw me my dictionary which hit me in the chest and landed on his filth caked floor.

I hated that place, Danny's place. The carpet was paper thin and beaten down to the point of basically being just the ground, there were bean bag chairs and beat up old sofas everywhere, and the best part, the walls were smothered in god-awful peeling, forest patterned wall paper.

The man was a millionaire and that's how he chose to live? Cups covered the entire surface of his counters which crowded the half eaten bowls of white rice and generic, yellow mustard. Who has that many cups and for God's sake who the hell eats rice and mustard?

I picked up my dictionary, lifted my eyes, and I begged my brother, "Please don't do this to me right now, Danny. I'm just in a lot of pain, that's all. I'm sorry I brought it up."

"Get out," Danny said coldly and with no emotion, his eyes completely fixed on an invisible target that he had no doubt painted on my chest. When Danny gets this look it's clear that his resolve has been met. Years of receiving this look had taken their toll on me. They had conditioned me and taught me that no amount of wailing or the beating of my face against his chest would cause him to fade. I would rest assured that he would never concede, no matter how bad I may have needed him to. So, in consequence I just turned and quietly walked out the splitting front door to greet the biting and utterly penetrating morning sky.

Once again I had seen in his eyes the vacancy and disassociation that had previously caused me to run. Again I saw the totality of his diminishing need for me. It was the same thing that had always happened between us. He would hit a point that hurt too bad and would just shut off and check out.

See, when Mom and Dad died he told me that he had decided to pull out his emotional wiring. He said he remembered the moment it happened and how the great and heavy burden was immediately lifted from his soul.

"I could see them clearly in my imagination," he said. "Three little wires: one red, one yellow, and one blue. They were all plugged into a fleshy, little hub clearly labeled *emotions*. So, I wrapped them up and I tugged them right out. Easy as that."

But, he soon found that there were drawbacks to numbing himself completely. The lack of pain had unexpected effects. For pain keeps you safe. Pain alerts you to danger. Without pain you would never know great joy or fierce adoration. And, you just might not be able to identify the exact moment that your little brother lost faith in you or the moment that he realized he was stronger than you.

And so, once again I stepped alone into the ever increasing, pouring sunlight and called back behind me, "See you soon, Dan. See you soon." The door shut quietly, a few sets of deadbolts latched, and I was cleared for take off.

I pulled a small beat up pepper tin from my interior breast pocket and enjoyed a pinch of mushrooms to prepare for the day. I had found that a modicum of low level mushrooms in a steady metered dose could make quite a difference in one's outlook on life. As I chewed and swallowed them down with a small swig of whiskey from my flask, I knocked the dust from the soles of my Doc's and set them to pavement.

To my left lay a crumbled mass of brick; the fallen infrastructure of a once great monolith known as Twiggy Toys. They were the reason that Mom and Dad had their hearts set on this complex and when the stars aligned they struck true and hard at their only local competition, delivering a crushing blow to the Twig family empire and squarely securing our family line in the great American record.

One morning Mom and Dad woke us early, just as the sun was coming up. They said they had a surprise for us. "Something big!" Mom said with her patented heart melting smile and her eyes all aglow.

Danny and I simultaneously sprinted to the garage, flung the cargo door of our spring-green VW van aside, flopped down on the maroon leather bench seat, and voraciously kicked our overly excited feet.

"Stop kicking my seat!" Dad whipped around and angrily screamed in his beautiful Czech accent then flashed us his trademark smile and peace sign combo.

The anticipation that filled that van was nothing short of electric. "Where are they taking us?" I questioned Danny, who was still wearing his favorite vintage Buck Rogers in the 25th Century pajamas.

"I don't know," he said, "but it feels like Christmas!"

Dad made no apology for the lack of safety as we careened far too quickly around autumn leaf curves, up and over small kicker-hills, and down through tiny little scenic valleys toward what he referred to as, "the Radezlav birthright". We traveled up, up, up a great spiraling hill, tall and slender, and there it was right at the very top, the future home of BA Toys, Inc.

As we came to a screeching halt in the loading dock, Dad proudly threw his hair filled nose in the air, tilted his big floppy ears from shoulder to shoulder and haughtily proclaimed, "Our family will work this ground for generations. You, my cherubs, will make toys and your sons will make toys!"

The day that wrecking ball fell the walls of Twiggy Toys was the single greatest day of my life. I remember watching the bricks let loose their bonds. Like old friends releasing from an embrace they tripped clumsily over themselves in their final descent. I gripped my dad's hand and squealed in delight as the concrete dust plumed high into the vast blue expanse of the sky.

Danny punched me lightly in the small of my back as our dad jostled his bowl cut hair between his stumpy sausage-fingers while Mom paced feverishly back and forth in front of us screaming,

"Isn't this fabulous? I mean just simply fabulous?" with her arms flailing in pure delight as the lightest flecks of gray, stone, ash fell softly upon our shoulders like industrial snow. Truly Christmas had come in October for the Radezlav family.

But, what seemed like Christmas to Danny and me was the worst case scenario for the Twig family. Like so many others the Twig family was finding it harder and harder to operate a business in an economy that could not recover from the bail-outs, the massive expansion of social efforts, and a battery of endless wars, known and unknown. Factories started falling off the market like flies, all the jobs swam away to other countries, and to stay afloat Mr. Twig sold the deed to the factory. Not only had the bulk of our local industries met an unseemly end, but the trend had spread across the entire United States.

Having inherited a tidy sum of money from his parents, Dad put together a whip smart business plan that included the purchase of the complex, but *not* Twiggy Toys. Instead he decided to discontinue their rental agreement, which for a business of its relatively large size meant the dismantling and relocation of equipment that would require time, money, and a crew; three things that the Twig family did not have and Dad had banked on it.

In effect our family had delivered a death sentence for not only Twiggy Toys, but for the Twig family itself. It seemed for the last few years Mr. Twig had been keeping a secret from his family. He alone knew that their factory was slowly becoming insolvent and that they would soon be forced to close altogether. But, Mr. Twig also knew that if

Mrs. Twig's credit cards were to stop accommodating her decadent desires she would leave him and their only child for another, more wealthy suitor, having been raised in opulence and being irrevocably accustomed to it.

Soon enough the well spring dried up, Mrs. Twig found out, and the wrecking ball fell the walls. As easy as pie Mrs. Twig packed her Chanel, her Versace, her DeBeers and the like and she was off to live the lavish life in the arms of another affluent lover, leaving Mr. Twig and their son, Jerrod Twig, with broken hearts and a severely delinquent mortgage.

When Dad had learned the effects of his whip smart power move he began to cry. "I have turned my back on my brother," he blubbered from behind his stout, cracked sausage-fingers. "In an attempt to elevate my family I have brought a man to his ruin. Surely I have shamed our family name! Our Heavenly Father will not be free to bless our business as it stands. I have tied his hands in the matter!"

Either out of fear, compassion, or both Dad arranged a meeting with Mr. Twig and Jerrod over steaks, fingerling potatoes, and local wine at our home in the quiet suburbs on the outskirts of Muddle.

Everyone was cordial, polite, and filled with anxiety. After a few minutes of pleasantries we all sat formally at the dining room table. We unfolded our napkins and placed them neatly across our thighs, passed the rolls and butter, then Dad called out abruptly with his knife and fork coming down harshly on his plate, "Come and work for me, Sir.

Please, I beg of you. Let me right the wrong that I have done to you so that I may clear my family name."

Right then and there at the dinner table, Mr. Twig burst into a wailing moan and sobbed heavily like a giant black cloud that had finally popped its seam, unleashing an eager flood. Mom the great emotional healer rushed to his side and pulled his ear into her gigantic, pillowy breast as she pet his head and rocked him back and forth saying, "There, there. There, there now. It's not so bad."

This all became too much for Dad who of course started back in with the water works, which eventually got Mom going too. It was quite a scene, the adults falling all over each other, all weepy and stammering in their nearly incomprehensible speech while us kids sat wide eyed in bewilderment with our mouths agape.

Danny and I shared a glance with Jerrod who winked as he took full advantage of the situation by inhaling the remainder of wine from his father's glass, silently slipping it back into place just as his father went for a drink.

"May I?" Mr. Twig asked while twisting the stem of his glass toward Dad and dabbing his cheek with his fine supper napkin.

Dad poured him another glass and continued in saying that Mr. Twig would be accepting residence in an apartment that he had built and furnished for him and Jerrod on the top floor of the Eighth Plague building. "This is not up for debate," he garbled while rudely chewing his steak.

Little did Dad know that he had started a tradition of grace and empathy that would imprint in the nature of his children and would continue in that same building for as long as our family crest should reside above the door.

With ketchup on his shirt and wine on his breath, Mr. Twig gleefully accepted the position of Vice Head of Operations for BA Toys, Inc. and upon an official hand shake a bond was formed between our families.

Over the years Jerrod proved to be a pretty good friend, but man was there ever something about that kid that made you want to break shit. It was his laugh, his slightly lazy right eye, crooked teeth set deep in a thick lipped mischievous smile, and a chopped mop of natural, stark-blonde rocker hair that all screamed t-r-o-u-b-l-e, trouble.

Danny and I spent huge blocks of time at Jerrod's apartment when the adults were at the factory. I think the adults somehow equated Mr. Twig's home being so close with us being safe. From time to time they would stop in for lunch, but for the most part they just stayed at work and well, we made nothing but stellar use of that.

Jerrod was a bit older than Danny and I and as such a bit more seasoned in the world. Nearly ever inch of the walls in his room was plastered with flyers from local rock shows. Cords and wires made a loose mesh that wove in and out of dirty dishes, band shirts, and records; eventually plugging into various guitars, speakers, and amps, making a beautiful mosaic dedicated to rock on his electric-blue shag carpet.

One day Jerrod sat us down in his room and made us watch a movie called *Suburbia* while we rolled and smoked Top cigarettes and drank Mr.

Twig's Pabst Blue Ribbons. I sat enthralled as I
watched kids spray painting their walls, drinking
booze, and taking care of each other. The aesthetic
struck a cord deep inside me and I knew that from
that moment on I wouldn't be the same again.

"I have to admit," I coughed in my adorable
eleven-year-old voice, "this lifestyle looks pretty
fucking cool." Danny and Jerrod laughed
hysterically as I took a sip of my beer, a drag of my
smoke, and thumbed through a few nudie
magazines.

As I sat there something welled up from deep
within me and I suddenly leapt to my feet, threw up
my arms, and shouted at the top of my lungs with
my voice cracking, "From this moment on I will be
punk incarnate! I am now a human porcupine!" I
then promptly did a face plant in a pile of Jerrod's
dirty laundry and blacked out.

OK Computer pounded from Jerrod's sound
system and filled the halls of the Eighth Plague
building, shaking the asbestos dust from the ceiling
as he shaved my hair into a Mohawk.

"What? What are you?" I wearily asked as my
eyes slowly focused on the bathroom mirror. "Oh,
cool!" I shouted and whipped my head toward
Danny with a shit eating grin on my face. Danny
just lifted his thumb in the air as he threw down on
another Pabst then out gassed in a terrific
esophagus vibrating belch.

"Me next," he said as he fell face first in a great
red splat on the pure white bathroom tile.

Without skipping a beat Jerrod said from
behind his burning cigarette, "If you thought that
first movie was cool, just wait until you see *A*

Clockwork Orange," as the adults ever so slowly crept into the room with their eyes growing wider and wider and wider.

"Hi Dad!" I noisily slurred as I squinted my eyes and raised my beer in the air with the clippers humming in Jerrod's extended hand behind me and my hair still falling to the ground.

When the adults showed up that night they were not pleased to say the least. We were drunk, shaven, bloody, and most importantly, punk as fuck. But, somehow they remained unimpressed.

Mom and Dad said I was an impressionable young gentleman exposed to a bad element and as such could not be held accountable. Danny however was to stay in his room again for no less than two months. Who knows if Mr. Twig spared the rod or not. Mom and Dad said that Danny and I would not be allowed to fraternize with Jerrod's caliber of company for quite some time.

Of course I was sent back to my counselor, that great fat androgen. Sometimes his advice was helpful, but for the most part I disagreed with him and even more than that, I was disturbed by the fact that I couldn't read him.

Most people I meet give off a sense so strong that their energy nearly makes an outline where they end and the world begins. Their scent, their demeanor, their words, inflection, and body language all make up a character in my mind that I can manipulate in various theoretical situations. If my sense of them is strong enough I can forecast events in their lives based on their past, the path they are currently on, and how my mental model of them behaves while running amok throughout endless scenarios in my head.

This automaton however gave off nothing. Just a homogenized, fat mound of human he was, completely devoid of any electrical signature that could be known as energy.

His silver soul patch bounced up and down, calmly and lightly below his lips as he spoke with the buzzing halogen light beaming off his beautifully waxed, bald head.

In a monotonous tone barely classifiable as communication he mumbled, "Asher, have you or your parents ever considered a well monitored, metered dose of medication? I know that we have discussed mindfulness and being truly present in the moment, but the techniques don't seem to be working for you. You seem to drift off and become unavailable.

"The disembodied messages that you feel you've been selected to receive are nothing more than dissociative, egotistical flights of fancy, my young friend. These dreams of yours aren't real, yet you persist in indulging them like some form of dogma.

"Either you are not applying my teachings properly or you have simply grown past how far I can take you on this journey."

He then folded his thin, meager forearms over his big, bloated belly and rolled rhythmically from side to side in his creaking leather chair like a gargantuan baby against soothing creamy-yellow walls with an ornate winding vine border hand painted at the top.

"Well, that's really not what an eleven-year-old wants to hear from an adult; from a professional! You can no longer help me on my journey? What is

it exactly that you *have* helped me with, Sir?" I
asked with my cute little voice shaking indignantly
and my lower lip quivering.

My high minded counselor displayed a burst of
energy by reaching nearly two inches to his left,
depressing the button on his intercom and saying,
"Suzie, please let the Radezlavs know that their son
is ready to depart."

Minutes later Mom and Dad and Danny and I
sat down in our living room on our white wooden-
bordered sofas to discuss the medication issue as a
family. Danny led the charge insistently.

"Is Asher going to be okay? Is there something
wrong with him? You can tell me. I mean, I know
he's a little weirdo, but is there anything *actually*
wrong with him?" he asked earnestly with fear in
his voice.

"That's enough, Daniel," said Mom.

"I'm okay, Dan. I'll be okay," I said quite unsure
of whether or not I was or would be.

After a few heated debates in which Danny
fervently voiced his dissent, and an initial medical
consultation, my handlers decided to give me
quetiapine, a heavy anti-psychotic. For weeks I
stumbled the halls of my school, the factory, our
home, like a creeping little sewer creature, sweaty
and sluggish. I complained to my parents that I
didn't feel quite right. I couldn't stay awake in
school and I'd fallen down a few times. They in turn
complained to my counselor that they were afraid
they were going to lose their baby boy.

"It would be dangerous to take him off his
medication now. It needs to cycle through his
system for at least one month to obtain its

therapeutic dosage. Come back in a few weeks and we can talk about any necessary adjustments. For now we'll give him something to help him concentrate, make him a little peppier," said my all knowing shaman, that sorcerer. "Just burn some sweet grass in his room to calm him at night and he'll be right as rain soon enough."

Well, for a period of about two years I received an ever evolving cocktail of noxious pharmaceuticals and for about two years I was not right as rain. But, everyday I rose to the occasion and I struggled through the fog. Sooner or later I managed to acclimate to the incessant urges to crash, the dizziness, the apparent inability to give a shit about pretty much anything, and my favorite, the sudden bursts of unabashed manic hysteria.

At times I found benefit in the medications, but every positive was balanced with a negative. The demons went away, but so did my dreams. My peaks and valleys all became plateaus, but I became bored and boring. My headaches were gone, but my creativity dwindled. It seemed that I was slowly losing me.

My small hands were once a flurry of explosive artistic expression. Paint drips, drops, and splats appeared sporadically on every article of clothing that I owned and nearly everyday a character was born of my brush. Dad took a special liking to one of my ideas and sent a copy off to the guys in the art department. About six months later, The Faceless rolled off our production lines and onto toy store shelves everywhere, making me the youngest conceptual designer in the industry.

Dad and I worked closely after school and on

weekends with our drafting tables facing each other. Dad said that he wanted three new ideas by the end of the week, but thanks to the pills I was all dried up. I could hear my characters screaming from behind what seemed like a wall of thick cellophane. Deep in the recesses of my mind they were stacking up in great heaping piles and slowly dying, creating a very unsanitary condition for the health of my imagination.

One day after school I was sitting alone at the tables and while feebly attempting to release my creations I dozed off for what I thought was just a moment. When I came to, the sun was down and my dad was standing across from me with a very strange look on his face.

When I looked down I saw that I had drawn an elaborate host of monsters, machines, and beasties all amassed and segregated in rank and size, long prepared for an impending battle for the planet Earth. I looked back up at Dad who had tears lightly streaming his cheeks. While wiping his face he softly asked, "How long have you been working on that?"

"I don't know," I replied with my eyes incredulously pouring over the page.

"That looks good, little man," said Jerrod clothed in shadow standing in the doorway.

"Jerrod!" I screamed giddily.

I hopped off my stool and ran to his prickly embrace. He grabbed my wrist, clasped on a fuzzy, cheetah patterned spiked bracelet of my very own and I instantly whipped my head around to Dad while holding my fist proudly in the air with my eyes all amazed and my chin on my collarbone. Dad just shook his head and giggled, still wiping his eyes.

"I was hoping to have a word with your dad. I have a bit of a business proposal for him and if you don't mind, dinner and the fam' are waiting at the casa."

Believing that Dad would be the hardest sell, Jerrod had decided to strike at his emotions while discussing his plan. So, he arranged a re-creation of the night that we met, right down to the fingerling potatoes and a very hard to find bottle of Sonoma Valley's finest red. It was difficult enough for a nineteen-year-old kid to find a bottle of beer, let alone this.

Like a piper Jerrod hopped and skipped and led us through our front doors, he danced down the hall and straight way to the dining room where he stopped and bowed, revealing Mr. Twig sitting on the left, Danny sitting on the right, Mom at the head and a beautiful steaming spread waiting anxiously to be devoured, covering every inch of our table.

Within moments it seemed like we had been together for hours as we delved deeply into our meals. Jerrod immediately poured the wine and began his presentation.

"This is what I'm seeing: a BA Toys freight truck that has been retrofitted as one-half gear storage and one-half bunk beds, barreling down the highway, rolling away the dew with the morning sun breaking just over the horizon. We'll travel from town to unruly town; delivering blistering, filthy punk rock to all the naughty girls and boys."

Jerrod passed out a document to each member

of our very exclusive dinner party and continued, "Now if you will all peruse your proposals you will find that the pie charts and bar graphs that lie in your hands are completely arbitrary. I just printed them off the internet. They mean nothing really."

We all simultaneously balled up our papers and tried our hardest to hit Jerrod in the face with them. "I assure you if I had actually taken the time to compile the necessary information, any information at all really, it would have been quite helpful," he said as he swatted away paper ball after tiny paper ball like King Kong atop the Empire State Building.

"Knock it off, Jerry," Mr. Twig joined in. "What Jerry is so horribly trying to illustrate is that his band has really got something that I think, well we all think, should be supported and as *these* charts show," Mr. Twig slid Dad an official proposal with signature line and all, "this could really pan out into something good for all of us. Give it a look, take a few days if you need them, and let us know what you think."

Dad squinted heavily, grunted and sighed, then began to speak, then abruptly stopped, then began again, until Mom screamed, "Come on already!"

He threw up his hands and slowly said, "We are a family. Who alone am I to say no?"

"Well, if you look at line number thirty-four you'll find that you're the main financier. That's who you are," said Mr. Twig.

"Yes, well, I saw that actually," Dad said under his breath.

Still squinting and flipping through the pages, Dad rose from his chair, slowly walked to Jerrod, and he grabbed him firmly by the cheeks with his short, beefy fingers while whispering in his ear loud enough for us all to hear, "I just want you to know how envious I am of you and that if you lose any of my money you will work as an indentured servant in my factory for the rest of your natural life. The answer is yes, Jerrod."

We all cheered as Dad kissed Jerrod's head. Retrieving the pen that lived in his pocket, the one that his father had given him as a gift when he left for college, Dad flamboyantly signed the proposal. He slid it forward a bit then hoisted his glass in the air and shouted, "Tonight we drink to health, to the success of Mr. Jerrod Twig, and to the glory of Yahveh. God speed, my boy. Nostrovia!"

"Nostrovia!" we shouted together with our wine glasses lifted and glowing like dark-red rubies under the crystal lighting of the chandelier.

We all got a large glass of wine that night and I have to tell you, it felt like an old friend had returned and was overfilling my heart and running free through my veins. I spent the rest of the evening seeking wayward goblets while Jerrod waxed on about his intentions to barnstorm America's bars, grange halls, back yards, and various underground rock venues. Soon enough I was hanging the corner of my jaw over the hard porcelain edge of the commode where Jerrod and Danny found me. They cleaned me up and dropped me in my bed while the adults roared and guffawed downstairs over their multiple glasses and their droll board games with their uncontrolled volume pounding in my head.

With Danny laid out on my bean bag chair in the

dark-black corner of my room, Jerrod sat down on the edge of my bed, sighed and said, "Hey Asher, I've been meaning to ask you, man. Do you think you can do me a really, really, like super huge favor?"

"Anything," I said far too eagerly, having a bit of an unhealthy obsession with Jerrod.

He looked me right in the eyes and bluntly said, "I need you to stop taking those atrocious robot pills, man."

"What do you mean? What does that mean, robot pills?" I asked nervously and slightly defensive.

"Asher, can I ask you something, man to man?"

I nodded rapidly, my head springing up and off my pillow. "Yes, yeah, sure. Man to man. Anything."

"How do you feel the medication is working for you, like in your life?" he asked with concern in his voice.

"Okay, I guess. I mean, the whole world is spinning, but I thought that was from the wine and I'm really tired all the time, but that's just what the pills do, right? They're supposed to do that, right?" I said beginning to feel a small, sharp twinge of panic growing in my chest.

"Asher, I've been watching you closely for quite some time now and I'm afraid that I'm just going to have to come right out and say it. You've been made the victim of a lecherous plan to corrupt the youth of America and control our minds. The governments of this world don't want us to think for ourselves. They know if we think for ourselves we can't be controlled.

"You know those pharmaceutical commercials, the ones with the guy blathering messages like, 'May cause rectal bleeding and, slash, or homicidal rage while sleep walking'? Well, just how long do you think they had to saturate the market with cheerful messages like that before we as a people stopped listening?

"Your parents have nothing but the best intentions for you, Asher. But, in the end it's *your* mind and *your* body, and it doesn't really matter who it is giving you those damn pills. It's wrong and it needs to stop."

Danny just sat in the corner with his arms crossed, slowly nodding his head with his eyes closed.

"So, here is what's going to happen next. I'm going to give you one more gift in addition to the bracelet; a medium-sized tin. You are going to take that tin and put it somewhere safe, away from those that may have certain preconceptions, including the adults. You are going to wait until me and my band-mates are all packed up and leaving town on that big rig, and then... you're going to open it."

Deafening moments passed like weights falling to ground. I sat dumfounded, speechless and drunk, shaking my head in indecision and silence.

"You got that, Asher?" barked Danny from the dark-black corner of my room.

"Okay," I replied sheepishly with my chin pressed back into my neck.

Jerrod leaned in and hugged me tight then ruffled my hair and said, "Don't make any changes yet. Just wait until you open that tin."

He slowly got up and as he began to walk down

the dimly lit hall he called back behind him, "I always liked you, Asher. You're a cool kid. Take care of Danny, alright? Danny, I'll see you soon."

We heard his chains jingling and jangling as he headed down, down, down the stairs and said his goodbyes to the adults who congratulated him profusely, loudly slapping his back and proudly presenting him to the biting expanse of the outside world.

Too soon after we heard the engine of his cherry-red Mustang roar and tear off into the night and Danny and I sat there silently until we both fell asleep right where we were.

A few weeks passed and I did just what Jerrod and Danny asked me to do. I didn't peek. I didn't even want to peek. But, the moment I knew that Jerrod had mounted that eighteen-wheeler, I flew to my closet and lifted the left corner of my toy chest which had a recessed bottom and with some difficulty I produced the tin and sprinted to the bathroom where I clumsily fumbled the handle of the door into the locked position. I heard my heart beating loudly in my throat as I anxiously pried the lid off the tin and poured over its contents.

Inside were a lighter covered by a metal sheath adorned with an American flag and a sweet diving eagle with a rainbow trout in its claws, an ornate hand-blown pipe with long glistening threads of gold and silver winding through its glass like mountain roads, one package of standard orange Zig-Zag rolling papers, and a small zip locking bag filled with a green leafy substance with a label folded crisply over its top that read, "High grade medical marijuana. 3.5 grams Trainwreck. As with

any medication, keep out of reach of children."
Underneath all this was a tattered black envelope. I
hesitated for a moment, took a deep breath, and
then tore into it like an animal.

"Hey man,

I am really glad to have met you and Danny. You
guys are hilarious and it has truly been my pleasure
knowing the both of you. Since the moment I met
you I knew that you would do great things; things
far greater than I could imagine. But, before you
can accomplish these things, Asher, there are a few
orders of business that you will need to take care of.
You are your own man, but here's what I'm
suggesting.

Continue taking your medication as directed for
an additional week and mentally prepare yourself
for a big change.

The second week, take half of your
recommended dosage and smoke a joint with
Danny. Danny and I have been smoking for years.
No big deal, really.

The third week, take half your recommended
dosage every other day and smoke another joint
with Danny.

By the fourth week you can see how you feel and
figure it out from there. Just make sure that we
keep this between us, okay? Just you, me, and
Danny.

Finally, and this will be my last request of you,
please talk to your brother. He needs you more
than you know. And, soon enough you're going to
need him too.

Take care, little badass. I'll send some files when
we have audio. The first album is eponymously

titled *Jerrod Twig and the Graduated Cylinders*, but I considered calling it *Asher's Experiments*. I think it's sure to be the biggest seller of all time. Just kidding. Maybe. I love you, brother-man.

Signed,

Jerrod Twig

P.S. I never blamed your family for making my mom leave. I always hated that bitch."

I neatly folded Jerrod's letter and stuffed it back in its tattered black envelope then shoved it blindly into my memory drawer where it landed naturally between a post card from Grandma's visit to the Bermuda Triangle and a signed eight-by-ten glossy photo of Count Dracula that read, "I hope your Halloween doesn't suck."

Isn't it funny how these memories, the triumphs and the failures, can all be triggered like a Rube Goldberg machine just by looking at something as seemingly meaningless as a pile of bricks?

Some pretty awful shit had happened to us over the years, but we always managed to make it through together. And, even though Danny wouldn't let me back in his apartment, I knew that we'd work it out somehow. I mean shit, he split my head open and *I* got kicked out? I should've been the one that was mad.

"But, I'm not," I randomly said aloud as I enjoyed another small pinch of mushrooms from my tin.

When I left that morning I thought, well fuck him, I got plenty of places to go; plenty of catching up to do downtown. But then there I was hours later, less than one-hundred feet away, watching my memories as they projected over the great mounds of broken, lifeless brick.

Again I rallied my poor battered body, brushed the concrete ash from the seat of my pants, and I shambled back toward Danny's place while I pondered what if?

What if I had decided not to follow Jerrod's suggestions to the letter? Would I have been normal? What if I kept taking those pills? Would I have gotten married and lived in the suburbs again with a family of my own? And, what if it turned out that Jerrod was simply wrong, too young, and over zealous? Would I have been able to accept responsibility for choosing to follow?

But still, there was one thing in particular that I knew he had hit square on the head. Jerrod said that Danny and I would soon need each other and unfortunately he couldn't have been more right.

When I was thirteen-years-old, Mom died of cancer and at age fourteen, Dad died of a heart attack. At the time of Dad's death Danny had just turned eighteen-years-old and since there were no relatives left to speak of, Danny by default became my legal guardian.

"Well, guess what," I yelled at the top of my lungs as I kicked in Danny's front door. "I'm home, mother-fucker!"

"Oh, no you're not," Danny screamed as he jumped from behind the door and dumped a huge bucket of water on my head while laughing hysterically as if he'd been waiting for me the whole time.

Chapter Three

The Eighth Plague

Silvery, pale apparitions formed and dissipated like
mist as my eardrums absorbed the horrifying
sounds of people going about their days. Internal
yet auditory, my mind swam in a sea of screams
and mumbles. Multiple time periods coated my
corneas like overlapping cellulous membranes and
I watched as a giant squid inked a defensive cloud
through prehistoric waters, while Native men
harvested the crops that once grew here, while Dad
and his hooligan friends took lunch and enjoyed a
few beers over talk of productivity as pertaining to
employee stock.

The last of my energy exited through my
fingertips and toes as my body cried out in an
inspired yawn and a stretch and my eyelids finally
collapsed under great duress with my lashes
colliding and interlacing like mammoth limbs of an
ancient cedar tree. I could no longer resist, so I just
let go and let it embrace me, what I had supposed
was a deep intoxicating sleep.

Ah, but no rest for the wicked. Like a sickness
comes upon its host it came upon me ever so
slowly, invading silently and without warning. It
was there in the midst of that affirming serenity,
that disingenuous promise of slumber, that I let my
guard down and was breathtakingly blindsided by
an epileptic seizure.

Every muscle and tendon locked, contorted, and
slammed against the floor as I kicked backward
against my body with all my might and slipped
down the tunnel of dreams, escaping and detaching
from my earthly tether.

Suddenly, I was floating free in a vast dark expanse of ominous reds, browns, and blues. Planes of perspective shifted and bent as my eyes focused and I beheld four far off points in space unfold and reveal four cloaked creatures of demonic possession, grunting and spewing oil from their gaping pores as they gathered four terrific lengths of chain which they pulled taut from out of the center of a dense, hollow void.

As they labored and strained, the void defiantly began to produce the body of a man. They eagerly encircled him as he floated between them naked and formless.

I watched as they laughed and prodded. I watched as they harmed and taunted, but it made no difference to the man for he had no spirit to command him. I felt a gentle nudge from behind and I was given the courage to approach and observe.

I floated forward to the beings in a defensive stance. I floated forward, but they did not care for me. I floated forward, but they had what they wanted. And, as I drew closer the man's countenance grew clearer, his make-up began to form, and sure enough it was I. The demons were greedily coveting none other than my empty husk.

Abruptly, I felt a strong, vacuous force grow between myself and my body. Like a dying star collapsing in on itself we merged with a dense gravity and again I awoke screaming and drenched in sweat in a pile of toys on the production floor of the factory with every muscle in my body taxed and torn.

"Son of a bitch," I grumbled as I slowly pried

myself from my makeshift bed and cracked my neck heartily. "Sleep be damned, I'm up!" I shouted to the rafters as I pulled my socks up tight and wrenched down on my boot laces. My body creaked and popped as I slowly made it to my feet with every vertebrae snapping and locking into place in succession as I rose. This happened nearly every time I stood. I suppose a real bed would've helped, but honestly who has the time for things like that?

I noisily cranked the chain on the giant roll door of bay-one, exposing my eyes to the glorious pantheon of cosmic happenings in the undulating night sky.

"Our past, present, and future written in the stars for all to see, plain as day," I called out to the street.

"That's beautiful, man!" a drunk passerby called back from behind his hand while his chortling girlfriend dropped her red plastic cup and clung to him as she tripped over her own inebriated steps.

I jumped down into the loading dock, sunk my rings and knuckles playfully into the decaying rubber bay bumpers, I shook me loose, and I was off to manifest another fantastic voyage.

Just like our commercials said, "Every fantastic voyage begins at The Eighth Plague," that towering inferno of disease and lust, that great overflowing lover waiting to shower you with booze, flattery, and an abundance of sheer unmentionables.

I decimated thigh-high weeds under my heavy and crushing stride as my chains jingled in the crisp night air with my jacket flowing neatly and gracefully in the cold breeze.

At times the Eighth Plague building seemed to

defy the laws of structural possibilities. When it was first built it was a two story tall luxury hotel that branched out to the left in the back in an *L*-shape. But, as time went on and multiple owners' visions shaped and repurposed the structure, the floor plan expanded in an exceedingly confusing manner indeed.

Sections appeared to be built on at random, some stacking precariously on top of others in a way that certainly could not meet building code. The final blueprint of the ground floor spidered outward like a broken windshield, staircases and door frames were left half built, and hallways splintered and converged at what seemed like impossible intersections, creating a very unsettling looking building to say the least.

So, what did two grief-stricken kids in their early twenties, heavy with disdain for authority and a seemingly never ending supply of cash decide to do with a beat up, old Frankenstein building? Why, make it a nightclub of course, silly. Hell, why not several nightclubs all labeled as plagues and given their own intricate themes?

In time this model proved to attract quite a quirky and loyal clientele and Danny and I spared no expense to please them. We had manufactured a refuge from the modern woe and it was pure decadence and entirely profitable.

Plagues one through four were Danny's creations. Plague One was a boring-ass cowboy bar, authentic down to its mechanical bull and line dancing cowgirls. Unfortunately, it was quite a success.

In what was a sweeping victory of Rochambeau,

Danny won all three of our basements: plagues two, a respected coffee house and jazz venue; three, an honor-system exchange post and lounge; and four, a stand-alone bunker completely separate of any structure above. Danny named that piece of shit The Discerning Palette; a room he had dedicated to fussy little scenesters obsessed with exacting cuisine and plating minutia. It was also quite a tragic success.

There was one formal dance hall that Danny and I shared, Plague Five, which we referred to professionally as Zinnia Hall after Mom's favorite flower. We reserved that rather large space for events like weddings for the obscenely rich or funerals for the poor and needy.

Plagues six and seven, however, were mine all mine. Plague Six was a modest, but lavish main stage which focused on natural acoustics through architecture and was equipped with a state of the art sound system designed by none other than the legendary Jerrod Twig. The backstage area boasted an extensive seventies themed pampering facility including a full bar attended by our house mixologist, a six table masseuse parlor, and an authentic shag carpeted conversation pit with low lit swag lamps hanging throughout. Now you tell me what bitchy little prima-donna rock star isn't going to just eat that up?

But, of course the main attraction was always Plague Seven, the adjoining taproom. Oh, the taproom; you vomit inducing taproom. How I loathed my dependence on you. Your tacky golden velvet walls call to me now, like a smutty siren to a love struck sailor. You are the clear favorite of all our plagues.

"But Plague Eight, let us not forget you, you collaborative effort. You respiring, living creature you," I called out as my boots pounded the pavement like a metronome.

Plague Eight was a never ending host of dimly lit corners, nooks, and hideouts where anything consensual goes. The majority of available rooms in the building were provided as low cost housing and were strictly set aside for runaways, transients, goons, artists, writers, and ne'er-do-wells. It was to this breed which we dedicated the overall moniker, The Eighth Plague.

The only policy that we had regarding prospective tenants was this: no person of wealth was allowed to buy, sell, or rent any space located within the property lines of the Radezlav Estate. Only those that needed it or those that deserved to be there were allowed to stay. We took care of our own and in turn, they took care of us.

We had purposely failed to provide the upper crust with overnight accommodations, so as to upset the balance of social classes while increasing mystique and exclusivity; a characteristic that the tremendously wealthy infuriatingly adored. Returning clientele however wised up and had long since established camaraderie among the tenants.

Although the wealthy could not buy, sell, or rent, there was no such policy that stated the tenants could not provide lodging of their own volition. Also, there was no such policy that stated patrons or tenants could not solicit one another for any reason other than lodging, including but not limited to the sale of elicit substances or a companion for hire.

Finally, the most widely utilized of our policies that did not exist: staff were expressly instructed not to inhibit patrons from ducking into dark hallways, storerooms, or other generally unsupervised areas for the purpose of taking themselves a little twelve or fourteen hour nap, though we highly recommended against it due to the nature of our tenants.

But, please don't believe us complete communal, anarchist hippies. We were also entrepreneurs and capitalists. We directly employed almost fifty people including one aggressively talented lawyer, one internationally acclaimed executive chef, two revered sous-chefs and seven speedy cooks, ten meticulous waiters, two ingenious lighting designers and three audiophile sound techs, four slippery accountants, nine curious security officers trained with the knowledge of what to pass over and what to swiftly extinguish, and a single florist who made stunning arrangements daily from only estate-grown flora that she had reared from the earth herself.

She was a runaway, a retro-eighties fashion punk, she was seventeen-years-old, and her name was Abigail Sutcher. My broken heart mends at the mere sight of you, Abigail. Just the thought of you quickens my pace.

From the glow in the dark jelly bracelets that crowd your wrists to your plethora of cut and tied Cyndi Lauper t-shirts, I adore you. From your skintight acid-washed jeans that have been torn and sewn so many times that they're more patch than they are pant, to your knee-high leather boots that you splatter painted because of your love for Jackson Pollack, I am entirely enamored with you. From your highest point to your lowest depth, I am yours and I am honestly and truly haunted by your energy and your every little detail.

Your long and healthy hair chopped into defiant locks of variable lengths and streaked from deep-indigo to jet-black at the tips bounced lightly in loose curls as you did your best to act like you weren't waiting for me under that buzzing neon sign with the frigid night air nipping at the shaven sections of your scalp, no doubt.

Your warm, precocious eyes, brown growing green from pupil to iris edge, lined in thick black eyeliner swept from outer ducts like cat eyes; mischievously pretending they didn't see me coming. Spitefully you hid them away as you raised your sweatshirt hood over your head and pulled the strings taut with both hands, making yourself look like a little boy. You knew I hated it when you'd do that, which is why you did it.

Your bright-red, high gloss lips pursed and scrunched, bound by a thick sterling silver ring which squeaked ever so lightly as it rubbed against that cute little gap between your front teeth that you're so self conscious about.

Thin, feminine, platinum chains that I had custom made for you draped gently off your curvaceous, bouncing hips and brushed across your thighs, alluring and beckoning me in without your permission. Whether furious or not, our inherent magnetism increased as I approached and we finally merged in an intertwining cloud of chemical reactions.

"We had plans tonight, didn't we?" I foolishly inquired as I twirled her around by her delicate hand.

"Why, yes we did. When did you finally remember, when you saw me from down the street or just right this very moment?" she asked while pulling her hood back with her face to the ground.

"Come on, Abigail, don't do this to me."

"Why, because you have a headache, or because you're hung over, or because you've been awake for three days, or, or, or?"

I fell to my knees, kissed her boots from spiked tip to eyelet covered shin, and I proclaimed to her under the eye piercing neon, "Red Queen, my Red Queen, what could but a lowly Seven of Hearts ever do to curry the favor of one as fair as you?"

She grabbed me firmly by my mop and pulled my head back with authority saying, "First of all, you know I greatly prefer the Cheshire cat, and second, you're going to take me dancing like you said you were going to!"

I pressed my right cheek hard against the giant tractor belt buckle that her father gave her the night she left home as I pathetically out stretched my grasping claw toward the glistening mahogany bar visible through the large bay windows behind her and mumbled, "Did I say that? That doesn't sound like something I'd say."

"Yes, you did! The Sock Hop at Zinnia, hello? Darn you, Asher," she pouted, having been thoroughly agitated as she ran her fingers gently through my hair.

"What the hell is this?" she hollered as her fingerprints scanned gracefully up and over and down each individual stitch.

I jumped quickly to my feet and pulled her in tight. "The Sock Hop, right. Of course I remember." I looked down at my father's watch. "Geez, we're really late. Let's go, already. Come on. What's your problem?"

She quickly put her hand over my mouth, dove deep into my massive pupils and lovingly said in a way that was both tender and matter of fact, "Asher, I just want you to know that you really are an idiot." Then she slapped me across the back of my head, sending what felt like a wave of bee stings spreading hotly across my cranium. "And, a jack ass," she added as she jabbed me repeatedly in the solar plexus.

She pivoted sharply on her heels and turned away from me, playfully shaking her gorgeous little behind from side to side, making her chains jingle and jangle as she swayed and swaggered down the short cobblestone path to Zinnia Hall, assuming that I would automatically follow. Which of course I did, but not before downing the contents of my flask.

"What are you doing, Asher?" she called out as I ducked behind a bush.

"Just taking a leak real fast," I yelled back as I quickly hit my pipe and then ran happily after her, suddenly reeking of weed and whiskey.

Before I met Abigail I was a wreck. I spent nearly all of my waking hours at Plague Seven drinking myself into a stupor or sewing wild oats and false pretenses in the tarts upstairs. Back and forth I would go, from one disaster to the next, imagining that my body was impervious to poisoning or making believe that those women were capable of separating anonymous intimacy from reasonable hopes of a relationship with a young, wealthy suitor.

Around that time I also developed the nasty habit of getting into fist fights with patrons or even staff, hence our abundantly talented and impish Lawyer, Harvey G. Arnold, who claimed to have the ability to, "charm rattlers, judges, or juryman alike".

One night as I was sucking on pills while sitting at the bar, especially transfixed on the purposely awful gold velvet wall panels and our collection of bejeweled, faux deer antler chandeliers, I called out to the bartender for a drink.

I see now that making the bartenders dress up for Halloween every night could become a bit of a bother if assigned a certain persona and I know that I was behaving like an entitled little rich-boy when I told him that I would shove a fifty-spot into his tutu if he brought me a bottle of Maker's Mark balanced on his head with a snifter in his mouth while prancing on his tippy toes, but for some strange reason the guy took it *way* too seriously and started barking at me about "standards" and "pride" and "professionalism" as the entire surface of his skin turned crimson like a plump and juicy vine ripened tomato crammed into a pink unitard that appeared about one size too small.

So, in response I turned to the guy's co-worker who was dressed as a Ghostbuster and asked, "What say you and I take good old Baryshnikov here out back and fuck him up?" again, totally kidding.

Well, guess who didn't think that was so funny. Before I knew it the guy lunged over the bar, grabbed me by my jacket, and quite rudely laid his knuckles across the bridge of my nose, knocking me clear off my antique, artisan made mahogany bar stool.

As I fell ever so slowly and gently to earth with the entire bar watching and wincing, I took notice of the odds and ends that needed mending or tidying up. Clearly the armadillo was in severe need of dusting, it appeared that the graffiti walls needed a fresh coat of orange paint and a restocking of art supplies, and it looked like our freaking Dig Dug arcade game was out of order again.

My nearly three hundred pounds packed the hardwood floor like a feckless side of beef, slamming my vertebrae violently into place. In a ridiculous thud I landed flat on my back and belted out a guttural, "Ugh!" as the wind was knocked out of my diaphragm and every patron groaned. Again I had been made the image of a frail-old-man, falling to the ground in slow motion, sending dust and ashes to flight.

I sprang up like a champ, gasping for air and struggling to refill myself with necessary oxygen. I choked and stammered while shaking off my complimentary chiropractic adjustment, then slowly regained my composure and sputtered, "That fucking armadillo needs to be dusted and for God's sake could we please call someone to fix Dig Dug?!"

My bartender's eyes grew wide as a canyon and he unexpectedly burst into a fit of nervous laughter as if he had been suddenly struck by the effects of some sort of panic inducing psychoactive. He ducked behind the bar for a brief moment and when he arose he had a snifter in each hand and a bottle of Maker's teetering dangerously atop his thick, uneven scalp.

He was still chuckling as he set them down in front of me, so I pulled up my stool, lowered my brow, and met my bartender deep inside his own eyes. Pushing and forcing my spirit past his optic nerves, neurons, and synapses, I dug down deep, burrowing into his psyche like a worm while a horror of blood flowed tremendously out of my nose and into my open mouth, dripping off my lips into gorgeous little piles that began to pool around the base of our glasses.

From behind a crumbling dam of ocular muscles he inevitably cracked and made with the tears as the reality of his ill-tempered decision fully formed in his head and I gradually grew calm. He shakily poured us both a drink and said, "This one's on me. I'll drink mine and go."

"No, you're fine. I got this," I said while spewing droplets. "And, in case you're wondering, you're not fired. I was being an asshole and you were right to call me on it. But, please know, if you ever touch me again it won't be getting fired that you'll have to worry about."

Without warning I struck out over the bar and buried my ringed fist deep in the dead center of his chest, bringing him heavily to his knees on the black rubber food service mats. I jumped over the bar, knelt next to him and whispered, "Now if you want to let bygones be bygones from here on out, that'd be just peachy. But, if you need to dance, well, I guess that'd be fine too."

He slowly looked up at me gripping his chest, gasping sharply, and with his eyes all bloodshot and his face shaking like gelatin he said, "How about another round instead, boss?"

I leaned into my bartender and whispered, "You know, I think there's a karate gi in the locker room about your size. Why don't you go check it out? See if it doesn't feel a bit more comfortable," then I slapped his back three times in affirmation and helped him to his feet. I raised his arm triumphantly in the air and shouted, "My man!" as the entire bar erupted into a rowdy and raucous debacle of liquid abandon.

This little incident, however raw and scandalous, paled in comparison to the night I met Abigail. The night we fell in love.

It started like any other night, with me obliterated and swaying terrifically on my bar stool while incessantly chattering way too loudly directly into Danny's left ear about how my home spun business models were going to save the economy.

I was all wrapped up in a double tall vodka tonic with grenadine and seven maraschino cherries, explicitly with stem in tact and body uncrushed, when I shouted uncontrollably in a thick sloppy slur, "First thing we need to do is bring the industries home. No more freaking sweat shops, no more outsourcing, no more greed, abuse, and slothful waste, no more turning a blind eye to sustainability.

"No longer shall we choose between products with little golden oval stickers on the bottom that read 'Made in China', 'Made in Bangladesh', or

'Hecho en Mexico'. I'm talking about made in America, made by Americans! There's your jobs right there!

"'But, the price of goods will go through the roof,' they'll snivel. But, if everyone has a job, guess what, all of a sudden we'll have money too; money that we'll be willing to invest in ourselves, in our future, in our country, and in our children.

"We'll bring our schools belatedly into the twenty-first century, which will produce more intelligent citizens who will be productive members of a free society, willing and able to be taxed in a higher bracket. And there's your revenue, damn it. There's your revenue.

"Now, you take that increased revenue and sick an incorruptible task force on the issue of misappropriation and theft by government officials and appointees, and you instruct small businesses on financial management and incentivize entrepreneurship and fiscal responsibility with tax credits and federal grants, and there goes the deficit, slowly but surely shrinking and shrinking as we grow and grow."

Danny just nodded his head and sipped his Pabst with the thumb of his free hand bobbing lightly up and down about three inches in front of my face saying, "Shrinking, right. Got it."

"I mean, is there something I'm not understanding here? Maybe these complex global monetary models are like, *way* too far beyond my feeble comprehension, but when I have ten dollars and I spend fifteen that's called debt. And, when Americans are out of work and cashing their government checks at Allmart so they can buy foreign goods while we slowly ship our jobs one-by-one around the world, that's just called crazy!

"Mom and Dad only spent what was in their wallets. Mom and Dad bought American and they sold American, damn it. That's how you do it. That's how you freaking do it!

"Sometimes I think we should get that factory going again. You ever think about that? Hire some more guys, make some more creatures? What do you say, man? Let's do it. Just you and me."

Suddenly I had Danny's full attention and he stared at me wide eyed. "Let's change the subject right now," he said with a fixed gaze and no emotion.

"Sorry to interrupt, Mr. Radezlav," Abigail said to Danny as she emerged from the crowd and assumingly wedged herself between us then slapped the bar and ordered a pint of Guinness and a shot of Bailey's Irish Cream and Jameson.

"I'm Abigail," she said turning her back to Danny and extending her hand confidently toward me with one long lock of lustrous hair hanging playfully over her right eye, running along her lightly freckled cheek, and curling down one side of her perfect young breasts.

"Yeah I know, I, um... Danny told me... about the flowers, I mean," I stuttered stupidly as I perceived her growing excruciatingly close to me, my nostrils deluged in her scent, her eyes hard-wiring into my mind and our pupils aligning like planets. It felt as if she were already mine.

She brushed her hair aside and said to me alone, "You know, I heard what you were saying about the economy and for what it's worth I think you're right on, I mean, really right on; except for the part about the foreign and migrant laborers. Please don't forget, Mr. Radezlav, migrants built this country too."

And with that she turned, dropped her shot into her beer, poured it directly into her stomach, and slammed a twenty dollar bill and the glasses down on the bar.

"Good night, gentleman," she said sweetly, clicking her splatter painted heels together and saluting us with that same lock of hair falling back over her right eye.

She glided gracefully through groups and stalemates as if she had foreseen the entire path from point *A* to point *B* before her departure, ducking and swaying through drunks and cretins like a dancer whose partner was the entire crowd. She stopped at the psychedelic hotel stairs in the back and turned to see if I was still watching as the light from my antiquated phone booth radiated her hair like fluorescents.

"That reminds me, man!" Danny said punching me in the arm, abruptly snapping me into a different frame. He tipped his goofy-ass cowboy hat to the side and with his eyes all wide and his dental work exposed he said, "You're going to shit yourself when you hear this!"

"What? Just say it already," I said half listening and half looking back to find that Abigail had already ascended.

"I forgot to tell you, man. That little purple-haired punk is into you."

My brow furrowed and I whispered, "It's indigo, not purple."

"What?"

"Her hair. It's indigo, not p-u-r-p-l-e," I said pretending to sign in the air about three inches in front of his face.

"Well, ain't you two just like peas and carrots; you're in love with her aren't you, you little perv? Jesus Christ, she's seventeen-years-old, grandpa!"

"Don't call me a perv and don't use the Lord's name in vain and don't call me grandpa!" I shouted loudly, eliciting queer reactions from those in our proximity, having uttered the random catch phrase of the year.

"Alright, calm down. As I was trying to say, she told me she thinks you're pretty hot, so there you go. How great is that?"

"No she didn't. Come on. Really? She didn't say that."

Danny just pointed to our bartender who was standing about ten feet away dressed as Pennywise the Clown, polishing a glass with his eyebrows arched high on his forehead and his neck intermittently forming double and triple chins as he shook his head up and down saying, "That's what she said alright. She said you were hot."

"Why would she tell you bozos that? She doesn't know either of you," I asked sensing a trap.

Danny finished his beer and then held his index finger in the air, signaling to Pennywise for another. He looked left, looked right, then leaned in and whispered, "Okay, last week she was signing paperwork at the bar and you were over there drawing in the corner, looking adorable as ever, and she asked who you were. So, I told her you were my brother and she said that you were hot and asked me to ask you to come up and see her sometime. You know, like the welcome wagon. Make her feel at home," then he lightly rabbit punched me in the gut while making a sour face as if sucking on a lemon.

"Now she wants me to come up and see her? Man, fuck you guys. I don't believe a word you're saying."

Little did I know that during this whole conversation Pennywise the Clown, formerly Baryshnikov the Ballerina, was drafting a very convincing forgery of an invitation to meet with Abigail at her apartment. Of course I missed it when he served Danny his Pabst with the invitation disguised as a coaster.

Like an old vaudevillian duo riffing off each other, sensing the next move like musicians, Danny seamlessly handed me the note and said, "Now either I had this planned out so far in advance that I fabricated this note, which I'm sure you'll notice is not written in my hand writing, or she actually asked me to give this to you. So, which is it?"

I snatched the note, hastily unfolded it and read, "You look like my kind of man. Maybe you can show me around sometime? I'm in room number two-thirteen if you ever want to party. Bring a twelve-pack, sailor. I'm ready when you are. –Abigail"

"Well, she *was* being really flirty with me," I began to rationalize; wanting to believe. I pulled my dictionary out of my breast pocket and placed the note at random in its pages.

"What kind of twelve-pack should I bring?" I asked while rubbing Danny's shoulders way too hard.

"Probably something really sweet. Little kids tend to like things *really* sweet," Danny said with his face contorted as he slapped at my hands in pain.

"I'm doing it. Screw it, I'm doing it," I said shrugging my shoulders, kicking my feet out, and flexing my hands as if I were preparing for a street fight. "One pack of Stella, my good man," I called to Pennywise and slapped the bar.

I chugged Danny's Pabst down in two gulps, crumpled it in my fist and threw it haphazardly over my shoulder, then ran off with my bottles clanking wildly as I knocked into nearly every patron in my path. I decimated dance floor darlings like thigh-high weeds as I neared the back of the bar and heard Danny and my bartender erupting in boisterous laughter, but by the time it registered I was already at the top of the stairs and was utterly incapable of deviating from my chosen path.

At that point tunnel vision had taken hold hard and was thoroughly at the wheel, driving me down hall after dilapidated hall. Right, left, right I turned. Left, right, left, until I realized that I was drunk, confused, and lost on the second floor of my own building.

I took a moment to catch my bearings and observe my surroundings and that is when I recoiled in disgust at the extent of our managerial neglect which had suddenly become all too apparent.

The majority of wall sconces and chandeliers were out of service, broken, or completely missing, leaving me to wonder why no one had ever complained of safety concerns. Also, none of the numbers ran in sequence. Who the hell designs a building like that? Had someone switched the numbers as a joke so long ago that it had since become the norm; two-twelve, then two-twenty-four, and across the hall, two-eighteen? And, why so many mirrors, damn it? Door shaped mirrors, wall sized mirrors, mirrors at head height. I found myself having to separate reflection from reality in the near dark through a thick haze of brain vibrating intoxication. Was my own building conspiring against me?

I continued this process for about one hour and ultimately admitted a dismal defeat as I ripped open my pack of Stella, fell hard into the wall behind me, and slumped down on the sticky, blackened, psychedelic carpet with beer flowing from the corners of my mouth which soaked my chest.

My beleaguered memory was growing dim and becoming tired of recalling a labyrinth that I had not mastered in ages and I dreadfully feared that I would not be able to solve the riddle in time, so I finished my beer, opened another, and resigned myself to live my life in solitude glued to the black, gummy, hotel carpet.

Just then a door slowly creaked open a few feet away on my left and Abigail stuck her head out. She smiled and quietly said, "Oh hey, Mr. Radezlav. What are you doing here?"

I closed my eyes, threw my head back lightly against the wall and sighed, "Abigail, what number are you?"

"Two-thirty-four. Why?"

I locked eyes with her, realizing that I had been tricked and was coming to terms with what I already knew.

"Because, I'm having an exceedingly difficult time finding apartment two-thirteen, that's why," I said with unwarranted accusation in my voice.

"There is no apartment two-thirteen, Mr. Radezlav. Rumor has it that you removed all the thirteens when you rearranged the numbers as a kid."

"Oh. Of course. Thank you, Abigail," I said fully dejected with my eyes to the ground, becoming uncharacteristically silent.

"Are you alright... Asher?" she asked in the sweetest, most concerned voice these ears could ever hear. I hadn't heard my name called in that key, in that tone, since the death of my mother and I embraced it wholly as the faint euphonious nuances danced from my active memory into my long-term mind.

"Finally," I said chuckling as I attempted to hold my emotions still. "I like that much better. Mr. Radezlav? Please. I'm not Mr. Radezlav," I said with my voice quivering as I rose to my feet with my bones cracking and ligaments popping back into place.

"Why does *that* happen?" she asked almost in disbelief and in slight revulsion.

"It's a really long story, but I appreciate the concern. Have a good night," I said attempting to spare her sympathy as I slunk away past mirror after lonely mirror with my Doc's peeling off the floor and reaffixing with every step.

I made it half way down the hall when she yelled

to me, "Well, you could come in and share those beers with me and maybe just tell me part of the story? That is, if there isn't someone else that you're supposed to meet."

I stopped and turned to her with my eyebrows rumpled up like a used blanket.

"Come on," she said turning her eyes to the ground and her feet in pigeon-toed, subtly waving me in.

The hall appeared to illuminate as I popped a bottle top with the bottom of my lighter. The cap ricocheted off the ceiling and lodged in an arrangement of golden leaves on the chandelier above as I slowly walked back to her with the beer foaming over and soaking rudely into the carpet.

She grabbed the beer at the threshold then took a dainty little sip and pushed me in, slamming the door behind us and shouting, "Welcome, friend! Mi casa es su casa!"

The first thing that struck me about Abigail's apartment was the absolute sublime order. Everything appeared squared at parallel angles, crisped and smoothed, ironed, pinned down, or secured in some fashion. Even though the plaster was falling off the walls, showing the wooden slats underneath like rib bones, even though the ceiling was bowing down from above, waiting for the worst possible opportunity to give way, even though the hotel furniture was stained yellow, brown, or black with age and its cloth had been eaten by time, everything was set at perfect, exacting, ninety degree angles and was as absolutely clean and pressed as it could be.

The few belongings she had consisted of one

large piece of rolling luggage that housed her art and art supplies, two medium sized bins that held clothing, shoes, and accessories; one small bag that cradled her precious memories; one standard issue Army pack containing only the essentials, including a first aid kit, a magnifying glass, a compass, a canteen, her make-up, and so on; and a few random tanks and aquariums that housed a multitude of various bugs and creepy-crawlies that she referred to as "her real friends". They were all happily feeding on her homegrown flowers and other assorted offerings of the field and she cared for them like children.

On her kitchen counter from left to right were a fork, a butter knife facing left, and a spoon atop a neatly folded paisley handkerchief, then a simple glass and one floral patterned dinner plate. Next to that was a rather large buck knife in a hand painted leather sheath, an old beat up salt encrusted fishing hat impaled mercilessly with rusted lures, a flint knapped chunk of obsidian, and on the wall at the end of the counter was a poster of Bjork standing in the woods with her eyes closed, licking up into the air while holding a gigantic leaf over her nakedness. It was made expressly clear to me that these items were sorted in order of necessity and were not to be disturbed in any manner, for any reason.

Her only other belongings were a phonograph accompanied by a milk crate filled with the greatest, most boiled down vinyl collection I have ever seen, which included a seven-inch of Stevie Wonder's *Superstitious*, a mint condition copy of *Yoshimi Battles the Pink Robots*, and of course a very rare original pressing of her heroine's *She's So*

Unusual.

Abigail happily dropped the needle on Beck Hansen's *Sea Change* and we sat and drank for hours as we spoke of her overbearing father and why she felt that she had to leave home, my mom and dad and why Danny and I are both still so destroyed, the economy, our hopes for the future, our passion for design, color theory, and visual weighting; and ultimately our own intricate and unconventional versions of spirituality.

Our pasts, paths, and ideologies seemed to merge and mesh like clockwork, while our differences and denominations were thrown off like so much slag in a melting pot. Our lives collided like atoms, merging us attractively together as if we were two gears joined in the great cosmic machine. And, that's when it happened. We actually ran out of beer.

I swiftly raced to the bar and collected whatever her heart desired and each time I returned I took the opportunity to move closer, ever closer. We continued this pattern until we were both entirely beyond repair and completely upon each other. I laid my hand palm up in her lap and became silent, looking to her to satisfy the starving void in my soul.

She reached out slightly then quickly withdrew, slapping her legs and whimpering in frustration and saying, "Look, I have this thing, okay. When I touch people I just feel too much. It's like I am already a full glass and if I fill anymore I just overflow and I don't know if I can do this, I don't think I can do this!"

I pulled my hand back slowly and looked her

sternly in the eyes attempting to communicate strength and comfort and then I grabbed her hand and pressed it against my chest above my aching, troubled heart.

"You can take it," I said. "It's yours. *I'm* yours if you want me."

Sure enough, she was a full glass and the water flowed freely from her eyes as she enveloped me. The spikes on my collar gently depressed her cheek as she repeatedly nosed into the crook of my neck, soaking my shoulder with her tears. She wiped her face on her sleeve with her nose scrunching like a little bunny, she sniffled, and then suddenly we met in an embarrassingly passionate embrace, our lips crashing roughly together, fitting perfectly as if they were created for one another. She placed her hand again on my chest and gradually pushed away, breaking our bond.

"I like you Asher, but I'm not so sure what's going on with me right now, you know? I took off to find myself, to find my life, and next thing I know I'm working and living in some beat down old hotel in California and I'm not really sure how I ended up here? I guess what I'm really trying to say is, I don't know how long I'm going to be able to stay and I just don't do one-nighters. I'm not like that."

I faced the floor and began to deflate, attempting to understand. "So, you don't do one-nighters and you don't know if you're going to stay, but where does that leave me, huh? What, are you afraid your dad is going to come looking for you or something, or you're not happy here so far? Why would you leave? What would make you leave? You just got here."

"I just need to be able to go when I need to go, that's all," she said as she snuggled into me, reaching her hand under my shirt, lightly caressing my ribs and scratching at my belly with her short black fingernails, making me tense and clench spastically.

"Oh my, you're ticklish aren't you?"

"No," I said with the left side of my upper lip lifting and shaking in an uncontrollable sneer.

"Oh, but I think you are, I think you are!" she giggled and snorted as she mercilessly laid into my stomach while I ineffectually attempted to cease her emasculatory assault, her fingers like little bolts of lightning always one stutter step ahead of mine. I lurched and seized at the waist, laughing like a powerless child, reveling in her friendship, her love, and absorbing her positive, healing energy as quickly as I could.

"What's this?" she said as she assumingly pulled the note from my breast pocket, dislodging my dictionary which fell to the floor in slow motion as my eyes followed it down. It balanced upright on its spine then landed open faced with the word *wormwood* staring back at me coldly, circled, highlighted, and underlined in bold thick ink.

My eyes abruptly exploded open as I jolted to my feet and screamed, "Holy shit, wormwood! That's it, that's what it was!"

"Is this supposed to be from me?" Abigail questioned while becoming increasingly upset.

"I got to go. I got to go," I said pacing frantically while collecting my effects as a minuscule, fleshy draw bridge in my mind dropped open, dosing my blood stream with epinephrine and enacting my fight or flight response as my pupils blasted to their capacity.

"You got to go? What the fuck is this, Asher?" Abigail screamed at me, shaking the note annoyingly in my face. The paper crumpled and scraped in my overly sensitive ears as I shoved my dictionary back in its home and headed purposefully toward the door.

Abigail blocked my path, clasped the note by its header and footer, and snapped it taut in front of my face yelling, "Hey asshole, I didn't write this! Did you think you were going to come up here, tear my shit up, and just bail out? Well, that ain't me, bucko. I'm not like you and I'm not like the other little whores that live here! You got that?"

I lowered my brow, collected my voice from the deep bottom of my stomach and said as nicely as I possibly could have, "Either you move or I go through you. One way or another I'm leaving right now."

Her eyes watered as they skipped back and forth and she stepped aside with her mouth hanging open, tensing and gasping for air. I barreled through her door, down the sticky steps, through the last-call crowd, and shoulder checked the door jamb of the main entrance with the word *wormwood* pounding darkly in my mind. I made it half way down the block and came to a halt under the buzzing orange streetlight, pressing my knuckles awfully into the sides of my head in an attempt to alleviate the raging pain that had consumed me.

I felt a terrific rush of energy approach me from behind and I was suddenly pushed to the ground with the asphalt scouring me clean. Instinctively I sprang up and faced my attacker.

Abigail stood before me with her backpack on, her big old bowie knife buckled to the outside of her right thigh, and she-was-screaming, "Come on, you piece of dog shit! You think you can treat me like that and then just walk out? What are you trying to pull here? I can have your heart? You're mine? You want to hurt me? You want to hurt me? Well, then I'll hurt you," she said as she struck out toward me.

I didn't bother to move figuring that she was just a little girl and that a big strong man like me could take whatever she had to give, but when she fell toward me and drove the heel of her palm sharply into my left ear while cupping her hand, making a concussive pop that created a horrible piercing tone deep within my ear canal, I quickly reassessed her as a serious threat.

With my eardrum feeling perforated and ringing in tremendous pain I jolted into her and wrapped her up in a lung folding bear hug, but I couldn't get a good grip around her because of her pack. And, was I ever surprised when she crushed her beautiful young forehead perfectly into the bridge of my poor abused nose. I staggered stupidly backward as my eyes focused through the water just in time to see her lean back as if she were going to take a seat on her left hip, her right leg extending and straightening upward with the heel of her boot lodging under my chin, pressing my jaw up and back towards my temples like a human reset button.

I fell hard to the ground, wilted and defeated as

her foot once again met the asphalt behind her with her arms held out to her sides, flexed and constricted like thin, rigid rods.

My eyes fluttered and collapsed as I tumbled down the tunnel of dreams, realizing that I had underestimated Abigail and that I had been knocked out clean and cold by a sweet, little girl.

Chapter Four

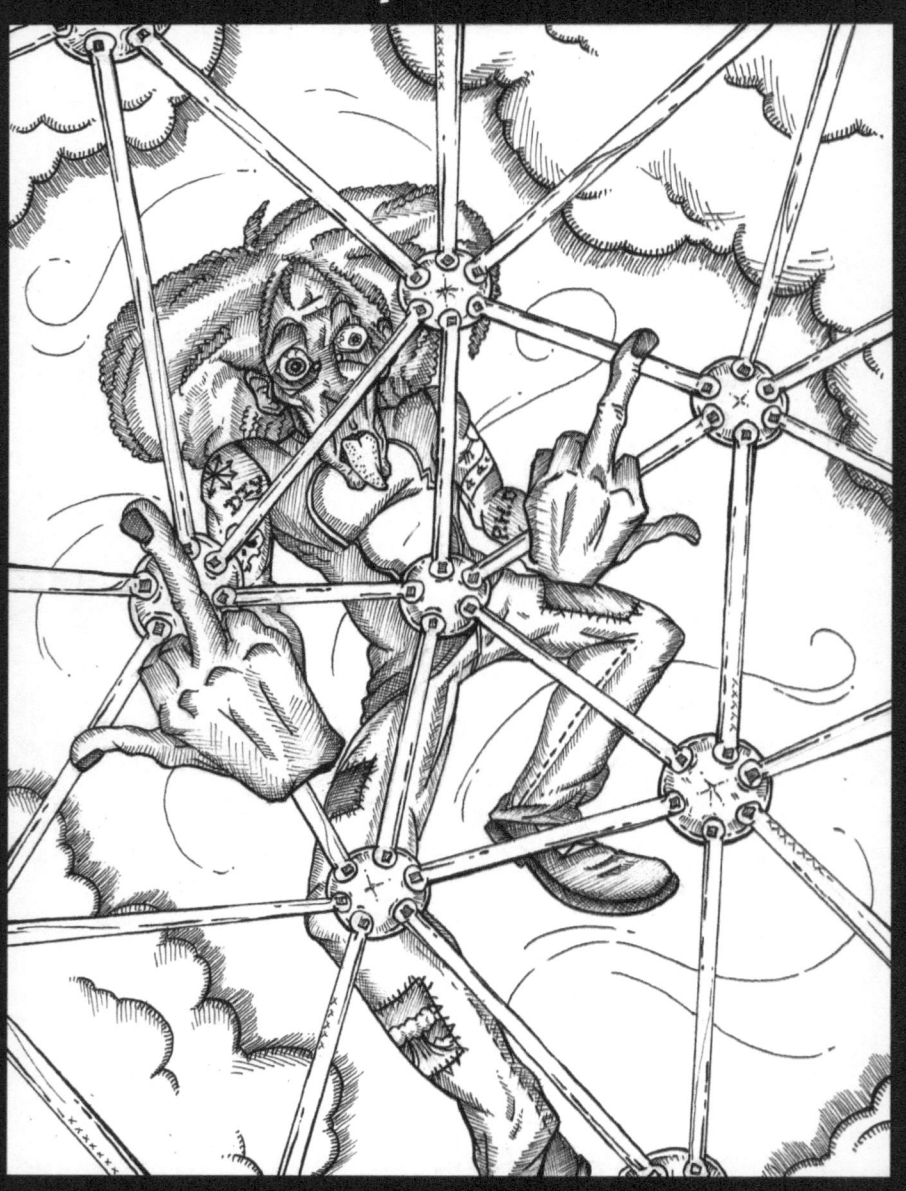

Danny and I

"Danny, wake up!" I screamed over and over as our house began to crumble down around us. Danny just laid there on the floor unresponsive with an ear to ear grin on his face which was smeared in a huge pile of puke. I grabbed him by his studded leather jacket that I had painted a horse shoe on across the back and dragged him down stair after head thumping stair, out the burning front door, and onto the lawn where we met with our dumfounded party guests.

Sirens cut through the frozen night air scattering juveniles from our property as red and blue lights pulsed inorganically, mixing eerily with the bright whipping spikes of scorching flames that licked passionately at the dark-black sky.

When Danny was hauled away by the EMTs for smoke inhalation and alcohol poisoning the last thing that struck me as the ambulance doors closed was his face pasted with that same ear to ear grin which was being covered by an oxygen mask that immediately fogged over. He had finally achieved pure bliss and was utterly unaware of his surroundings and the fact that our childhood home was gone, never to return again.

Just a few hours earlier the party of the year was under way and I have to say, we were all having a really tremendous time. It seemed as if our entire high school was in attendance and Danny was our chaperone.

Well, I suppose Danny was on a self-destructive mission, because our chaperone blacked out within the first hour. He was a slobbering, useless, weepy wreck hanging from my neck like a heavy and volatile orangutan.

"Asher, they're gone. They're really gone," he kept spitting in my right ear as drool and alcohol dripped off his lip rings and soaked into Mom's prized beige carpet.

"I know, Dan. I know. We got each other. I'm here," I said in small consolation as I wiped my eyes and the crevices of my ear clean.

Danny tipped a handle back and sucked down the last of the bottom shelf whiskey. Danny inhaled chamber after chamber of hot, rolling marijuana smoke. Danny swallowed pill after pill and tab after tab in an attempt to obliterate his pain and escape his incessant memory, but as long as he was coherent he could still see their faces and could still hear their voices calling out messages of love and resolution; messages that would not cease from breaking his heart.

Soon enough he was gone, vacated from his body and unable to attend to our guests who consisted of Seniors, Juniors, Sophomores, and other large and angst-ridden youths that I could not possibly control or subdue if necessary. These fuckers ripped through our cabinets and devoured what was left of our food. These degenerates consumed our parents bar and created a heaping pile of ash where our stash once was. The reckless and violent behavior ensued and grew like impending flames, watching and waiting for the right time to simply explode.

Before Danny made himself scarce he thought it a fine idea to light the fire place, it being the dead of winter, and leave the supervision of a hoard of disaffected deviants to a child that had been sheltered and coddled to the point of being inept.

Cowboys from Hell blasted from our speakers inciting an impromptu mosh-pit in our living room that caused the females to scatter. Pictures were broken, dirt was stomped into Mom's carpets, and a drink was spilled on the toughest, most arrogant kid in school who of course elevated the rowdy dance into an all-out fist fight that angrily spread like a hungry virus across the entire downstairs.

Kids pushed and punched and shuffled about in their pathetically inflated cock struts; some ran for cover while others dove in. The crowd kicked and swayed knocking our furniture around the room and inching one of our white wooden-bordered sofas closer and closer to the fireplace. I ran in and tried to break it up, seeing the future unfold in my mind, but as I entered the pit I was instantly knocked unconscious by a random sucker-punch and fell to the floor, useless like Danny.

When I awoke I was alone and the house was engulfed in flames. I sprang to my feet and panicked, running in circles and calling out in a horrific howl, "Dan, Danny, Daniel!"

I frantically searched the house, yelling and screaming, until I came to his locked bedroom door. I commenced with the blows to the handle and as the lock gave way the door sucked opened as if the room had inhaled and a small explosion burped back in my face. When I ran across the threshold, the flames ingested the majority of my dark-brown hair, including my eyebrows, eyelashes, and what sparse amount of pubescent fuzz I wore on my young face that I proudly showcased as my first beard.

As the sirens ripped into the crisp early morning air and the last flame was extinguished, I knew that the entirety of my short life had been undone and that I had been wholly decimated.

I was fatherless, motherless, homeless, penniless, singed, bald, and alone. I filled out paper after paper, first at the hospital, then down at the police station until I put down my pen and simply refused to be party to a system that was cold, sterile, and ineffective.

When the police officers weren't looking I floated out the precinct doors like a dead little ghost-boy and was off to begin my new life as a porcupine. My first order of business was to escape like Danny did, so I walked to the curb and put out my thumb.

As if pre-ordained, a gray primer sprayed pickup truck screeched to a halt next to me. A scroungy old man with teeth the color of butter and a nose the texture and shape of an avocado flung the passenger door open and eagerly offered me a pull off his peppermint schnapps; shaking it like an enticing treat.

I wondered if he was sent by the devil, then stupidly I grabbed the bottle and inhaled it to the last drop. I told him to fuck off as I smashed it across the inside of his windshield to which he smiled a crooked little smile and then suddenly lunged at me screaming, "You little limp-dick!"

Fast as fast, I pulled my father's knife from behind my belt buckle, snapped the blade into place, and sliced gracefully across the top of his hand which was affixed to the lapel of my jacket.

He shook his scruffy jowls vigorously from side to side and recoiled his grubby paw in pain. With a wild snarl he let the hammer down on the accelerator and peeled off into the sunrise with his rear bumper striking me on the left side of my thigh, catching and ripping my jacket up the back.

In this moment I stood victorious and I found a sense of comfort in the fact that my jacket needed mending. I felt the embrace of my parents fall lightly on my shoulders and then suddenly I began to violently ralph into the gutter as I grew weak in the knees.

Either the bottle hit me all at once or it had been spiked. After fully evacuating the last food that my parents would ever provide me, I found myself crawling along the exterior wall of the precinct like a dripping sludge monster, ultimately collapsing in a heap under a bush with my stomach all twisted and puckered.

My eyelids sealed disobediently as sirens ripped into the distance and I began to hear the broadcaster in my mind proclaim the AM news in that classic old-timey voice as he loudly tapped a superfluous stack of papers on his desk and I slid contemptuously into a dream.

I furiously thrashed my head about attempting to wake myself and as I began to rise the broadcaster broke the fourth wall and seized me from behind. He clamped down hard on my shoulders like vice grips and pulled me speedily down an ever narrowing hole in the earth, until I could descend no further and was completely wedged into a deep, dark grave.

That son-of-a-bitch appeared above me at the

end of the corridor and continued obnoxiously tapping his papers on his desk. Unable to move or free myself, I listened for what must have been at least four hours as he mumbled incomprehensibly.

"Message not received!" I yelled at a passing police officer from under the bush.

"Get moving if you know what's good for you, kid," he commanded as he nervously buttoned his formal shirt cuffs with his freshly shined boots pounding the pavement in the direction of the precinct.

With my young joints free of pops, snaps, and cracks I rose to my feet and fearfully beheld what appeared to be the entire police force swarming toward me like bees to their hive. They were all wearing their Sunday best which they continued to smooth, tuck, and fasten as they came. So, of course I made like a tree and promptly got the fuck out of there.

As I walked aimlessly for hours and miles under bridges, down train tracks, past business districts, in parking garages, through fields and neighborhoods, I took stock of my worldly possessions which now consisted of everything on my person and nothing more.

My knives were safe in their sheaths, my dictionary was warm and cozy in its home, and the hidden interior pocket that I had sewn under the lining of my jacket above the bottom left hem housed my pipe, a small tin made air tight with a thin rubber seal, and my American eagle lighter. My jewelry and accoutrement were affixed, my chains hung heavy, my boots were laced tight, and the sense of my parents returned to me gracefully, making me ask myself, what more could I need?

I descended upon my abandoned grade school like a solitary locust. I headed straight way to the playground, climbed directly to the top of the dome shaped jungle gym that had always frightened me as a youth and thrust my fists in the air, calling out to the empty classrooms with my breath steaming and my voice echoing, "I carry my mother in my dictionary and my father in my knives. A lifetime of friends and acquired family have I affixed to myself with a needle and thread. Each bracelet, chain, and bottle top is a person. They are sacred to me and I carry them in my heart and on my sleeves. I am a walking memory, damn you. We refuse to be erased! We will not be undone!"

I jumped down into the cold, shifting gravel and rolled my ankle a bit, then crawled between the interconnecting knurled bars and collapsed in the dead-center of the dome with my face to the clouds which drifted handsomely behind the geometric pattern of aluminum triangles.

I floated off in thought and climbed up my own spine like a ladder into the tree house of my mind as I set flame to green leaf, self-regulating my psychology and puffing great fluffy clouds of my very own while reliving my brief and tumultuous life.

I reviewed what I knew of our family tree and pondered the effects of my branch being severed. I considered my demise and weighed death against an eventual stasis and inevitable joy. I continued to take stock of what it was that I truly had now that I was but half of the Radezlavs left in the United States and I decided to remain in this world, realizing that adventure and recklessness were far better options than suicide. I also became convinced that Danny's new bias would not allow him to tell Dad's story properly; a story that Dad desperately wanted his children to continue.

We could always see it coming a mile away, Dad's story. He'd get all quiet and take an exceptionally long pull of his deep-red merlot, he'd stare off into the distance smacking his lips a few times and squinting his eyes, and then he'd begin his nearly verbatim recitation.

"In the year of our Lord nineteen-hundred and forty-eight, the Radezlav family and the entire world entered a penultimate phase. Israel had once again become known as a sovereign nation unto itself, marking the last generation to inhabit the earth; my homeland of Czechoslovakia underwent a coup-d'état transfer of power to the Reds prompting my family's migration, and more importantly, it was the year that the Radezlavs became honest to goodness Americans!

"Your grandparents were woodworkers, painters, and artisans. They added fine decorative trim to wealthy walls, painted vast sweeping murals on the ceilings of decadent homes, and built stunning mahogany bar sets for top businessmen and lofty entrepreneurs.

"They became the crust of the artisan community and quickly amassed a fortune built solely of their talents and unparalleled work ethic. They labored long and they labored hard. They scrimped and saved and invested their fortune in an economy free from depression.

"Soon enough they were creating these

masterpieces in a decadent home of their own in the land of their choosing. This home took three generations to build and as they gave it to me, so I give it to you, my cherubs."

From out of nowhere I was rudely ejected from my mind by a big ass, wet loogie plopping square in the middle of my forehead. My eyes focused to find a young, lanky, tall drink of gutter-punk sprawled out across the bars above me with his arms dangling down and his middle fingers extended out toward me.

From head to toe he wore only black and white clothing, zero jewelry, and had plenty of poorly executed black and gray tattoos running down his bare goose pimpled arms. He had a single piercing through the top of the bridge of his nose which made his wide, constantly surprised eyes look even larger. Long, kinky curls of thick black wire-hair protruded from his scalp, bopping back and forth comically as he jutted out his chin with his tongue flicking crudely as if he alone were privy to the greatest music the world would ever know; music that it would never hear.

"What's up, fucker. Let me hit that weed," he called down like an old friend.

I sprang faster than he could react and pulled him hastily through a triangle, making him land on his neck and shoulders to which he laughed manically as he writhed about in the gravel like a bug on its back, working up a mighty cloud of choking dust.

He suddenly stopped, sat up with a look on his face like he had just remembered something important and said, "Early."

"Early for what?" I asked unknowingly enacting an old Abbott and Costello bit.

"No, I'm Early," he said.

"Early for what?!" I shouted.

He thrust his hand out to me saying quite civilly and with a surprising manner of sentience in his immature yet gravelly voice, "Pleasure to meet you. My name is Early."

"I'm Asher," I said as I wiped his spit from my forehead and slapped it roughly across his face.

Early turned and ran toward the triangles then made like a straight arrow and all but materialized on the other side of the dome. He laughed a disconcerting, high-pitched laugh as if in a nervous panic and then he abruptly burst into an all out sprint toward the classrooms yelling back at me as his hair thrashed about wildly, "Come on, man. I want to show you something. It's going to change your life."

Well, since I didn't have much of a life to speak of I guessed that didn't sound half bad, so I followed after Early who had at least a fifty yard lead on me. He waited all nonchalant-like, propped against a wall with his arms crossed like a badass as I met up with him, huffing out great chuffs of hot lung air into the brisk afternoon.

"So, why do they call you Early?" I inquired as I caught my breath with my hands on my knees.

"I guess I'm just ahead of my time," he said confidently while trying his hardest to hold back a proud sneer from his pale and gaunt skull-face.

"That's stupid, man. I mean really, you shouldn't say that anymore. I should be the last person you ever say that to. Seriously."

"Alright, alright," he said as he peeled himself off the chipping, lead painted wall, shaking his hands spastically in front of him like they were on fire.

"My name is Cal Early, are you happy now, geez? Just follow me and try not to suck anymore of the wind out of my sails, will you?"

Early sashayed like a drunken pimp toward a sky-blue, glossy metal door stenciled with the word *Lab*. He produced a rather large keyset from his pocket and to my complete surprise, unsecured the deadbolt and simply entered.

"I got a client who's a locksmith. We did a trade."

"Trade for what?" I asked under my breath wondering what useful skill this premature burnout could possibly possess as we entered an all-out mad-scientist lab and my eyelids swelled in disbelief. The classroom was equipped with full sets of cylinders and beakers, stoppers and tubing, ambient red and green lighting, and even a Jacob's ladder; all running on free, renewable solar energy collected by the panels installed during the green-jobs rush following the collapse.

Gigantic cans of corn and outdated chemistry books were strewn across a crappy old mattress next to a small pile of black and white clothing that lay under an inspirational poster of a sperm whale leaping triumphantly out of arctic waters with the saying *Reach for the Stars* printed above it in a garish spray of glitter and gold.

"The stuff was already here, so I figured hell, why not," said Early as he stared deep into a beaker which began to excite and glow green as he swirled it.

"White phosphorous," he said. "There's really no application for my purposes, but it sure as hell looks cool, don't it?"

"What are you making in here?" I asked.

"A little bit of this, a little bit of that and a whole shit load of LSD; which is what I wanted to show you."

He took me over to a table that was covered with a large sheet of perforated squares that each had a tiny black mushroom stamped on it, which Early found side splittingly ironic. Each square retailed for the ungodly price of just four dollars and was extremely potent.

"You only need one," he said as he meticulously tore off a couple of squares with a pair of tweezers. So, of course I snatched both of them and popped them in my mouth.

Early and I spent the next few days climbing the walls, eating canned corn, and getting up to speed on the tragedies that had befallen each other.

"What happened to your hair?" enacted my story.

"Where are your parents?" enacted his.

He told me how they never loved him and how they constantly said he was a mistake. When he would go to sleep his mom would sit at the edge of his bed with an exposed light bulb hanging in the hall behind her, making her an ominous black silhouette. She would tell him stories of the great adventures that she and his father used to have before he was born and how they all came to a screeching halt when she became pregnant out of wedlock. So they came home, got married, and Dad got a j-o-b.

His last name was supposed to be Lowenberg, but his dad wanted to name him Batman Early as a prank. His dad would break into fits of convulsive laughter as he imagined people asking why he doesn't just go by his middle name and thanks to his father's wonderfully irreverent wit he would be forced to hang his head in shame and answer, "Because, it's Spider-Man."

Luckily for Cal when his father set eyes on his newborn baby boy he was graced with a sense of pity and wrote in the state that he was born in as his first name. Unluckily for Cal his father was resolute that they would not be sharing his surname.

I began to cry lightly as I wondered what it would be like if my father never loved me, then suddenly I felt it well up inside me, growing uncontrollably, and all at once I erupted in a horrible wail as I let loose a tsunami of emotion. I cried for about the next hour and a half as we debated whether it was truly better to have loved and lost than never to have loved at all; each of us being a member of the respective camps.

I told him how Mom died of lymphoma and how we watched her deteriorate in her own bed under the guidance of hospice. I spoke of the utter hopelessness of witnessing her grow ever weaker and the crushing guilt of not being able to save her, until she no longer occupied the same space and was simply gone.

I told him of the factory and how our father shut it down, how Mr. Twig begged him to relinquish operations and how Dad said, "No. It dies with her," as did our relationship with Mr. Twig.

I told him how Danny and I found our father the next year in that same bed and how he had died of a heart attack and quite literally stepped out of his body, because his heart was torn and refused to mend. Stealthily in the night he stole away to become one with his bride, selfishly leaving his sons in the world to fend for themselves.

Suddenly Cal began to feel his emotions as well and he started to cry solemnly to himself from behind a thick wall of coiling raven hair. I scooted up next to him, threw my arm over his shoulder and California Early and I cried together as we lanced our demons, undertaking the treacherous stroll through the darkness that had taken root in our souls, a journey that had illuminated a newly acquired family member and had bound us in camaraderie.

In his honor I affixed a rough draft patch of denim to my jacket with safety pins and sketched a stopwatch on it to commemorate our trip and as a show of thanks for his warmth and hospitality I gave him his first piece of jewelry, a studded bracelet that he immediately stuffed in his pocket.

Then for reasons I am unaware of Early leapt to his feet and screamed, "We got to go!" and from out of nowhere we heard a thundering crash and the walls shook terribly, dislodging years of stagnant, infectious dust.

We bolted outside to see what it was and just as we exited the glossy-blue classroom door, a huge black wrecking-ball came through the walls with wood and glass and canned corn exploding around us. If we had stayed seated for just fourteen seconds longer we would have been pulverized. Instead we were merely sliced, shaken, and impaled with shards and splinters.

"Damn it, my whale poster!" yelled Early as we ran for our lives and paused at the triangle dome with a flood of demolition men pouring after us yelling and beating their chests.

In a panic we turned and hopped the fence behind us, running through a backyard that of course had a huge Pit-bull in it. As I hopped the fence into the neighbors' yard I hastily pulled Early over it with the Pit-bull hanging hilariously from the butt of his jeans, ripping the entire ass off his pants. We laughed hysterically as we made it to the street, down the cul-de-sac, and through the woods that Danny and I had played in nearly everyday as children. Just on the other side of this quarter square-mile of dense scrub pine, oak, and manzanita lay the charred remains of the Radezlav homestead.

Early and I stopped briefly in the center of the woods and fell down next to a giant poison oak bush, heaving and gasping for oxygen. And, just like that Early's life was once again undone, so I felt comfortable sharing with him the torched wreckage of mine.

Every step I took toward the dark, burnt mass that was my home became more painful than the last. As the acid and adrenaline and weed all wore off I said my last goodbyes and we were off to find a more permanent squat. So, we made our way around frozen leaf curves, down through shimmering valleys, and up, up, up the great spiraling hill as the sun went down.

When we arrived at Plague Seven our feet were pummeled, we were completely sober, and Danny was sitting in the dark at the hotel concierge counter that would be the bar, drinking off a lone bottle of vodka. He turned slowly toward us as the buzzing streetlights kicked on with the light pouring through the front door, covering him in a bright-orange wash. Then he looked up at me indignantly from under his brand new cowboy hat that was shading a painful burn that ran up the left side of his face.

He had stripped himself of his jewelry, shaved his head, and sealed himself inside a pair of tight blue Wrangler jeans that were tucked into Dad's old cowboy boots. He didn't speak at first. He just stared into me with his eyes shaking and glowing red, believing that he had been betrayed. Tears streamed down his cheeks and a slow fire in him grew and finally ignited into a furious blaze as he stood and approached us screaming, "Where the fuck have you been, Asher, and who the fuck is that?"

"I'm Early," said Cal as he walked toward him with his hand outstretched.

"Early for what, asshole?" said Danny as he slapped his hand aside. "Beat it, guy. My brother and I have some shit we need to iron out."

Ignoring Danny completely I turned to Early, the only person that had been there for me, the only one in the world who seemed to understand me and said, "Go ahead upstairs, Cal. Go find yourself a room and consider it home. I'll be up in a minute to find you."

Early headed up the psychedelic stairs as Danny

exploded into me in a barrage of anger and saliva and like always I just took it, because he needed the release and I was still strong enough to supply him that. But, something in me changed and time slowed as I heard him say, "You will abide by my rules. I know what's best for you. I am your guardian."

A single, ordinary moth flew directly between us, momentarily redirecting my rage, then suddenly I blew my stack and screamed, "My guardian? My guardian?! I'm *your* angel, bitch!" and I picked up a chair and hucked it through one of the giant bay windows, making the tattered brown velvet curtains whip strikingly in the incoming night wind.

Danny's jaw dropped and he immediately became silent. A few moments passed and he simply turned his back on me and took a long, hard swallow from his bottle. This was the first time that I ever stood up to him and unlike the countless fantasies that I'd had as a child this was real and was absolutely gut-wrenching.

Danny screwed the lid on his bottle then threw it perfectly to me over his shoulder and asked me calmly, "So, are you going to run off with your boyfriend now? Huh, brother-of-mine?"

I happily unscrewed the lid and took a mighty pull. With the vodka burning my throat and running down my chin I replied, "Can we talk about this tomorrow, Dan? I'm pretty tired, you know?"

Danny just walked to the front door, stopped with his back to me and said, "I love you Asher, even if you don't love me."

"That's not fair, Dan!" I shouted as he walked

past window after bay window, until I could no longer see him and could no longer hear Dad's cowboy boots clicking along the cobblestone path.

The next day Danny was nowhere to be found, so Early and I left town on the rails and each year I returned on Danny's birthday to wish him well and see if we could begin to move past this, our mutual animosity. I continued this pattern for five years and on the sixth year Danny asked me to stay. He said he needed help decorating and that he didn't understand color schemes or visual weighting.

"You know, all those faggy things that seem to come so naturally to you," he said.

And, with an apology as eloquent as that, how could I possibly say no? How could I?

Chapter Five

Asher and Me

Asher's limp body lies in the middle of the road as I walk away unsympathetic into the dark and I hear that same small voice whisper, "Help him, Abigail."

"I don't want to help him!" I shout out insolently at the stars while stomping the ground, with my hands balled up in tight little fists.

"Help him now," whispers the small voice gently as always.

I pause briefly then turn and begrudgingly walk back to him, kicking small rocks with my fists shoved in the pockets of my hoody and my hair in my face. I speak harshly to my prince as I straddle over him, take a seat square on his chest and say, "You certainly are one pathetic fool, aren't you?"

I grab him by his long, silky goatee and pull down repeatedly, making his mouth open and close like a mindless goldfish as I mutter out the side of my mouth in a high pitched voice, "Yes I am, Abigail. You sure got my number."

"I bet your poor Mom and Dad would be so proud of you and all the resources that you've squandered. Just look at you, Asher. You were given everything and you've wasted it all, haven't you?"

My prince replies something in his sleep, but the only word I can make out is *bitterness*, so I lean in closer to listen. Just then he belches a giant, disgusting cloud of alcoholic gas right in my face and it fills my nostrils. I jump to my feet and throw up in my mouth a little bit as my privileged prince unknowingly fades back into oblivion with a look of comfort and a faint smile gracing his lips.

I throw my hands in the air and yell, "That's it! I'm out," and then I turn and storm off. Suddenly my vision goes black and a giant, red thirty-four outlined in a thick white stroke flashes in my mind and I come to an abrupt stop. I stand still, silent, and shocked.

I slowly face the stars and fearfully ask, "Really? This is why you had me leave home? For him?" I turn and scan him up and down, and then I sigh a deep cleansing breath and ask, "Him? You got to be kidding me."

A delivery truck barrels down the street and pulls to a grinding stop in front of us. The bright, intense headlights burn into my eyes as I drag Asher's dead weight into the nearest alleyway with his coat tails trailing behind him like some kind of wannabe fallen superhero.

"Everything alright, Ma'am?" the delivery man yells out the passenger side window.

"Yeah, my boyfriend just hit the sauce a little too hard, that's all. Thanks for the concern. Everything's fine," I feign as I wave him on.

"Well, tell your boyfriend that he needs to stop passing out in the middle of the street. That's the second time this month that I could have turned him into a pile of mush," the driver says as he blares his air horn and roars off toward the bar.

I pull Asher roughly into a peculiar mound of rotten old stuffed animals, I crash down next to him with my weight making him press against me tenderly, and I get right in his face and confess, "I felt something for you earlier, Asher, but looking at you right now just ain't doing it for me and I got to tell you, I think I've lost that loving feeling.

"Well, at least you're warm. I guess you can't screw that up."

I snuggle into him and cover myself in his jacket as I stare contemptuously at my chivalrous knight and say, "You know, I want to thank you, Asher. Thank you for the lovely accommodations. Really, I mean it. Thank you for taking me into your gorgeous home."

I tug at his goatee making him say, "You're welcome Abigail, my sweet. Welcome to Muddle Town. Where everyone is your friend and no one lies to you or takes advantage at all."

Why is everyone so out for themselves these days? What ever happened to community? I'm so damn sick of this world and all of the scumbags in it, those greedy sons-of-bitches. Half my shit was stolen on the way here, I was nearly raped in San Francisco, and now I'm lying in a heap of decaying dinosaurs and teddy bears with a psychopathic alcoholic. Look at me, God. Look at where I am. Is this *really* where you want me to be and who you want me with? I'm not questioning you, but am I hearing you correctly? This is Joshua's father?

I look at Asher in near disbelief and say, "I came a long way and went through a lot of shit to get to you, Asher. You better be worth it. And, you better be a good dad. Not like my dad.

"I mean seriously, who lets a seventeen-year-old girl run half way across the country totally unsupervised? He didn't even try to stop me."

And again the tears roll down my cheeks, smearing my make-up this time for sure. I bury my face in his chest, the steam rises from my tears and I sob in that same stupid, weak voice, "Oh God, I'm so lonely. Am I building a fantasy world around a drunken imbecile to mask the pain of my daddy issues? Am I making this all up? Please help me to hear you clearly."

I look up again at Asher and I clearly hear, "It's him," and I see that same red thirty-four superimposed on his forehead.

All the bourgeois Bible-belt kids back home say that I'm crazy or that I'm a false prophet and a fake clairvoyant. But, I know what I've heard and I know what I've seen. Just because they're deaf, blind, and pedestrian doesn't mean that I'm crazy. I'm not crazy.

So, because of what I've seen and because of what I've heard, I pull him in tight and celebrate our future. As I speak into his unresponsive ear of the beauty of our children and the glory of our mission to come he awakens slightly. Still asleep, yet coherent enough to relay a message, he gets a pained look on his face and whispers, "You know you're full on bonkers, right? It's kind of sexy though."

I pull him in tight and use him as my pillow as he blacks back out. I nuzzle in deep for stolen warmth and affection, eventually falling asleep in the protected cocoon of his big, heavy arms and I dream of our wedding day and how gorgeous and festive it will be.

My daddy holds me tight and against his will he slowly lets go and gives me away. In my nervous grip I'm holding the bouquet I've always wanted to make and Asher slips the ring that his father had custom made for his mother on my trembling finger. Then, of course, we have the best after-party ever with tons of live music, a boatload of scrumptious tummy filling delicacies, and all the liquor necessary to keep the dance floor hot.

It felt like an eternity passed and I watched us grow old together. And, now our three kids, an overly mischievous beagle dog, and a slew of grandkids run wild in our house, spilling their drinks and breaking precious antiques. Asher jokingly yells at them from his favorite chair, "It's been really nice seeing you kids. Isn't it about time you all went home?"

My visions slowly break away as I yawn and stretch like a waking cat with the morning sun beating down on my skin. I open my tired eyes and reach out for him, but of course he's gone. I guess the moment had passed, but I was just getting started with that beautiful boy, the future father of my children, that totally inconsiderate asshole.

I throw myself back into the pile of stuffing and sigh heavily, filled with love and spite, feeling tricked again, and fully ready to utilize the violent wellspring of creative energy that is overflowing from my bleeding heart.

So, what will it be then? Maybe a poem about Sheol and Gehenna or a swirling painting done in burnt reds and an unforgiving shade of chocolate or a feverish sketch that wears my charcoals down to a nub.

Or maybe just a few more minutes of sleep? These stuffed animals are actually *really* comfortable. And for once, imagine if you will, I just might be too pooped for the drama.

I watched her like a hawk from the second story window above as she curled into a cute little fetal ball. She dozed back off and a wandering derelict walked by the mouth of my alley home and did a double take on my sleeping beauty. He looked around to see if he was under surveillance, but the coast appeared clear to him, so he licked his crusty lips and advanced.

I fought every paternal instinct inside me as he looked down at her in lust and disgust, but after being power-booted in the chin I figured she could handle herself and I wanted to see what she was made of.

So, I observed in excruciating pain as the derelict touched himself and continued toward her. He reached down, grabbed a lock of her hair to smell and breathed it deep as it were the fragrance of a rose. Just then the dull shimmer of canvas stuffed full of presents caught his eye and a choice emerged. Go for the backpack or go for the girl? The suspense of what lay inside was all too much and he mistakenly turned his back on her as he rummaged through her pack.

Like a boy on Christmas morning his eyes lit up as he pulled a small bottle of rum from one of her inner pockets and he flashed a familiar metallic grin; all the while Abigail was rising and unsheathing her knife from behind. As he stood and turned to view his would-be assassin he lost his grip on the bottle and urine soaked his pant legs as broken glass flew up around his shins. The happy look was lost and fear was found.

Her face with shimmering eyes violently penetrated him as if he were a piece of meat to be carved. She slid her tongue up the blade and to the point and a single drop of blood ran down as she playfully wrapped her tongue around it.

"You like how I smell, mister?" she asked. "You want to be my boyfriend? Because, I just love smelly old men who dream of raping little girls."

He turned to run, but quick as a flash she blocked his path and screamed, "Hold up, now! You ain't going nowhere."

She took brave steps toward him, intrusively entering his personal zone and inching him backward as she brandished her weapon, whipping it carelessly to and fro.

"You know I've been waiting for you, or at least someone like you. Someone to take my anger out on. Someone to hurt. Someone to share my pain with. You look like a nice single boy. What's your name?"

He grew a pair and replied, "Now you better put that down before someone gets hurt."

Before he knew she would strike he had been struck and she slowly lowered her quivering open palm to her side as his eye socket began to throb and swell and she asked him again, "What is your name?"

"Muh, may, my," the derelict stammered, defensively covering his now blood filled eye with both hands.

"Muh? That's a nice name, Muh. Pretty little name. I like you, Muh. Do you want to know why?"

"Yuh, yea, yes. Yes, I do," he said.

"Good, because I was going to tell you anyway. I like you because you are a man and for some odd reason men don't like me. They get close to me.

They touch me. They tell me that they love me and then they leave me. They all raise my hopes only to smash my dreams. They just-don't-like me."

She closed the last few inches of distance between them and got right in his face. She held the knife to his throat and whispered in his ear seductively in a low breathy way, alluring him into a false sense of sexual engagement, "But you like me don't you?"

"Yes Ma'am, yes Ma'am, I do. Very much so, I do. I didn't mean any disrespect."

"Oh, but you did. You did mean me disrespect and you meant me harm as well. But, it's okay, Muh. Because, every act has its price and everyday we learn a lesson." Then suddenly she sank her teeth into the top of his ear, ripping and tearing at it like a jackal thrown a steak.

I yelled out, "Holy shit, Abigail, what are you doing?!" and the derelict wriggled in pain as she ripped his ear half off. In the commotion he swatted the blade from her hand and all motion slowed as I heard the knife clanking loudly on the soiled asphalt. He drove his fist deep and hard into her stomach and she doubled over for him.

Just then she looked up at me, directly at me, and she flexed and screamed and launched back into him.

"Just say the word, Abigail," I whispered as I looked on in horror, still believing she would be able to recover and rectify the situation.

They struggled and wrestled and scampered about, both scraping feverishly at the ground, trying desperately for the knife, but he was the victor. He firmly grasped the hand-carved wooden handle and slashed violently at her breasts once, drawing two thin slits and a perfect red line across the top of her hoody which was still connected in the middle by the zipper.

She stood amazed and confused as he screamed through a thick foamy mucous that had developed around his mouth and collected in his beard, "You bloody little whore! You are so dead! I'm going to whoop you like, well I don't know what, but it's going to hurt a lot and you'd better believe you won't be forgetting the likes of me anytime soon.

"But, before I make you bleed were going to have some fun, you and me. You're going to see what a real man does to his meat and I ain't going to need no knife!"

The derelict, that sewer dweller, licked the blood off her blade, threw it over the wall to his left, and then he slunk up and enveloped her with the top half of his ear spurting. And, that was when I started to get a little uneasy, wondering if she had what it would take to prevail.

She struggled greatly with the derelict in a one on one competition, unable to land any substantial blows. He dropped back momentarily and when she rushed in to attack, he saw his opportunity. He swooped under her like a great diving vulture, lifting her off the ground and smashing her head into the wall behind her, knocking her unconscious. He undid his belt, exposed his desecrated genitals to her, and closed in clambering to defile my gorgeous flower in that most heinous, soul squelching act. The darkness of his shadow consumed her and I lost sight of my Red Queen. At that moment I became someone new, someone much darker.

My shaky hand and Dad's wristwatch came into my own view as if I were disconnected from my body and not the one raising my arm. I was bombarded by wave after wave of assaulting déjà vu, Dad's watch read seven-fourteen AM, and a glimmer shot off the face of it, constricting my pupils and directing my attention back to the derelict. All at once, I knew what I had to do, as if I had done it a hundred times before.

I could have opened the window if I had been thinking clearly. Instead I woke my knives from their slumber and turned them upside down with the blades held flat against the suicide veins in my wrists. I cleared a runway and jump-kicked through the thin glass pane, floating ever so lightly to earth with a host of shards falling with me and the morning sun illuminating them brilliantly as they spun down in a shimmering hail, making that filthy fuck piss himself once again as I stuck the landing.

"I bet you wish you hadn't thrown that knife now, huh?" I inquired of my enemy with my eyes heavily bloodshot, my body charged and buzzing electrically with my hair standing straight on end and my blades twirling playfully in between my fingers. The derelict stumbled backward and fell square on his naked ass next to the knocked out Abigail and I advanced as my blades came to a halt with my fingers tensed around their handles and my knuckles white as snow.

The sun grew brighter as I approached and I heard a rumbling grow from deep inside my bowels. It rose slowly as the derelict shook in terror, awaiting the righteous retribution that would befall him. It was the sound of rage, the oration of fury, my human roar. Without my permission it burst forth from my diaphragm and out my mouth in a terrific sonic flood. I was a mighty lion protecting its future, I was a wild animal marking his territory, I was the embodiment of justice and at that exact moment I became the executioner.

I slid forward as if my feet were affixed to free-rolling casters. The deviant derelict feebly raised his hands in defense and I crossed my blades in an *X* and simultaneously lacerated both his palms to the bones.

I heard the screams that Abigail deserved to hear and I crouched in front of him and explained, "See now, you are an antichrist. You are the evil in this world, chum, and now it is my distinct pleasure to dispatch you to our Lord."

A simple, "No!" he screamed as I pounced on him and pried his gushing hands away from my pulsating target. He slipped and slapped at me like a weak little sister, but I eventually got what I needed.

I slit his throat.

It was awful. The pain in his eyes, the spray and the gurgle, his final wind releasing from his lungs and escaping from where it ought not, were all necessary atrocities. The terrifying details scraped and cemented in my mind, clawing into the same folder that housed my memory of Danny and the potato shaped rock. So, I dragged him across the street as he bled out and faded from this world, this heartbreaking world.

I unclipped my keys from my chains and

unsecured the padlock on the side door leading into one of our abandoned storehouses. I entered and pulled him inside, along the frigid concrete floor, and I shoved him into one of those crates that had been filled with extraneous bright-white men's briefs.

It was amazing, the absorption. Like a thick red pen pressed heavy against a thirsty slice of paper, the underwear appeared to drink him in, until he simply was no more and they were dyed crimson.

I will not pretend that I was unaffected or that I was proud of myself or that I felt nothing, but I was confident in my decision and as the adrenaline cleared from my veins I nailed him inside that crate, but not before making absolutely sure he was dead. I may have supposed myself a dispatcher, but cruelty does not reside within me.

Thick black ominous clouds hurried and pushed in off the coast, covering the entire valley, and they poured and poured and poured, washing away the blood and the pain as if mine architect had sanctioned the act.

I secured the storehouse and ran back to her as she lay unconscious. I slouched down next to her and sat her up against the red brick wall with the torrential rain soaking and cleansing us both. As quickly as they came, the clouds parted and the day shone bright with a symphony of chirping blue jays and the rustling of gray treetop squirrels filling the air as if I had never left her side.

I sprang to my feet with a pop in my step and I climbed over the east wall of my alley home. I jumped down into the fresh mud and collected her knife which stuck perfectly upright into the body of a fallen tree. As if I were withdrawing Excalibur, I twisted and wrenched it from the log and held it high in the air with the sun glinting and gleaming off its blade as I looked out over the vast fields and plains of tall amber weeds. I climbed back to her, sheathed her knife on her thigh, put her pack on my back and I scooped her up like a good little bridegroom.

I carried her to the factory and stripped her of her sopping wet clothing and hung them on a line, then I gently dried her off and inspected her for damage. There was nothing too major; just some abrasions, some swelling, and that unfortunate slice across the top of her chest. Thankfully it wasn't too deep. It would be the emotional injury that would be the worst and take the longest to heal.

I cleaned her chest wound with an antimicrobial solution and taped it shut with medical adhesive strips which I kept on hand due to my excessive altercations. I rushed to a stack of boxes and knocked them over. Pulling out bag after bag of brand new plush toys, I constructed her one of my make shift beds. She whimpered a bit as I laid her down and I whispered in her bruised ear, "I just want you to know that I heard everything you said, Abigail. I think you're tops and I'm not going to leave you again. I'll keep you safe."

Other than the occasional shower I did not take my jacket off and Lord knows I would never have let another wear it, but for her love I would've burned it if necessary. So, I whipped it off my shoulders like a matador and draped it over her gorgeous, shivering body. I paced back and forth, filled with stress and anxiety as I watched over her and before I knew it the sun had gone down and the moon had come up. It poured soft light in through the solitary window and flowed over her beautiful young face in a low, diffused glow as she slept and shivered. And, even though my jacket didn't have sleeves, having had only myself to consider, I'd never noticed just how cold it was in the factory.

ꜩ

I feel my face scrunch tight and I wake up screaming, "No, no, no!" It's pitch black except for right under this window and I can't see a damn thing. Adjust eyes, adjust damn you! Where the hell am I? Oh God, I'm in my bra and panties. That pervert has me in some dungeon or something, I just know it! My mind begins to race and confusion turns to panic. I scatter myself back against the wall like a cornered animal and I search the room for him. My eyes stop on the darkest part of the dark-black room and I can barely make out his outline, but I see him there. Oh shit, I see him there.

He's sitting hunched over with his golden eyes glowing and his sharp, jagged teeth chattering in excitement. He's getting up and coming for me, what do I do? What do I do?

For the first time in my adult life I stupidly back down and bury my face in my hands as he approaches. I curl into a ball and I scream bloody murder, flailing my arms in a feeble attempt to stop my assailant's onslaught. He runs to me and grabs me firmly by my shoulders saying, "It's me, Abigail. It's only me."

"Asher?" I ask in a disoriented voice, feeling small and traumatized. Wait a minute, his jacket is over me and I'm sitting in a pile of stuffed animals. Are those my clothes on the line?

"You're okay, Abigail. Everything's okay."

I look up at him with tears in my eyes, huffing and puffing. I throw myself into his arms and I sob a harder sob than ever before as he strokes my hair and kisses my forehead.

"Just let it out. I'm here. No one can touch you now. I took care of it. He's never going to touch you again," he says in empathy with an undertone of menacing vindication.

"What do you mean you took care of it? What did you do to him?" I ask fearfully.

He backs up a little and gets a guilty look on his face. "Nothing," he says. "I just took care of it, that's all. He ran off before I could do anything."

"I don't believe you," I say coming to the realization that I'm locked in a warehouse, next to naked in the dark with a more than capable young male who had recently proven himself untrustworthy. I spy his knife tucked away behind his belt buckle and I snatch it, hastily flicking the blade open with one hand and turning it against him.

"What are you doing?" he asks seemingly disaffected.

I reply, "You killed him, didn't you?" with the blade shaking wildly in front me.

"No I didn't. I already told you that. He ran off."

I begin to shout, coming thoroughly unglued, "I don't believe you! I don't know what to think, I don't know what to say, I don't know what to do and most of all I don't know you! I can't trust you. I can't trust anyone."

I start to break down again and Asher comes in to console me, but he gets too close too fast and I instinctively shove the tip of his knife firmly into the crotch of his worn out, black jeans and stare deep in his eyes, meaning nothing but business.

He relaxes his posture, slows and lowers his voice and very convincingly says, "Look, I'm sorry I left you. I honestly am. It will never happen again, okay?"

I scream at him, "Liar! You stop talking, liar! You don't get to talk. Let's review the situation here. You leave me, I almost get raped, you kill him, and everything is just ducky now? Well fuck you! Everything is not ducky. Everything is all fucked up and it's all your fault!

"Did you leave me because of what crawls around in your brain in the middle of the night or because of the evil that you call upon yourself and your parents' property or is it because you can't make it through the night without a drink? How do I know you wouldn't just kill *me*?"

The anger visibly swells in him and his eyes lower. Magnetically the blade appears in his hand and he turns with precision and power and throws it about thirty feet behind him. It makes an audible whipping sound as it spins through the air, ultimately sticking and vibrating in the face of a gigantic wooden clown head that hangs from the rafters. He turns to me and says with conviction, "Trust me. If I wanted to kill you, you would already be dead."

I retort, "You can't just kill someone and not

expect to pay for it, Asher. That was someone's son, maybe someone's brother or father."

Asher yells back, "I don't pay for it? I don't pay for it?! I pay for it every night of my life by way of a bone locking seizure, a soul crushing night terror, or how about a week long debilitating bout with insomnia?

"Besides, after what he did to you I would think you would want him dead. But, instead you probably want him to have access to free psychological care, room and board in a facility far nicer than *your* abode, and emergency medical treatment whenever he gets a case of the sniffles. You people are completely cracked! You got it all wrong you precious little social-worker, you. Sewage like that deserves to be killed and if I have to do it, I will. Gladly! Besides, like I already told you, he-ran-off!"

He abruptly stops talking and turns and walks into the partial darkness with his chains jingling like a box of screws. I watch him climb up onto the roof of a forklift and squat down on all fours like a cement gargoyle perched high on a ledge, surveying his dominion; or a sulking little baby boy with a bruised ego. You take your pick.

I genuinely ask him, "What makes you think that life or death is your decision? You could have subdued him and called the cops or maybe just beaten him up. It's not up to you to decide who should live or die."

He replies, "Well evidently it is up to me, because I assassinated his crusty ass with a cold-hearted vengeance. Is that what you want me to say?"

I slant my eyes, cock my head to the side a bit, and I answer with a question, "Was it fun for you? Did you enjoy it? And, you say *I'm* cracked. How do you enjoy something like that?"

"French-fried, mother-fucker. French-fried," he says as if he's the coolest thing to walk the earth since Miles Davis.

I stand enticingly in the moonlight in my undies to make myself feel less intimidated and more authoritative; playing the same card that got me kicked out of my dad's house time and time again. I stick my boobs out, raise my nose in the air, and I gather my strength and goad him in asking, "You're so damn clever aren't you?"

"Hells yes, I am. Thanks for noticing." He jumps down off his perch, walks right up to me threateningly, and without hesitation continues on to his window where he stares out at the stars, making me sink back into myself and die a little more. So, I just stand there crumbling like a dismissed, naive child and a few quiet minutes pass before he launches back into me.

"And, what were you going to do, Miss Morals? Why do you care what happens to someone that doesn't care what happens to you?"

"I don't know. I just do," I reply as I lower my eyes and my voice.

He steps into me with his speech growing in his stomach and says, "So, basically your plan was to get raped. You were just going to let him tear away at you and dent your soul? Let him rip away with his grimy old-man paws shredding at your breasts? Or are you going to cut that sicky fuck and take his life from him?"

"No. I would have... I mean, I was going to..."

"Fuck yes! You were going to pick up that knife and slash away, slash away. No rest for the wicked, dear girly. They must die!"

And now, silence. Dead silence. If looks could set men ablaze he would be burning. I push off against him and slam myself into the wall behind me. I slip through my plush stuffed animal bed and hit the floor full flesh. I strain my throat in a coarse howling as I tear at my chest wound while disturbingly rocking back and forth. Asher drops to me and holds me from myself with blood and tears melding into one and rolling down my chest and stomach as I desperately mumble into his ear, "Why did you say that? I can't take this all at once, damn it. It's too heavy."

"I said it because it's the truth, Abigail. Because, it's what I would have done. And, if God will hate a man for protecting his wife then let him hate me."

"Your wife?" I ask.

I lunge into him and kiss him full and strong on the lips in my unspoken thanksgiving, but he stops me and whispers, "Go back to sleep, Abigail. You've had a lot to deal with today. I'll be here when you wake up, okay? I promise. We've got nothing but time.

"And by the way, I really didn't touch that guy. He ran off before I could get to him and I didn't want to leave you again. Lord only knows what I would have done if I had caught him."

And with that, he lies me down and he lies down with me in the heaping pile of stuffed animals. He pulls me in tight, this time of his own free will, and I choose to believe him against my better judgment.

I sigh as I lay my battered head on his hot inviting shoulder and I shut my eyes, immediately falling back to sleep and dreaming not of fear and hostility, but of love, of progeny, and of the beauty that is soon to come.

Chapter Six

BA Toys, Inc.

Hammer strikes reverberated heavily within the factory walls as construction workers pounded long sharp nails through two-by-fours, connecting new frames to the existing structure with the western wall torn out, exposing my horrified eyes to the terrific amber plains behind. Electricians scurried about and mingled with contractors who poured over enormous blueprints and as I looked down on the puffy mounds of sawdust I realized, no one ever notices when you vacuum.

All they see is the floor. They don't recognize that it is clean or that it took a concerted effort, nor will they necessarily consider the positive, calming effects that a pristine floor has on their mental state. But, they sure do notice when you *haven't* vacuumed. "Look at this filthy floor," they'll say. "What a terrible and disturbing effect this is having on my poor, fragile psyche."

And, that is my relationship with Abigail. All the blame for the things I do wrong and none of the recognition of the things I do right.

"It's not about money, Asher!" she shouted snapping me out of my deep, transfixed gaze. "You know, for someone so disenchanted with the monetary system you sure have been dwelling on the subject lately."

"That's really easy for you to say, Abigail. You didn't have to work for that money, my parents did. It's not yours to spend how ever you damn well please. I mean shit, look at this! How much is this going to cost?"

She answered my question with a question,

completely ignoring my inquiry as usual. "Why did you even give me access to your accounts then? So far it's caused nothing but strife between us."

I paced back and forth in front of her, looking at the ground and saying, "For the bare essentials of life, that's why. Not for the purpose of buying out Pier 1. I guess I stupidly expected you to be like me, but you're not. You like *stuff*, while I find possessions to be a burden and a clutter of the mind; a veritable mind killer."

She splintered her attention as she flipped through endless swatch books and caressed countless bolts of fabric saying over her shoulder, "I like stuff? Damn it, Asher. I'm investing your parents' money in our future and their namesake by building us a home where I can raise their grandchildren while motivating you to get their business back up and running and all you have to say is I like stuff?"

"You're not building us a home. You're building *you* a home," I said under my breath with a smart ass smirk on my face.

Her selective hearing kicked in, our eyes locked and she went off on me yelling, "I heard that you freaking ingrate! Can you try to think of this process like I do please, as an investment? It's like my dad always says, 'Every sound investment meets a proper return,' and if you can find it in your heart to trust me, not only will I replace your parents' money in the very same account that you find to be such a monumental burden, but I'll double it and even triple it. I guarantee you.

"And, if you still think I'm just some crackpot bimbo or another adorable fly-by-night plaything to placate then look out mister, because here comes Mama. I'm ordained by God himself, buster, you'll see.

"You know what, let me ask you something. At what point exactly did you stop believing in yourself and your skills? I asked you to take a leap of faith by giving me access to the funds that you've totally neglected, so I can build something for you, for us, and you agreed to do just that. And, now I'm going to ask you to do one more thing for me. Go get your pretty little ass back in that studio and draw me some more monsters so I have something to sell, damn it, and I mean like now! Go!"

"Yes, my liege. Your will is my command, my magnanimous queen," I said as I backed into Dad's office continually bowing at the waist until I slammed the door in front of me, locked it, shut the blinds on all the windows and peeked through the aluminum slats with my middle finger pressed against the glass and my smitten heart all in a frenzy.

I flopped down in Dad's maroon leather office chair and lit up, blowing billowing plumes of smoke into the same space where I'd have been backhanded if Dad had caught me as a youth, and I slipped off into my mind.

Even though I had previously planned a night of whiskey fueled debauchery, the Sock Hop at Zinnia was actually a blast. It was just a few months after that whole unsightly derelict incident and Abigail and I had become inseparable. She moved into the factory with me and immediately my makeshift beds turned into a dark-cherry sleigh, the nighttime chill became a grip of central heating and air vents, and the void of empty cupboards in the break-room overflowed with fine teas, nuts, hearty breads, dried fruits, and other assorted shits that just didn't interest me. But, she loved them and that was enough.

We made a belated visit to my local bank and were nervously greeted in the humid vestibule by an elderly branch manager who tripped and fell over his words. I assumed he feared that Abigail and I were there to stick the joint up, but it quickly became apparent that he was genuinely nervous to be in my presence, as if I were his favorite star.

"How about a cappuccino for you and the lovely lady, Mr. Radezlav?" he asked through borderline inappropriate, anxious laughter as he shook my hand vigorously.

"Yes please," said Abigail who hopped giddily and wrung her hands in anticipation.

I replied, "Can't say that I drink the stuff, Sir. It makes me sleepy. And, might I ask how in the world you knew my name?"

"You're joking, right?" he asked. "Follow me, my boy. It has been quite some time."

As he parted the large, glass double doors and we entered the bank our eyes were deluged in a host of BA Toys memorabilia. Framed photos of the manager with me and my family hung on central pillars, life-sized promotional cutouts were at every desk, and I ran to a wall that was lined with lighted curios that housed every toy we had ever made and they were all in mint condition.

Of course I teared up a little as the manager showed us around while narrating, "At one point the entire economy of this town was held in the palm of your father's hand. From the factory workers to the delivery men to the bank employees; we all hinged on his decisions. He was a great man and a very close personal friend of mine."

He too began to get misty-eyed as he continued, "You know, you're his spitting image, son."

"Oh, please don't say that, sir. He was a beefy man."

"Well, you are. You have his way about you. Your Dad continually bragged about his boys in the off times that you weren't attached to his hip and while I would never tell this to Daniel, your father always knew that it would be you who would continue his legacy and now that you're here to take up his mantle we expect great things from you, Asher."

I quickly interjected, "I'm sorry, I think you may have gotten the wrong impression about my visit here today."

As if he heard nothing he seized my shoulders with my spikes poking out from between his fingers, then he looked deep into my eyes and attempted to plant a seed in my mind saying, "I see Daniel a few times a month and while you certainly won't be winning any games of hide and seek dressed like this, I can't say that I've seen you even once since you were that little boy building Lego castles on my office floor. My conscience simply won't let you go until you've been back in that office and familiarized with your accounts so you can get this town back to work."

"Wow, that's a heavy burden! I'm sorry, sir, but no thank you. Just a simple addition to my accounts will do," I said shaking my head and waving my hands in front of me.

Out of a sense of duty to my elder we indeed did sit down in his office and we talked intently for hours about my father and not so intently about the mind-numbing minutia of financial capabilities that lay desperately at my fingertips.

Abigail listened quietly and supportively during the family portions of the conversation, but when it came to fiduciary matters her ears shot up like a coyote and she could not get the questions out fast enough. Maybe it was the coffee, but she became a whole other person and was completely alive. She reminded me of my mother, that captain of industry.

At the time her fervor and unabashed interest squelched any doubt that I had about her intentions and I authorized her full access to my accounts. The manager scanned her fingerprints, I signed my life away and with every signature I became more worried, more wary, and ultimately remorseful and ill in the stomach.

We parted company with the manager and for the next few days Abigail shopped online and swiped her fingerprint. She shopped in-store and swiped, and ordered services and swiped, and managed deliveries and swiped. She was very passionate about it and she did appear to have a genuine vision, I'll give her that. Danny however was none too pleased about my decision and especially the alterations to the last bastion of the memory of our parents, the factory.

I awoke from my fog in Dad's leather chair and I drew a stick figure with boobs and an arrow pointing to it that said *The Boss*. I went out and stealthily taped it to Abigail's back who immediately reached over her shoulder and ripped it off shouting, "Hey!" as I jumped down through bay-one and ran off to the bar to meet Danny.

Don Julio and Danny and I had a pow-wow that night and I spilled the beans to him saying, "This is my future wife, Dan. It's not like she's just some random chick that I met at the bar and handed the keys to, you know?"

Danny's jaw dropped and he incredulously replied, "Are you freaking serious, Ash? That's not only what it's like, that's exactly what it is! Have you even considered the gold-digger aspect? In ten years you've barely touched your money and the same day you give this girl the reigns she drops like fifty *G's* on a bunch of fruity-ass pillows and foofy curtains and a slew of out of work chuckle head contractors that I see drowning their sorrows every night at The Horse Shoe."

"Oh, you mean Plague One?" I asked.

"The Horse Shoe," said Danny.

"Plague One and she's not a gold-digger, stupid. She has a plan."

Danny threw back another shot and said loud as shit, "Oh, she's got a plan alright. Phase-two of Abigail's big plan? Get pregnant. Then you'll really be waist deep in the big muddy."

"His name is going to be Joshua," I said as I dropped my full shot on the bar and got up to leave.

"What did you just say to me?" Danny asked in anger.

I pulled his hat off, kissed him on the faint burn scar that ran up to his temple and replied, "Don't worry, Dan. I know what I'm doing." I staggered to

the front door and turned and very softly and
sloppily finished in saying, "By the way, I'm not
listening to your advice anymore. It's often wrong
and usually has some sort of self-serving black
lining to it. So guess what, I'm going back to the
factory to officially ask her to marry me and there
ain't a damn thing that you can do to stop me."
Then suddenly everything went black.

꒰ꓕ

I woke up hours later on one of Danny's many
disgusting couches with a pounding headache and
the words *obligation* and *artifact* looping in my
brain. As per usual in situations such as this I
pulled out my dictionary and attempted to look
them up, but I was having trouble reading, so I
stood and walked out alone into the great night
light of the full cheddar moon with one of our many
local metal bands grinding brutally behind me at
Plague Six.

Leather clad meatball, head-bangers milled
about on the street, chain smoking never ending
cigarettes and snorting copious lines of life
derailing twack out of their vintage T-top Camaros
and I wondered, why hasn't Security noticed any of
these savory details. As I walked through them they
seemed to congregate toward me while growing
strangely darker. They closed in like the ever
starving undead and I inquired of them, "How is it
that I became this monster? I haven't always been
the scum of the earth. I used to be a good kid."

I looked down one of our alleyways and thought
I saw a woman breastfeeding her baby next to a

dumpster as the head-bangers crowded in and began to vibrate, creakingly stumbling forth as if infected with some sort of motor inhibiting neurological disease.

I was instilled with a heavy sense of impending doom and I lifted my chin to the moon and cried aloud, "Mom always used to say I was her good little baby boy. If she could have had ten babies just like me she would have, but if she had to deal with ten of me as a youth she would've snapped."

Far off at the end of the block a hairy, lumpy image fell from the sky and crashed through the roof of the defunct corner market. The ground quaked increasingly as it emerged from the side door and it sat down in the middle of the road, spilling out over itself like a morbidly obese dog.

"Does anyone else see that?" I asked, but suddenly I was alone in the stark, dead silence.

The monstrous heap sat heaving and morphing nebulously in the dark. All I could make out were a pair of glowing golden eyes and a set of wet hog nostrils spewing mighty clouds of thick, green sulfur.

Suddenly, the demonic heap took form and it shot off toward me as it were a lion after its prey. Instinctively I turned to run and I did not look back. I ran as fast as my legs would go, but I was too late and too slow. The Heap climbed creepily out of the deep, dark shadows ahead and without warning it leapt forth and shattered the asphalt beneath my feet as it stood with me, face-to-face.

The creature smacked its spongy lips revealing a mouthful of steaming, putrid, decaying fangs. "Do I know you?" dripped the creature's words from its forked tongue as it slowly morphed and became my image. And there I stood, face-to-face with myself.

"Do I make you feel sexy?" it chortled as it became the form of Abigail. "Or maybe this is more your bag," it said as it turned into Jerrod.

I stood petrified as lightning severed the atmosphere over the violet mountain tops in the far off distance, making the image of Jerrod cower and shutter at the light. Thunder crashed like a mighty rack of cymbals and it writhed in pain as it clawed at its ears and snapped back to its original form. It hastily backed me into my alley home where Abigail was again sleeping and I stood boldly in front of her in a protective stance.

The lightning rippled through the air and struck my arms, leaving them singed and blackened with an ancient, curvaceous sword whipping serpentine in my grasp like a living organism eager to fulfill its purpose. As the torn sky collided in an enormous rolling cacophony of thunder I turned to witness a hoard of girded angels. They descended on heavy steeds of war out of a glistening heavenly window with their terrifying voices raised high and their swords drawn and illuminated like giant crystals refracting the sun.

My facial muscles grew tight and my expression evolved from fear and helplessness to courage and conviction. With all my might I plunged the whipping sword into the stomach of the demon as the thunder rescinded and my heavenly window faded from my eyes. The disgusting heap hit the wall and exploded into a flood of candy bar wrappers, banana peels and other rotten garbage that fell lifeless at my feet. I was ejected from my mind like a spent round of ammunition and I awoke from my visitation a delirious and broken down wreck in our bed, held tightly in Abigail's arms.

I brushed my hands down along my sides and I soaked in the soothing experience of fine silk. I looked around our finished bedroom and I saw that Abigail had effectively merged our styles, the old and the new, our collective art and music swag and everything else in between. There were large area rugs atop the stained and polished concrete, two walk-in closets, a razor thin television surrounded by plenty of verdant plants, matching easels, her bug filled aquariums, and multiple stacks of amplifiers next to an old reel to reel tape recorder and a vintage Ludwig drum kit. I actually felt like I was home.

With a mass of nighttime crickets calling out messages of love to her just outside our window I looked into her watery eyes which glinted in the moonlight and she whispered with fear in her voice, "You wouldn't wake up. You just kept thrashing and thrashing and I didn't know what to do, so I just held you." She shivered a little and sheepishly confessed, "I honestly and truly love you, Asher. I want you to know beyond a shadow of a doubt that you are not, nor have you ever been, a meal ticket. You're my man and I'm your girl. Who else is going to put up with your bullshit? I mean, really? So I like *stuff*, get over it already."

I stopped her while I was ahead and abruptly burst into her, kissing her passionately as I caressed her soft, blessed body from head to hips. For the first time our matter merged as one and we collided terrifically like crashing automobiles and repelled repeatedly like polar magnets. She pulled me in tight and we stayed tied in each other all night long and did not let go until the sun rose the next day.

She covered her naked body with my jacket as I exited our cherry sleigh and with the sunrise pouring through our big open window she asked, "Where are you going, Ash?"

As naturally as I could muster I replied, "To work, Abby. I'm going to work."

I put on my underwear and as I approached the hanging wooden clown head in the production room I was struck by a memory. I suddenly realized why The Heap had asked if he knew me. It was a clue. When I was seven-years-old it had visited me in my waking life and tried to talk me into building that clown head a body, so it could inhabit it and we could play. It was then that I realized The Heap was an appointed demon; the photo negative of my guardian angel. So, I ripped that fucking atrocity off its chains and ran it through a band-saw until it became a pile of drum sticks.

I didn't sleep after that for about a week and I struggled terribly with a bout of sobriety as I feverishly drew out our entire first line run of toys complete with production specs, package script, and graphic design. The saying "go with what you know" rang in my head and I wrote out a list of contemporaries from my life.

The Faceless V2 was my leading man, an idealized version of the demon-slayer inside; Wormwood the Fallen was his nemesis and leader of the heaven realm rebellion, followed by an unruly sorcerer named Nevada Lately, a vigilante rock star named Jacob Branch, and a tomahawk wielding punk rock heroine by the name of Sydney Chopper. Each character was drawn with a mini-zine, weaponry, alternate battle versions, and a host of ancillary sidekicks and minions.

After I submitted my material to the boss-lady the process snowballed and I was free and clear of any further responsibility. Abigail rode the construction crew into the wild blue yonder and under her supervision they surprisingly met both their budget and schedule. To be quite honest I think they wanted to get the hell away from the boss' fearsome whip-crack.

Abigail held a few open interview sessions and the line ran down the block. From the factory to the bar, people of all walks and types stood hopeful, brimming with desperate enthusiasm and rejuvenated by the prospect. We collected countless resumes, chose the best and brightest and immediately got to work pouring and pressing and packaging. Abigail took me on a wild ride for the next few months and it took everything I had just to keep up with her. Her combination of youthful electricity and precocious application proved to be an asset that I was sure did not exist in another her age, or maybe not at all.

Evidently the factory became self-sufficient far too quickly for Abigail's liking and the high of supervision had worn off all too soon, so she thought it a swell idea to organize a gala affair to commemorate the grand re-opening of the illustrious BA Toys, Inc.

As if she were some sort of inter-dimensional

being I held onto her tightly as time flew by my head. I spun nauseatingly and the next thing I knew hors d'oeuvres and champagne were at the ready, the wait staff was there in triplicate, and Abigail had surprised me by contacting Jerrod's manager who said that Jerrod had been eagerly awaiting an invitation and that we could count on The Cylinders to turn the place upside down.

I stood mortified outside the bar as the sun went down and my heart thumped in my chest like a small woodland creature that was trying to escape a hole too tight. I stared down a tunnel as a disapproving Danny sidled up on my right and threw his arm around me, an absolutely beaming Abigail clung proudly to my left arm, and the local news arrived with multiple senior bank executives and the entire cast of Eighth Plague players, including my most beloved tenant, California Early, who took it upon himself to sneak up behind me and drop a single liquid dose on my scalp.

"What the hell? No, no, no, bad idea!" I yelled and distractedly pushed him back and slapped at my head like Curly Howard as the posh tour busses arrived through the parting crowd.

"Oops, sorry man. Too late now, I guess," he said as he guiltily scrunched his shoulders up to his ears with his palms face up and his afro bopping about.

We made our way to the backstage lounge where we met with Jerrod and as word spread, both the crowd and my anxiety grew to a fever pitch. The acid came on strong and the immense pressure I was under imploded in booze and exploded in throw-up as I collapsed on the floor of the conversation pit.

"Still rocking that same vibe, hey bro?" asked Jerrod as he handed me a towel and wrapped me up in a manly embrace.

"I missed you, Jerrod," I said as the shag carpet grew up around me and caressed my flushed cheeks lovingly.

The media had an absolute field day as The Cylinders took to the stage. They threw out boxes of signed Jacob Branch figures to the overflowing audience and of course I absolutely had to take off all my clothes and run around backstage like a lunatic. It was only a matter of time before the camera crew caught wind of my finest hour and documented it so the whole world could behold my ridiculous majesty.

Abigail tried desperately to claw me away from my inevitable spotlight, but at that moment I was absolutely positive that mankind was meant to live in the nude and I was destined to lead the way. So, I threw on my jacket and hit the stage as the crowd burst into great rolling waves of applause and uproarious laughter with the band churning out visible notes of sonic destruction behind me.

Seeing the camera crew walk up stage-right stairs, Abigail decided that there was only one way to stop me; she had to drop the bomb. She rushed up next to me and yelled something into my ear, but I couldn't hear what she was saying, so she grabbed a microphone and yelled matter of fact over the top of the music, "Asher, I'm pregnant!"

My feet turned to concrete and I stood cemented in my steps as a slow hush fell over the crowd and the music died off. All of a sudden, the place erupted into a raucous cheer, immature catcalls, and many heartfelt congratulations as the band tore back in like a motorcycle ripping down a dirt road.

Danny just stood there in the shadows off stage, shaking his head at me with a shit eating grin on his face and his arms crossed as I bumbled over to the camera with my wedding tackle flapping in the breeze. I grabbed the cameraman and smeared my face across his lens, screaming, "Did you hear that? I'm going to be a daddy!"

In a matter of minutes that son-of-a-bitching footage went viral and instead of this great society segregating its masses from the threat of obscenity, it bestowed upon me an instant cult status and the orders came flooding in. I had effectively put the entire city back to work and secured my name in particular as the biggest boob in Muddle's history, and all it took was an amazing little girl from Arkansas and my family jewels banging around on the internet.

Chapter Seven

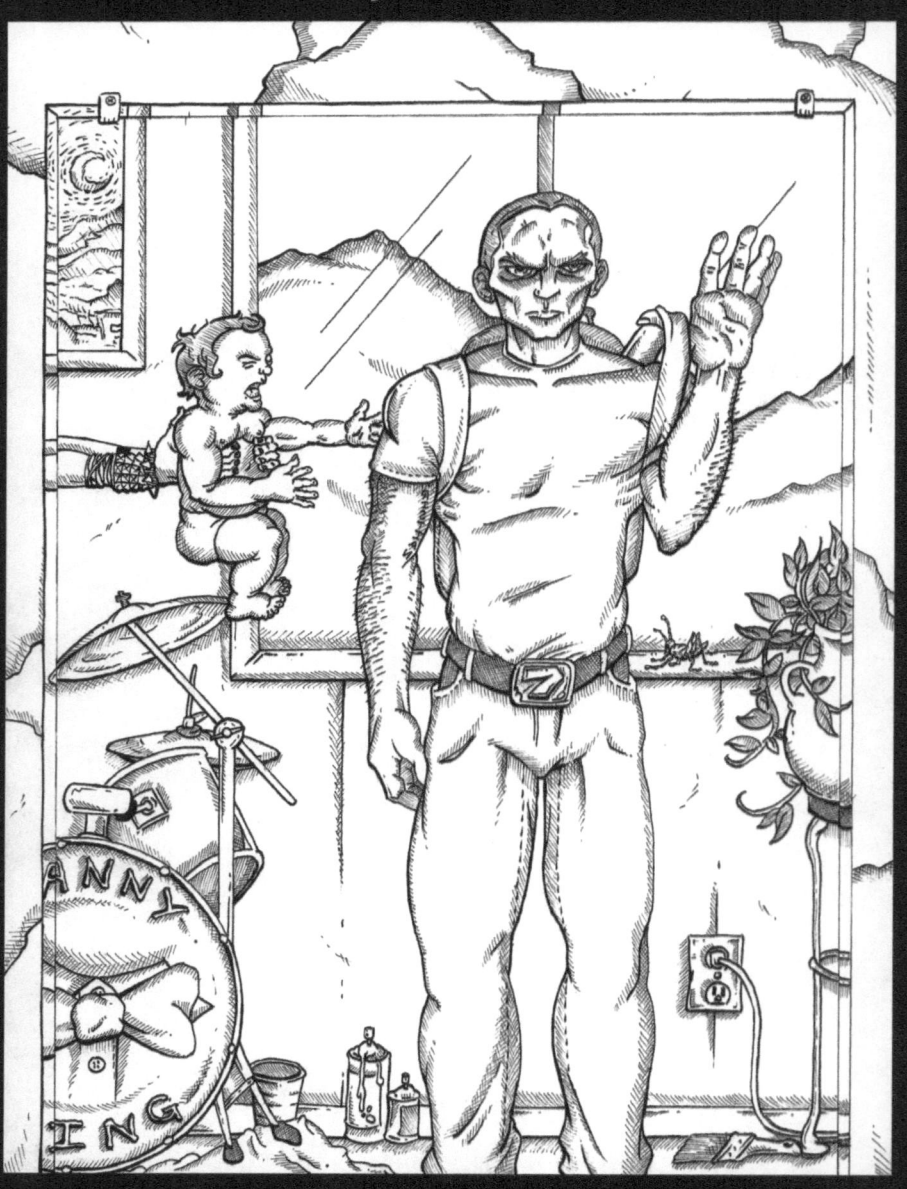

I Put My Left Arm in the Right Arm Hole

"Can you please make him stop screaming?" I shouted at Abigail as she warmed Joshua's bottle in the break-room sink. She bounced him lightly and lovingly in her nurturing arms as his shrill little voice struck out against me in aggressive, penetrating rings.

"You can't be serious? Please tell me you're not serious. Since it's so easy to quiet him, why don't *you* make him stop?" she asked as we walked to our room where I folded and packed my stencils and spray cans in my bag and threw them on my back.

"I got to go," I said emotionless as I looked myself up and down in our full-length mirror with Abigail hooting and hollering in the background.

In an effort to take parenting seriously I had decided to go the route of Cowboy Danny and dumb myself down with a new persona. I had put away the intoxicants, shaved my head, taken out all my piercings, stripped myself of my jewelry and chains, and defeatedly shoved my jacket in my closet in the back. I wore only a plain white t-shirt, standard black jeans, a pair of brand new Doc's, and a simple backpack.

I figured if I were going to lose myself and my character to make way for the new star of the show, my gorgeous little man, I would have to create a new me. And, if I were going to dilute myself at all I may as well just let go completely and present myself as a pure, untouched canvas free of any misleading outward advertisements. Plus it helped to be nondescript as Cal and I ran from our latest public installments of street art, often with the cops in hot pursuit.

Cal and I had been hanging out a bit too much for Abigail's taste and she certainly did not like the direction we were heading in with our new found pastime of graciously bestowing our marks upon the city. Cal's was a grayscale, wheatpasted beaker with a solid black mushroom floating in a sloshing liquid that he would affix at an angle so that the liquid was parallel with the ground and the beaker was tilted askew. Mine was a stenciled black and white blocky tuxedo body with gloves, a red bowtie, and the name *Manny King* stacked on its shoulders in cursive, all atop a solid white rectangle surrounded by a thick red stroke.

We hit the majority of the state and flew our tags next to the rooftop greats, billboard beatniks, subway prophets and the like. Before we knew it people in the art world were talking and asking, "Who are The Black Mushroom and Manny King?"

I can't speak for Cal, but I'll tell you who Manny is. He's a sorry excuse for a businessman, an ineffectual father, and a boring-ass sober version of the maniac within. He was my statement on what the world makes us and how it violently and humiliatingly strips us of our innocence and decency. He was the picture of a sinking ship, the embodiment of a failed experiment, and the personification of our once great and noble society which had been brought to its ruin by greed, sloth, and the commercial enslavement of the so-called lower classes. Like me, he was all dressed up with nowhere to go and because of him I had become self-aware and was forced to ask myself, why am I dressed like this, is this look still working for me, and beneath all these layers and adornments, who am I really?

As my literal chains fell away, the metaphysical ones latched on and I immediately knew that becoming Manny would not save me. He could not erase the harm and ugly truths that I had manifested, but as with all my endeavors I tried to make the square peg fit, so I created inside myself a ticking time-bomb wrapped in a spray painted tuxedo.

"Hello, anyone home?" inquired Abigail as I gawked at myself in the mirror wondering who it was that was staring back at me. Her reflection broke through my inattention and she asked, "Why are you in such a foul mood lately? If you need relief then go smoke a bowl or drink a beer for God's sake. Maybe you needed to scale it back a bit, but no one told you to go cold turkey and get all crabby and weird. And, by the way, Asher, I liked you better before the upgrade. Now you're just, well, kind of plain and boring like everyone else."

I took offense to the truth and harshly snapped back at her, "Can't you see for the first time in my adult life I'm doing something for someone other than myself, for my family? We can't be freak shows forever, Abigail! No one takes a burnout seriously. I've lived a laborious life and everywhere I turn I'm laughed at like some sort of clown. When I sign for a delivery, when I meet with an executive, hell, when I buy a fucking soda I'm made to feel like a deceiver or some disingenuous half wit. I don't want to die early like my parents. I have obligations now and I want to be here for you and our baby boy instead of buried in some fucking hole too soon!"

Abigail hid Joshua away from my anger and vulgarity and pulled his face into her breast. Again she turned her feet in pigeon-toed, looked to the ground and whispered, "Is that what I am to you, a freak show?"

I begged of her, "Please tell me that isn't the only thing you heard me say. I just need you to understand me right now. You don't need to turn it around or fix it or do anything other than just understand me."

"Asher, I do hear you and I understand what you're trying to say, and while I definitely do support you in your decision to be healthy I want you to know that I'd rather live happily with a drunken creative than miserably with a sober depressive."

"Manny is not a depressive! Manny is reserved and in control!" I blurted out like an insolent psychiatric patient.

Evidently that was the nudge that had put her one step over the line and evoked the lioness from her meek and tender den. I had made it impossible for her not to answer my call and she laid it all out in one screaming breath. "Asher, you are not Manny! I did not fall in love with Manny! I fell in love with an asshole who would not compromise, who never backed down, and who could levitate if he actually tried. I don't know who this Manny character is and I don't think I like who you're becoming!"

She abruptly whipped Joshua around and thrust him in my face. He smiled and cooed at me as if he found our argument amusing, then she asked, "Are you even excited about your son or is he just another *obligation* to you? Look at him, Asher. Manny is not this boy's father. You are. Now, are you going to be able to do this or not?"

I scooped up my baby Joshie and pulled him in tight. I tried to look my boy in the eyes as he wriggled and wiggle-wormed about, but he kept shying away as if he knew something that I did not. He opened his gummy mouth and smiled huge and bashful for me as he nuzzled in with a thick glistening strand of slobber extending from his bottom lip to my chest. Then he looked up, our eyes locked, and I uncontrollably fell into a feedback loop, feeling as if time had folded and I had simultaneously become my father and my son. Then I got lost, nearly fainted, and almost dropped him.

Abigail swooped in, snatched him up and shouted, "What the hell is wrong with you, Asher?! You're not going to run off with Cal today; oh no. You're going to the doctor, mister. And, I mean like right now."

And so, once again I sought counsel of the big minds in the ER. They ran me through CAT scans and drew vials of blood and called case management to come and chat me up. Next thing I knew the androgen came bobbling into my room, looked down his miniscule glasses teetering on the tip of his bulbous, veiny nose, and he barely parted his lips to say, "Mr. Radezlav, we meet again."

Because I did need help and because he was familiar to me and because I simply could not muster the strength to acquaint another with my ridiculousness, I broke down and told him how my night terrors had increased, how my stress levels were inappropriate, how my self-medication had reached an apparent end and my blackouts and seizures had not, how I still heard the voices and how the dreams were becoming more consequential and syncing up with the news, and on and on and on.

He replied, "Uh huh, I see. So, not much has changed then."

Without batting an eye he haphazardly wrote me a repeated prescription for quetiapine then stared blankly at me as he handed it over.

I looked down my nose at the scrip and asked, "And, what about the stress?"

Without breaking eye-contact he scratched and scribbled me up a pleasant little side of what would become my new drug of choice, alprazolam. Then he struggled to his feet and slithered out of the room without another word.

This quickly reaffirmed my conclusion that greater modern psychology was not for me, but I did like the fact that now that I was a full blown respectable, adult citizen looking to get hooked on legal drugs, all I had to do to obtain my fix was to research a set of symptoms and like the commercials say, "Ask your doctor about..." then you just fill in that pesky little blank and voila, here's your drugs.

From that point I hopped from doctor to doctor, creating myself my very own noxious pharmaceutical cocktail and it soon became evident that my work began to suffer. My characters became formulaic and nonsensical. I began to pull too heavily from my backlog of ideas and I realized that while I loved each and every one of my childhood drawings, they had no business being forwarded to the newly reformed art department, whom under Abigail's instruction had no choice but to take over in my stead.

Within the matter of about a year I had been ousted from my position as creative director of BA Toys, Inc. and as the record will show, it was for good reason. I was drying up again and becoming a prematurely agitated and bitter old man whose only passion consisted of repeatedly spraying a can across the same old stencils, and eventually I even stopped doing that.

"Have you seen what these freaking peons are proposing now?" I shouted from my bed at the broadcast news as the factory staff buzzed noisily outside my room like worker-bees and my pajamas stuck to my skin from the putrid sweat of inactivity.

"Our currency is devalued? Well, then maybe you should just print some more. Just print your way out of it you fucking stooges! Print it up! Ah, to hell with it," I shouted as I popped another pill.

Right then and there, in the middle of the work day, I closed my eyes and non-triumphantly fell asleep. I did not pass out from a horrific binge nor did I fall prey to a drug fueled coma, I just fell asleep. I had become the status quo. A tired, crotchety bastard I was at the age of twenty-five, falling into a warm and cozy slumber with the sun up high and a plethora of unused art supplies weeping and gnashing their teeth on my drafting table, begging to be torn into and abused. But, it wasn't documentation of my right brain that I was after. I yearned for the last frontier of creativity in my mind and our purest form of self-manifested escapism. I craved the liberty of the dream world.

꓿

"Rise up, now! Rise up! Rise up!" cried Wormwood from behind his pulpit, dressed in dapper, stately attire with the fallen masses exciting like fidgeting apes while seated in their pews. They jostled around in their business suits and harrumphed while passing collection plates as they made show of their vast generational wealth. They shuffled about random legislative propositions and earmarked bills from paw to filthy paw as they cackled like hyenas making their authoritative marks on the dotted lines.

With his wings bursting through his suit like a tattered butterfly emerging from its dusty cocoon, Wormwood escaped his pulpit and again approached the available golden seat which he now openly coveted, but he was still bound by his rank and he reassumed his position crouched at the fourth corner of the seat, anxiously awaiting the end of another thousand year period.

The seat crumbled and reformed to become the image of the rapidly progressing earth and it became clear to me that the seat was the world and whosoever occupied it was its master.

"Then that would make the four winged creatures the keepers of the four winds of the earth," I spoke aloud as I floated freely in the vast black expanse of deep-space.

"Very good," said The Heap from behind me as my feet planted hard on terra firma and I turned to witness a tumbling mound of colorful candy-coated pills falling out of its mouth and collecting around its bubbling stump feet.

I softly woke from my restless snooze feeling confused and violated, then I walked purposefully to my medicine cabinet and poured all my pills down the toilet. I immediately walked to my closet and threw on my jacket, strapped on my chains and roughly shoved my rings and studs back in my face, then I loaded up and took a long, deep pull off my pipe and screamed triumphantly through a choking cloud of thick gray weed smoke, "Daddy is back!"

About one week later Daddy was gripped by the reality that a gradual deceleration is absolutely necessary when dealing with the matters of brain drugs. I spiraled down in a terrific psychotic break as I trembled in cold sweat and writhed about on all fours on the bathroom floor with sputum flowing freely from my lips, soaking into Abigail's beloved Elvis bath mats. It was in this swirling torrent of crushing madness and fragility that I finally grew tired of my own bullshit and came to terms with the fact that I had a real problem with addiction. Not with alcohol or marijuana or LSD or pills, but with addiction itself.

Abigail found me later that night after she had put in a full day's work and picked up baby Joshie from proud Uncle Danny's and guess what, she was not at all happy with what she found.

"Why should I have to put up with this, Asher? Tell me why," she commanded from my all but reserved room in the ER.

"Because, my punch card is almost full and if I end up here one more time this month I get a freebie?" I snorted trying to lighten the mood.

"Stop it, Asher. Just stop it. This isn't funny anymore. It never really was," she said as she got up, left the room, and simply went home without me.

During my mandatory seventy-two hour psych-hold in the ER I plotted and planned how to make it up to Abigail. I considered flowers, but that's a crappy gift to give a florist. I thought about writing her a poem, but knowing me it would eventually end up discussing despair and loathing. Then I was suddenly struck like a frying pan to the head by the mother of all forgive me pleas.

She had since turned eighteen-years-old, we had grown a business together making us financially inseparable, and we had a child for crying out loud. It just made good sense to make that tenacious little girl my ever-loving bride, so I decided to re-create the Sock Hop that we loved so much, with three variations. One: I would remain relatively sober this time. Two: our child would be present. And, three: the evening's music would be carefully orchestrated selections from her collection of vinyl and the song of the night would be Al Green's *Let's Get Married*.

I called out to Danny through the ancient tethering landline at my bedside and we prearranged all the precious little details. Danny was surprisingly supportive and it was a pleasure to watch him work and to be his client.

"You know what, Dan? I can see why you're so successful and why everyone in town loves you and gushes over you so much. You're really great at this."

"Come on, Ash. Knock it off," he choked back.

"No Dan, I mean it. Mom and Dad would be really proud of you."

He quietly sniffled a few times and abruptly changed the subject. "I guess you were right about Abigail not being who I thought she was. She's just like Mom and you're just like Dad."

"How do you figure?" I asked.

"Well, Mom came from a poor family and she laid into Dad's money pretty good too. Just look at all the expensive crap we had growing up. The crystal chandeliers, the designer furniture, the fine dinnerware; Dad didn't care about any of that shit. That was all Mom's doing.

"And come to think of it, the factory was all Mom's doing too; again just like Abigail. Dad didn't shut down BA Toys because of his grief. He shut it down because he didn't know how to run a business, just like you. All Dad ever wanted to do was sit around and draw with his boys, just like you're going to do with Josh.

"It's kind of freaky how everything comes full circle and I get it now. You and Abigail were meant to be together, like some kind of cosmic happening or something. So, I'll get Mom and Dad's rings ready for you, but you have to promise me that you won't screw this up and that you're going to be able to hold yourself together for once. As long as you keep your head above water I'll be there for..."

And, from out of nowhere the phone hung up and my knives and clothes and chains and jewelry landed heavily in my lap with my heinous sow of a nurse bellowing, "Time to go! Get out!"

I looked up at her lovingly and softly said, "I just want you to know that the service here has been absolutely sublime and I plan on making a sizable donation to the Mildred Ratched Foundation in your honor." Then Security mobbed into the room, scooped me up, and dragged me out the front door as I hung limp like a possum in their big, strong, man-arms.

"You know it's really hard to get these chains unknotted once they're like this!" I yelled at them as I dressed myself in the ambulance bay with a slew of onlookers laughing and pointing at me.

So, I tucked my tail between my legs and made the long walk home in the punishing summer heat and as I approached my forlorn girl holding Joshie at the entrance to the factory, I poured tears like a helpless whelp and apologized to her profusely. Of course she accepted me back, but not after laying down a few new ground rules. Not since living under my parents' harsh totalitarian regime had I been subject to rules, or even guidance for that matter, and for just a split second I was less than receptive. But, one stern look from Mama Abigail straightened me right out and I gladly accepted her terms for re-entering my own home.

"I love you my Seven of Hearts," she said as we embraced in a family hug and she set her head against my collarbone with Joshua pressed between us, squirming about and grunting.

Later that night I told Abigail that Danny had planned some lame-ass cowboy event at Zinnia and he wanted the three of us to drop by. As I emerged from the shower, I wiped the fog from the bathroom mirror and stared at my shaven head and my piercings. All at once it clicked and it occurred to me that change does not need to be drastic and compulsive. The all or nothing approach that I was so accustomed to was slowly but surely dying in me and was giving birth to a steady and evolving maturity.

I wrapped myself in a towel and stepped into our bedroom where Abby was sitting cross legged atop her dresser with her face focused deep in her mirror as she applied her signature cat eyes, Joshie was having himself a ripping and gurgling scream session in his bassinet because he hadn't felt the comfort of his mom's affirming touch in nearly three seconds, and I looked around at what we had built together. Suddenly, I began to smile huge and wide and I laughed and cried like an unhinging goon.

"Oh, great," said Abigail through the reflection, naturally assuming that I was losing my mind again.

"No, no, I'm fine. I'm just really happy, that's all," I said as my chuckles faded and I wiped the tears from my face.

We finished getting ready and loaded Joshie up in his stroller then headed down the road with a gorgeous sunset lighting the skyline in vibrant red and purple sherbet tones. As we approached the large archaic double doors of Zinnia we were greeted by Danny who handed Abigail a single white rose and said, "Ms. Sutcher, please accept this rose as a symbol of my thanks for all that you've done for our family. Little Joshua is nothing short of my hero, you're kicking ass at the factory, and somehow you've managed to continue on with my brother and for that I am eternally grateful.

"With that said, I am proud to introduce you to

your evening here at Zinnia Hall. Please do enjoy."

I scrunched my face a little, entertaining the slightest inkling of jealousy as Danny dramatically lowered his eyes, bowed at the waist and pulled the door open to reveal the Sock hop in full swing, making Abigail's eyes blast open in amazement with her full red lips separated and silent.

"What's all this? I thought it was stupid cowboy night," said Abigail.

I laughed and put my arm around her as we soaked in the scene and I explained, "This is for you, sweetie. Because, an apology just wasn't good enough."

Everything that night went absolutely according to plan. Danny happily held Joshua as we danced to Prince, then California rocked him as we ate, then Danny reluctantly held him again as we sidled up to the bar. Exhaustedly, Cal set him down in his tableside highchair as we collapsed into our seats, full up, tuckered out, and satisfied as Al Green crooned in like a saxophone and I popped a cork, pouring us two flutes of fine Cristal.

Abigail looked up at me from behind her napkin and asked, "Is this *Let's Get Married*?"

I suddenly grew very serious, nodding my head knowingly, and she immediately began to tear up. It was then that I took her hands in mine and I promised her, "Abigail, for you I will learn to maintain myself. For you I will no longer entertain insanity. Never again will you need to visit me in the ER and if I fail or falter, you will have every reason necessary to divorce me."

"But, we're not married, Asher," she said as she burst into tears and shook with glee.

So, I got down on one knee, I held my mom's glinting diamond and platinum ring before her and I asked her earnestly and truly, "Ms. Abigail Sutcher, will you do me the great honor of becoming Mrs. Abigail Radezlav?"

With tears streaming her cheeks, she clasped her hands over her mouth, shook her head lightly up and down and whispered one word through her fingers. "Yes."

Chapter Eight

All My Dreams Come True

"How is this escaping you? You take the REAUX portion and spell it phonetically as ROW, add a W, then add the MOOD back in and piece it all back together in the proper order. Moodreaux, moodroww, wormwood, it's all the same, don't you see? It's a puzzle, an anagram!" I shouted at Abigail as I scribbled incessantly at my yellow legal pad, undertaking the most important word jumble the world would ever know.

"Asher you're scaring me," said Abigail. "You need to let this go, please. It's past five AM and you haven't slept in days. You're just getting mixed up, that's all. Come to bed."

"No, Abby. I'm not getting mixed up. I'm seeing things clearly for the first time in my life."

"Well, now that you woke Joshua up with your crazy-man routine I guess I won't be getting any sleep either!" she shouted as she exited Dad's office and slammed the door shut with Joshie screaming his poor little head off across the factory in our room.

Earlier that night Danny and I had made a visit to our friends, slash, competitors in the downtown bar scene. We had already been kicked out of a few places, but our buddies down at Brew Sleaze were always there for us. As we sat next to each other, not speaking a word, downing vodka-bulls and staring at the mesmerizing wall of blaring televisions, my mind was suddenly assaulted.

The tumbling chatter of the crowd rang in my ears and my eyes snapped to the upper-left-most screen where I saw a commercial for an emergency medical product. A man was clutching his chest and then fell over, then it cut to a bald woman at home in her bed being consoled by her two sons. One of the boys was holding an early BA Toys plush bear as the product information scrolled across the bottom of the screen. I had seen other shows and commercials with our toys in the background, but it just seemed odd to me, the synchronicity of the whole commercial.

Another screen featuring a Cylinders performance in Japan caught my eye, then another was showing a bad science fiction movie about demons, on another a mad scientist was swirling beakers of glowing viscous liquid, and another featured the movie *Suburbia*. Each screen that caught my eye was a personal reflection or snippet from my life and they had all led up to the last screen which wholly gripped me. It was Wormwood in human form, wearing dapper attire and shaking hands with our president. Across the bottom of the screen was written, *Congressman Louis Moodreaux Accepts Award*. And, that was when I lost it.

"Holy shit!" I screamed and jumped down from my bar stool, knocking over my drink and running out through the saloon-style front doors with Danny yelling something in the background as the doors swung shut, then open, then shut again.

I hailed a cab and went straight home where I grabbed the nearest phone and frantically searched Congressman Moodreaux, expecting to find a laundry list of atrocities under his name. To my surprise he seemed to be an extremely squared away guy, having been a founding member of his neighborhood Boys and Girls Club and a regular volunteer at his local homeless shelter. He was an advocate of peace, a pillar of his community, and here's the kicker, he was an outspoken proponent of one-worldism, which he believed achievable through "social outreach" and more importantly, "the abolition of The Fed, the decommissioning of hard international borders, and the elimination of paper and coin currency."

"The fingerprint and credit systems that are currently in place and that are being used daily have proven themselves vastly superior to the antiquated papers and coins of our grandfathers' fathers. Are we really still Neanderthals trading sticks and stones for bricks and loaves?" said Wormwood in an interview with The Washington Post entitled, *Louis Moodreaux, The New Face of Change?*, with the word change cleverly spelled out in coins.

He continued, "We've lived in a world market for far too long to tolerate obsolete systems that deter and convolute international commerce. At the bottom of the Great Seal of the United States are written the words *Novus Ordo Seclorum* or in the English, *New Order of the Ages*. Feel free to check the reverse of your dollar bills if you still carry any. In short, folks, it's time for our monetary system to shed its training wheels and grow wings. And, if we so choose to take this bold but necessary step I guarantee you the eye of God at the top of that pyramid is still going to be watching over us."

"Don't you think you're jumping to conclusions a bit?" asked Abigail as I reluctantly crawled into bed wringing my hands and shaking in worry.

"No, I do not. The man's first action as a Utah Congressman was to draft an energy bill called *The Four Winds*, which he says he named after the Four-Corners states. But, I know better. That's a reference to biblical prophecy."

"So what, maybe he's into the Bible or the book of Mormon or something," she said flippantly.

"How about this one then? In an interview with USA Today he refers to Utah as, 'the golden seat of the United States'."

"Maybe it's just a coincidence," she replied.

"He affectionately refers to his obese dog as The Heap."

To that she sucked her chin in, got a strange look on her face and pulled away from me saying, "Okay, now that's a little weird."

"Yeah, you think?"

We both slowly slunk down under the covers and held each other as we fell asleep with the sun coming up and I slipped down the tunnel of dreams, filled with anxiety and paying close attention to the instructions that I was no doubt about to receive.

*

"Watch this. Major concurrent earthquakes in Chile, Turkey, and the region of Micronesia," I said to Abigail as I pointed at our TV just before we saw footage of earthquakes in Chile, Turkey, and Guam. "Close enough. United Nations formalizes International Disaster Relief Task Force," I said just before those exact words scrolled along the ticker at the bottom of the screen.

"Is that on DVR or something? How are you doing that?" Abigail asked fearfully.

"I told you, my dreams are syncing up with reality. Everything that I thought was just a story or a hallucination or an error of the mind? It's all coming true. Earthquakes in diverse places, wars and rumors of wars known and unknown, Wormwood as Moodreaux and his eventual revelation as the supreme world leader, soon to be known as the antichrist. It's all coming to pass and God has chosen me as a conduit to inform the world."

Abigail's mouth hung open in absolute shock as she lightly shook her head side to side with her palms faced out toward me. "Come again? The antichrist? God has chosen you? Just for giggles let's say that you're not bat-shit insane and that you're the conduit for God himself..."

I interrupted, "No, no, no, not *the* conduit; *a* conduit. There are many others like me I'm sure."

"Okay, *a* conduit. What is it exactly that you plan to do about it?"

I walked to our bed and pulled my sketchbook and charcoals from under my pillow and answered, "Hell if I know, Abby. Hell if I know."

As I sat on our bed and began to draw, I felt as if I were a tuning radio picking up the entire world's signals and impulses through my buzzing, magnetic, antennae-head. The B-52's *Channel Z* played loudly in my mind and I just opened up and let it pour in through the top of my skull, down through the tubes and troughs in my brain, through my veins, muscles, and sinew, and out my hand onto the paper.

At first it appeared as one straight line and a series of parallel circles, then another set of lines and circles interconnected with the first, then I filled the circles with dates of prominent world events along with little drawings of the world leaders that starred in each, surrounded by simple scenes signifying their situations. It appeared that I was constructing a map of prophetic events replete with splintering branches that illuminated alternate outcomes dependant on key details. Thanks to this I remained awake and sober for another week's time.

I had holed myself up in Dad's office as the factory churned outside like a chugging locomotive. When I finished filling up my sketchbook I tore it apart and affixed each page to the wall or to another page with push pins or tape or glue, plastering the entire north wall with past, present, and probable futures.

I frenetically searched internet archives, news stations, maps and globes, theological works and forecasts. I dug in and verified my claims and all evidence pointed to the same conclusion: Wormwood's globalist rhetoric was the integral piece of the puzzle that would situate him as the usurping king of the world united.

I lamented over every probable outcome and came to the conclusion that the only way to save the world was to kill Wormwood off from his current form. I would not allow him the satisfaction of emerging from his human cocoon transformed as the great red dragon.

If you could have foreseen the rise of Hitler and the genocide that he spawned, would you have stopped him?

As I was putting the final touches on my timeline that I had labeled Project Six Six Five, Abigail quickly came through the door holding a stack of invoices in one arm and baby Joshua up the other, making the aluminum blinds crackle and shake in a loud and intrusive shuffle.

"Don't you ever knock?!" I shouted at her.

Joshua, who had entered with a smile, was now crying and Abigail vindictively let loose on me yelling, "Great, thanks for asking. That's how we're doing. We're doing great! Asher, where the hell have you been?"

"What do you mean? I've been right here."

"No, you've been off in Bonkerstown, USA constructing a half-baked end-times timeline and totally neglecting your family. That's where you've been!"

"Please don't do this," I pleaded with her. "Not only is this the most important thing I've ever done, but when I finish this it may just change the course of history. I've been given the unique opportunity to save people, Abby. That has to mean something to you."

"You know what means something to me, what means everything to me? Our family, our business, all that we've built. Not the rest of the world. Not the liars and the cheats and heads of state that are game, set, and match above us steering the machine. *This* is what matters. *This* is what's real. Now I'm going to ask you again. Asher, where have you been?"

And, because of her I finally got it and I fell back into my body and closed the conduit. I stood up and my hips popped back into their sockets, I limped feebly over to her and I swatted the invoices out of her hand and wrapped my girl and my little guy up in a daddy bear embrace.

"I realize that you and Joshie are the world. I just want to save you," I said as my eyes skipped back and forth between them, watering over.

"Oh Asher, you don't have to save us. You just have to be available," she said, then she slapped me playfully across the face to which Joshie hopped in delight as he shook excitedly between us, then to my horror she asked, "Do you remember what today is?"

My fearful voice cracked and sold me out as I pretended, "Of course I do."

She asked skeptically, "Then what did you get him?" and I sharply recalled that it was indeed one of the most important days of my life, Joshua's first birthday.

"I'm designing him a new toy, it's just not ready yet. I'm almost done."

"Oh, okay," Abigail said half believing what she needed to believe and half knowing what she didn't want to.

I felt a gradually growing, piercing pain in my head and I briefly clasped my eyes shut. When I opened them we were at the nature conservatory where we spent the rest of the day having a family picnic and opening presents next to the cool, clear creek that bumbled and jived over submerged rocks and roots, singing a happy birthday tune just for my little man.

"Are you alright?" asked Abigail as I fended off intoxicating sleep under a great, thick oak tree with acorns and leaves strewn about on the lush green grass below. All the while a congregation of popping grasshoppers bounded happily about us with a colony of fearsome gray squirrels barking down epithets at us from overhead.

"I guess. I just... I mean, yeah I'm fine. I'm fine." I answered as I laid my defeated head down in her warm, inviting lap. Every time I closed and opened my eyes it felt as if a day had passed and we spent what seemed like a month out there in the warm summer air; a month that I will always treasure down to the depths of me.

When we returned home that night my baby boy eagerly hit his crib like a satisfied potato sack and instantly fell asleep. My fiancé eagerly hit our bed like a satisfied potato sack and instantly fell asleep. And, I eagerly hit Dad's office like an obsessed insomniac and resumed my all important work on Project Six Six Five.

With the moon staring intrusively through the front window I crashed into Dad's leather chair and compiled a list of key players in the end game scenario. The list included Congressman Moodreaux at the head, followed by the US President of course, the Secretary-General of the United Nations, then it was rounded out at the bottom by a host of talking-head broadcasters, miscellaneous cave dwelling intelligence agents, various nefarious imps and orcs, and an assortment of political boogie men. I pulled up a browser and entered the term *contact* and then each individual's name or title and I catalogued the information next to their names on my list. But, what to send them? Oh, I know. How about a warning?

"Dear Mr. or Mrs. (enter name here),

I would like to take a moment to familiarize you with my findings. It has recently come to my attention that you and many others like you are part of a tight knit world syndicate set on global domination and I sincerely urge you to cease and desist immediately.

I feel it my duty to warn you that there are those out here that are willing to do whatever it takes to stop you. For we are they that engulf you in heavenly fire; we are they who cause you to turn to blood; we are they that were left behind in the field still working and we are watching you.

A dreadful day of retribution has been set aside for those of you who disseminate works of damnation and it is waiting hungrily in the hands of the oppressed and downtrodden common man. We may not yet be formed and amassed in rank and file but rest assured, if you fools keep prattling on behind your podiums and pulpits, deciding what is good and right and just for a people who are not your own, we will rise up and come against you like a terrific wave of destroying locusts.

It is true; many of us have yet to realize our destiny. But, we know that a steady itch has long since been growing inside us causing a palpable daily tension that manifests itself as debilitating knots or clawing ulcers or digesting cancers and it's only so long before we wonder where to place our righteous indignation. So, because of the current state of things we've been looking around a bit more than usual and guess what, we've spotted you hiding in the periphery. We're slowly waking up Mr. or Mrs. (enter name here) and we're placing the blame squarely on your shoulders.

Please be aware that there is nothing you can do to slow this movement, nothing you can say that will cause us to fade or rescind from this, nor will you be able to abate your impending share of wrath and bitter recompense. But, listen friend, until we come for you please do have a pleasant day and enjoy your dreams. That is, if you can still sleep.

Signed your brother in morning,

Valzedar Rehsa"

Right after I hit send from my anonymous email account I thought to myself, maybe I should have encoded that name a little better.

"Oh, who gives a shit? They're going to find me anyway," I said aloud as I relaxed into a six-pack of Sierra Nevada Pale, threw my feet up proudly on my drafting table, and unlaced my Doc's feeling satisfied that I was finally making a difference in the world.

Suddenly my boots were kicked off the table and hit the floor in a knee jarring thud. When I looked up Abigail was standing over me with her arms crossed and her foot tapping nervously with the sun up high, blazing through the front window directly behind her head, illuminating her crown like a beautiful vexed angel. Evidently I had fallen asleep again.

"What have you done?" she asked.

"What? Done what? What did I do? I did what?" I stammered defensively like a child caught with a can of gasoline.

"Your little email? It's still up on the screen, dumbass. You know you're going to jail, right?"

"For what?" I shrugged innocently.

She contorted her face and mocked me in a dimwitted way saying, "Oh I don't know, maybe for threatening multiple government officials, members of the news media, an international emissary, and the President of the United States for God's sake!"

"Oh boo-hoo, I threatened them? How did I threaten them?"

She stomped her feet with her fists balled up in tight little rocks and yelled, "Stop playing stupid, Asher! You said you were going to turn them to blood and set them on fire!"

"First of all I'm not playing anything and second that wasn't meant to be taken literally. It's hyperbole, a simple metaphor that's all."

"A metaphor for what exactly," she said slowly.

"For... um... killing them?" I inappropriately snickered from behind a mischievous sneer that I could not smooth from off my face.

"You know you're ruining this. You're trying to destroy me, our family, and everything that we've worked so hard to create here. Case in point, how's Joshua's toy coming along?"

"Oh shit, the toy!" I jolted in remorse as I fumbled through a stack of papers.

"You know what, Asher, don't bother. Danny warned me that you might do this, but I didn't believe him. I didn't think that anyone could be so selfish and self destructive, but here you are."

I looked up from under my brow with that same twinge of doubt and jealousy becoming a small growing fire in me and I snapped into her. "Wait a minute, what? Danny warned you? Why have you been talking to Danny? What business do you have talking to Danny?"

And with that, any patience that Abigail still harbored for me was gone and she simply exploded, "If you think you are going to turn this around on me or put me on the defensive then you got another thing coming, asshole! Am I the one fucking up your life or is it the other way around? Excuse me if I sought the advice of an actual professional businessman when I ran into problems getting this factory up and running. Lord only knows where you were; probably off in some storeroom getting high while I was changing Joshua's diaper or getting drunk while I was reconciling the books or frying your brain out on mushrooms while I was breast feeding or doing God knows what else while I was managing shipments or bathing your son or meeting with inspectors. I don't know what you expect from me. I'm a nineteen-year-old farm girl reject, Asher! What the hell do I know about running and maintaining a full scale toy factory?"

I squared my shoulders to her and callously yelled back, "Well, no one asked you to restart the factory, farm girl!" then I crossed my arms, threw my feet back up, and I closed my eyes and began to fall back asleep as she started to gently cry.

She stood there for a while and watched me as she wept, then she slowly walked to the door and just before she exited and lightly shut it she said in a whisper, "Asher, Manny, Valzedar, whoever you are; I never knew you. I must have been mistaken. And by the way, you may want to check your email. The FBI sent you a reply. Your name has been added to the terrorist watch-list and Federal Agent

Benjamin Torrez wants to meet with you on Monday morning. So, how awesome are you now you smug piece of shit?"

Chapter Nine

Torrez, Big and Tall

"What do you mean he just took off?" asks Danny in a panic that is definitely not calming me down.

"Well, he woke up screaming like he always does, but this time he got up and started packing everything he saw."

"Packing? What does that mean, packing?"

I snap at him, "Daniel, why do you keep asking me what everything means?"

He snaps back defensively like a lonely dog chained in a yard, as if I were a stranger entering his territory, "Because Abigail, the last time he took off like that I saw him six times in six years and I'm not willing to go through that shit again with that fucking little prick! That's why. Does that answer your question?"

Okay, that just floored me. Not only has Danny never talked to me like that, but he basically just told me that Joshua could be without a father for six-long-years.

As Danny and Joshua and I sit down on my bed and look out the window that Asher just jumped out of, over the hills and valleys that he is now running through, and then back at each other, we both realize that we may not be seeing him for a really long time and I'm starting to feel extremely guilty. What if the last words I ever said to him were anything other than, I love you, I need you, and you are my heart? Asher if you can hear me now, please come home. I promise I'll try to respect your space more.

"Alright, back it up. What the hell happened?"

asks Danny as he reaches out toward me and grabs Joshua's little hand.

"Well, like I said he woke up screaming."

♪♫

"Abigail, wake up! We got to go. Get Joshua, get everything you need, pack your bags, we have to move! Up, up, up!" I shouted at her, feeling that old familiar wash of dread coat me like a thick desensitizing layer of wax.

"What? What time is it?" she whispered from under the covers as Joshie started to stir and sputter in his crib.

I got up next to her, shook her head a bit and said, "I'm deadly serious, Abigail. I just had a dream, now get moving." I ripped open the curtains, letting the bold clarifying beams of pure radiant sunrise burst through our window, making our pupils slam shut like the precision instruments they are as Abigail bolted under the blankets like Nosferatu.

She squinted and shielded her eyes as I tore her clothes out of her closet and she sat up and rudely replied, "You just had a dream? Asher, I was having a dream too, but you don't see me freaking out about it."

I stuffed duffel bag after backpack after suitcase full of anything we would need while shouting, "Well, the difference is I'm tuned in and you were merely asleep, now get up and get mobile or I'm going to prison."

"Going to prison? Why would you go to prison?" she grumbled in a scratchy, foggy voice while propped up on her elbows, apparently having zero intentions of moving any further.

"For murder. Now are you going to get a move on or am I going to have to tie the two of you up and strap you both to my back?"

A look of utter horror plastered her face like an unchanging mask as she pulled the blankets up to her chin and I knowingly asked, "You're not coming are you?"

She just shook her head side to side ever so lightly with her mouth hanging open in shock again and I looked over at Joshua who was wide awake and staring at me silently with his eyes big as saucers as if he too could see that my aura was set ablaze in holy fire.

Having already seen beforehand that I would be going it alone, I stopped packing and checked myself for what it was that I truly needed. Jacket: check, dictionary: check, knives: check, chains: check, jewelry: check. Fuck the pipe, fuck the flask, and fuck her; I'm out. "I'll be back for Joshua."

꒰꒱

"Then he jumped out the window and that's when I called you."

Danny winces and asks apprehensively, "What did he mean when he said he could go to prison for murder?"

I quickly break eye contact and guiltily stare at the floor, then turn my toes in toward each other and reluctantly answer, "Did Asher ever tell you about me getting him into a fight with a homeless guy in his alleyway?"

"He may have mentioned it briefly, but we get stragglers around here all the time and he made it sound like it was no big deal. Why?"

I unzip my hoody a little and reveal to Danny that big hideous memento that was carved across my chest and his eyes swell as I become increasingly upset. I uncontrollably cram my words together with my speech and breath growing erratic in my stomach and I just let it all spill. "Well, that particular straggler gave me this scar when he tried to rape me and I don't really know for sure what happened for a period of a couple hours after he bashed my head into a wall and Asher was so adamant that he didn't touch him and I was so mixed up that I just didn't want to think about it anymore and, well," I momentarily collect myself and look Danny in the eyes, "now that I think about it I guess he may have killed him." A few seconds pass and I bury my face in my hands and erupt in tears, "Danny, I think he killed him."

Danny calmly breathes in a great big gasp of air and quietly says, "Oh God, Abigail, that's not good. Where was Asher when the guy cut you?"

"Danny, it's not how it sounds."

"Not how what sounds?"

"Look, he thought I could handle myself, okay?"

Danny leans in and zips my hoody all the way up, he tenderly presses his lightly burnt hand against my cheek and asks me firmly, "Abigail, where was Asher when the straggler attacked you?"

I shy away from him and unwillingly answer, "He was watching me from the second story window above."

Danny jumps to his feet and starts to pace

feverishly around the bedroom yelling, "That is absolutely unacceptable! Who do we call? We have to call someone. Who do we call?"

I hold my phone out toward my TV and bump Asher's email and Agent Torrez's reply onto the screen while whimpering sheepishly, "I think I know who to call."

Danny approaches the screen on the wall and quickly scrolls through the text saying, "Wait a minute, what is this? Okay, we got to think about this. Oh man, what's the right thing to do here? What if he did kill that guy, Abigail? He could get locked up for the rest of his life."

Suddenly, a deep Latino voice calls into my room from out on the factory floor, "And, who might you folks be referring to?" and I scream out as Joshua finally starts to cry and Danny plants in front of me in a protective blade stance.

Like something out of a bad dream or a view into another dimension, a lumbering Aztec giant crawls through my bedroom door, taking up the entire door frame. A flood of cheap department store fabrics pour sloppily off his awkward skyscraper body, portraying him as a bad impression of a private detective stuffed in a khaki suit and dark-brown overcoat. He takes a few steps forward and shrinks a little as he enters my room, removing his matching fedora and whipping his jet-black eighties wedge hairdo out of his face. Compulsively smoothing his pencil thin mustache with one hand, he holds his badge and ID out in the other saying, "Pardon the intrusion, folks. I didn't mean to startle you. I'm Special Agent Benjamin Torrez with the Bureau of Investigation. It's

Monday morning and no one returned my calls so I thought what the heck, I'll just catch the next plane across the country real quick and you know, pop on by and say hi."

"Sorry, we don't really use phones around here," I reply snottily in contempt of his unwelcomed presence as I clutch Joshua's tear soaked face into my neck and groom his hot little head.

"Oh, you don't? Then what's that in your hand?"

"What, my son?" I ask as I shove my phone under my thigh.

"No Ma'am, your other hand. Look, I'm not the bad guy here and I certainly don't have time for childish games, alright? I just need to speak with a Mr.," then he pauses coyly and flips open a tiny dollar-store notebook that appears even tinier in his gargantuan hand and continues, "Valzedar Rehsa? No wait, I'm sorry, Asher Radezlav. How did I get those two mixed up? Anywho, I just have a few questions for him about the poem he recently submitted. It's very good by the way. I personally like the part about the destroying locusts, but it's the section about the blood and the fire that my boss seems to be having a problem with. See, the president doesn't take too kindly to threats."

"What's he talking about, Abigail?" Danny asks angrily, not taking his eyes off the giant.

"Yeah, what's he talking about, Abigail?" the giant asks snidely. "Say, you folks own a bar, right? So, where are all the cervezas at?"

Danny yells indignantly, "Oh, how trite. Just because we own a bar means we have a beer tap on every wall?" Then the giant looks behind Asher's drum kit and spots his kegerator.

Danny shakes his embarrassed face back and forth in the palm of his hand as Torrez points to it and asks, "And, what about the cups?" He looks just to the right of the keg and spies Asher's red cup dispenser mounted on the side. "How about we use these until we find them, huh?" he asks jovially as he pulls one down and pours one out then slams it and proclaims, "Ay Dios mio! Very good, very good. Extremely tight carbonation. What is that, Delirium?"

I clasp my eyes shut with my thumb and forefinger pinching the bridge of my nose in frustration and say in tremendous annoyance, "Actually, it's Asher's house beer."

"Asher has a house beer?" asks Danny in a bewildered and injured tone.

"Indeed he does and you weren't supposed to know about it because guess why, it's called 'Cowboy Danny'. He was working on it for your birthday, so happy early birthday, Dan. Sorry to spoil the surprise. And, thank you for that Agent Torrez. Are you supposed to be drinking on the job?"

He leans in toward me as he pours himself another and with his eyelids flexed open aggressively he whispers, "As a duly appointed federal agent it falls within my power to do whatever it is I deem necessary, ma'am." Then he chugs it down and continues to stare at me as he pours himself another, another. "That reminds me, my bags are outside. I hear you all have a hotel here. I'll be staying on the first floor until we get this whole mess sorted out."

"The hell you are, Torrez! That's against

company policy!" shouts Danny as he takes an ill-conceived offensive step forward.

Agent Torrez reactively bucks his jacket off his shoulders and onto the floor, revealing his holstered Glock and his intimidating, bulging physique. Suddenly, it becomes very apparent to Danny and me that we are outnumbered by this one man. He closes proximity and shouts at Danny, "Sit down!" and as if Danny were under a curse of compliance he automatically sits.

Torrez wags his scolding finger at us as he goes off in a preachy tirade. "Look I didn't want to have to do this, but with the position you all are in here, I've had certain special authorities extended to me by the president himself and if you feel the need to get all official up in here then let's get all official.

"The authorities extended to me by the President of the United States include, but are not limited to: the auditing of all financial ledgers, the immediate freezing of both of your bank accounts, the search and seizure of records or paperwork in any format, an extremely complete and invasive exploration of this and any other premises that may be attributed to the Radezlav and/or Sutcher families, and pretty much anything else my imaginative little heart can conjure up.

"You folks don't seem to be appreciating the gravity of the situation you all are in here. Little Abigail isn't even twenty-one, but oddly enough I seem to be enjoying a beer from her tap. I wonder if I asked around if anyone would say that they'd seen her at the bars, or any other number of juveniles for that matter. What do you think Child Protective Services would have to say about little Joshua there being raised in an environment like that, or would they be more interested in finding out that he lives and plays around industrial machinery?

"And, what if I chose to examine the unique lifestyles of your tenants and conduct random searches of their domiciles? Would I uncover any illegal activities there; perhaps the production of controlled substances or unlawful sexual services or the harboring of runaway minors most of which are still unaccounted for?"

"How do you know all this?" I mutter under my breath, stupidly verifying his accusations.

Thankfully he ignores me and slowly pulls up a chair. Whipping it around backward he drapes his massive forearms over the top saying, "Long story short, folks, I can make things tremendously difficult for you or you can learn to trust me and just go with the program."

Danny and I shrink into ourselves as he continues to dress us down while enjoying Asher's beer and it begins to thoroughly sink in that although this man is in *my* home I am not the one in charge here. He's bigger, stronger, meaner, strapped, and imbued with all the ungodly powers that the world's largest and most powerful mafia has to provide.

"Look, here's a little bit of my background, just for posterity," he says and then launches into what seems like more of a counseling session for him than a disclaimer for us.

"I was raised in a poor family in a bad neighborhood in south-central Los Angeles with a slew of snot-nosed brothers and sisters to look after. Our mother was severely addicted to pain

pills and pretended to be disabled so she could
Minnie-mooch the system. But, thanks to the pills
her imaginary pains became real ones and they
multiplied until she was no longer ambulatory, so
us kids had to grow up too quick and raise each
other. Soon enough we all joined gangs and sold
drugs and ran the streets where we found a pseudo
network of support. So, believe me when I say I'm
aware of the importance of community and the fact
that each family situation has its own unique set of
variables to consider. In this day and age it seems
the nuclear family has finally reached complete
meltdown and after that you take what you can get.
Isn't that right? You take what you can get."

He begins to zone out as he draws a long,
bottomless breath in and stares deep into the
reflection of the polished concrete as if he can see
his siblings running to and fro on the streets. He
gets a pained look on his face, snorts like a bull, and
abruptly snaps back in.

"I am a globalist, which means I do not believe
in borders, but I do believe in government. It also
means that I believe people should be free to move
about as they please and is a precursor to my belief
in the abstract and nearly unattainable concept of
freedom itself. I believe that which does not hurt
another is not another's business. I work for the
people of the United States, the real people, which
means I serve the greater good not the greater
authority. That's why I got in this game in the first
place; to uphold the truth.

"But, please feel free to take all of this with a
grain of salt, because you never know who's a
counterfeit. You have to hold each individual up to

the light and look for that watermark, don't you?" He leans in a bit and gets an almost whimsical look on his face and says, "And, that's what I'm asking you folks to do. You don't have to believe me now, because you will eventually.

"But, on the other hand I'm also a federal agent and as such I'm bound by the obligations set before me to satisfy my investigation and to satiate my bosses. So, I'm going to put it to you like this. Should I go get my bags and have you show me to my room like the adults that we are or shall I put the kid gloves back on, forget all that lovey-dovey bullshit I just spouted, and go back to getting nasty?"

Torrez gulps the rest of his beer down and drops his empty cup on the floor. He leans back with his swollen arms folded over each other like a super macho-man and I just sit there silent and fearful. Danny, however, boldly stands and steps to him with his chest all puffed out, then quickly averts to the keg and pours himself a cold one. He throws the whole thing back in one great gulp and stares off into the distance with a well deserved look of peace and contentment saying, "Wow. That's actually really good, little bro'," then his momentary solace turns to sour disgust and he continues by speaking through clenched teeth, "Agent Torrez, follow me."

I wrap up baby Joshua and strap him to my chest as we exit the factory. Agent Torrez grabs his great big duffel bags from off the porch and were off toward The Eighth Plague, filled with apprehension of the various illegal activities that may currently be taking place there.

As we stroll together Agent Torrez asks point blank, "Daniel, where's your brother?"

"Can't say that I know, Agent Torrez," he replies nonchalantly.

Point blank he asks, "Abigail, where's your fiancé?"

"How did you know we're engaged?" I ask.

"The same way I knew everything else. I know what I need to know and after reviewing Asher's files there are only two things that I can say I know about him for sure. He is sick and he needs help. If we can find him, we can help him."

Apparently Torrez's comments had released a lifetime of pain and worry from Danny's subconscious and he steps in front of us bringing us to a halt. He begins to tear up and shake a bit as he asks from behind suddenly bloodshot eyes, "Do you mean that, Agent Torrez?"

The giant stands cold and unflinching as the sky begins to rumble and darken with an army of thick black rain clouds marching in like a bad omen overhead. He puts his hand over his heart and says in a cheesy way that Daniel needs to believe and can't help but eat up, "I certainly do, Daniel. I have resources."

And, with that I think the tide may be changing between Danny and the giant, but not with me. I don't trust him for a second. Maybe there's something that can be done for Asher, but deep down inside I know this colossal banyan tree of a man does not have his best interest in mind.

Danny and I look at each other and non-verbally weigh our options, and against my better judgment we both silently agree, so Danny starts in, "I can't tell you where he is, Benjamin. I can only tell you where he's been." And, again we start to walk.

"When Asher was fourteen-years-old he left town on the rails with his friend, Cal. We got into a fight the night before where I was busy telling him how I had been named his guardian and that I only wanted what was best for him, but he seemed more interested in the moth that was flying between us. It landed on his lapel and stuck there like a pin and he became transfixed on it, not responding to much of anything I was saying. I can't really be sure that he was listening to me at all and he seemed to drift off as I asked him what his plans were and if he were going to stay with me or not. He seemed to wake up as the moth released from his lapel and he got all indignant with me, telling me that all he had to do was follow his God's will and everything would turn out for him in the end.

"So, I asked him if God had instructed him to leave me by myself in the Intensive Care Unit or had he come to that conclusion all by himself? I asked him, if God is so great and omnipotent than why did our parents have to die in pain? And, I asked him above all else, why do you persist with the outdated notion of a personal God who will lead you and guide you on your very own egocentric path to enlightenment? As the moth finally flew out of his view he started shouting something about an automatic system and the importance of choice, then he lost it completely and threw a chair through the front window.

"Just before he stormed off he looked at me in a way that I'll never forget. It was as if he were already gone and reaching back to me from beyond

the grave. He seemed to look right through me as
he said, 'I am your angel'.

"Fairly recently Cal told me they left the next
morning at dawn after Asher woke up screaming
from one of his prophetic nightmares. He insisted
that God had sent him a message in his dream
telling him and Cal to leave town on a train headed
for Berkeley. He told him they needed to leave right
away with only the clothes on their backs, so that's
exactly what they did. For years that's where they
squatted; in abandoned buildings getting high, in
the hills getting drunk, and on the streets frying on
Cal's homemade acid and panhandling for dollar
Chinese plates. That still makes me laugh, a
millionaire street-kid begging for change.

"As you probably well know, Torrez, and as you
most likely do not, Abigail, one night while they
were sleeping in one of those abandoned buildings
Asher and Cal were attacked by a bum. He said he
wanted to cut their heads off and eat them. So,
Asher slipped his knife between the derelict's ribs
and they ran out onto the streets and flagged down
a college campus policeman who took them to a
substation and filled them with coffee and donuts.
The very next morning they met with a judge who
acquitted them of any wrong doing as it was
deemed self-defense."

I butt in, "You're damn right that's news to me!
I'm starting to realize there's a whole lot about
Asher that's going to be news to me. Is there
anything else I should know about?"

Danny hurtfully passes me off with a,
"Probably," and starts right back in. "Since Asher
was still underage and had made it abundantly

clear to the court that he was not going to be staying with me, he became a ward of the state. He was placed in home after home and program after program, but he ran away from every last one of them and inevitably ended up in juvenile hall. It was only so long before he disappeared from there too and when he did, they finally gave up. They just stopped looking for him. It's like his entire life he's been able to slip right through the cracks.

"Even when Mom and Dad were alive Mom would call him her little ghost-boy. We would all be cleaning up as a family after dinner, washing dishes and wiping down counters. He would be standing next to us with a rag in his hand one minute and off drawing in his room the next, but we would never see him leave.

"His medical records would get misfiled in storage, his court records got corrupted during data migration; even his first social security number mistakenly contained too few digits. Sometimes it's almost like he never existed at all, like the system just rejects him.

"He's never owned a car, he doesn't carry a phone, he pays for things with cash only or he barters. Hell, his clothes don't even have RFID's in them because he only wears shirts and pants and boots that he pulls out of the crates in these old storehouses made before RFID was even invented. So, I guess what I'm trying to say is, good luck finding him Agent Torrez."

As we approach the Eighth Plague building the sky opens up in rows upon rows of heavy pouring buckets and Danny's words begin to nestle down into the crevices of my mind. Like an old fashioned gentleman, Torrez removes his coat and spreads it aloft Joshua and me in a great big canopy as we stand on Danny's porch. Looking up, we watch and listen to the rain drops *tipping* and *tapping* on the yards and yards of fabric above us as they slowly trickle through a dense lattice of inexpensive cloth like a sieve. Danny coughs loudly and kicks the door a few times as he fumbles his key into the lock to warn Asher to flee should he be seeking sanctuary inside. Then he stalls for a moment longer and faces the ground filled with emotion, knowing as I do that he's long gone.

Danny opens his front door and the giant immediately pushes past him to introduce himself to Danny's collection of beat up old couches. He yawns and stretches taking up the entire room and crashing down into the repulsive embrace of the filthiest couch, creating the sound of breaking wood. He riffles through his bags and feigns a tone of sympathy saying, "I can see you folks have been through a lot here and now that we've shared a bit with each other I only feel it fair to inform you that finding Asher isn't exactly the only aspect of our case. We think he may be part of something larger, possibly a newly forming terrorist cell. Any information is good information as far as I'm concerned and I sincerely appreciate your openness, I really do."

With so much new *good information* and with all of these condolences I'm starting to wonder if I ever really knew who Asher was in the first place. This is all becoming too much for me. Oh God, why did you pair me with him? "Okay that's enough, just stop it. Asher isn't a terrorist you fucking phony! I know what you're trying to do and it's not going to work on me. Maybe you have Danny here fooled, no offense Daniel, but I'm not buying it," I scream at the giant hoping that Danny too can smell the blood in the water, at least on some level. But, instead they just stare at me as if I'm a child interrupting the big kids who are at work, so I lower my eyebrows and head straight out the door saying, "You know Asher may be an asshole and a criminal, but at least he doesn't patronize me and make me feel like an adolescent nuisance."

"And, just where do you think you're going, missy?" shouts the sedentary Aztec.

I gaze back fiercely over my shoulder through dagger eyes, staring out across the threshold in the dumping rain and yelling, "You know what, fuck you Torrez! And Danny, I expect more from you than this. I think I've subjected my child to just about enough slander and neglect for one day thank you very much. So, either you arrest me right now or I'm going-the-fuck-home." And, with that we're walking.

I jut my chin out over my sweet baby boy's head and he instinctively pulls into me for warmth as I whisper down to him, "Don't you worry about a thing, boy, don't you listen to a single word they said. Daddy's going to be home real soon, you'll see."

We make it to our room and both crash down in complete and utter exhaustion, falling fast asleep in our soaking wet clothes in a sleigh built for three. Suddenly, I jolt awake the next afternoon in a sweaty panic with California feeding Joshua in his highchair at the foot of the bed and Danny watching over me looking extremely worried and disheveled. Before my eyes can fully adjust, Daniel is apologizing to me and he just lets it all flow out of his big stupid mouth: the drug charges, the assaults and batteries, the previous threats, the concern of their parents and the like. He claims that he hadn't told me beforehand to protect me from the pain of truth, but somewhere deep down I know it was to spare his brother a life of lovelessness.

I guess I really didn't ever know who Asher Radezlav was. But, as I look over at Joshua Radezlav who's now laughing and spitting stewed carrots all over California, I can't help but feel a bit remorseful. But, I'll be damned before I feel anything but this entirely engulfing and insanely heart-wrenching love for my son.

Danny tells me how he's going to be taking over the factory in Asher's absence because, "it's my birthright and it's the right thing to do," and how Cal will be taking over the bar because, "well, who else do we know really?"

"Everything else is shutting down," he whimpers as he actually begins to cry. "That goliath is over there right now drinking all our booze, eating all our food, and screwing all the whores upstairs. I mean hell, he freaking lives in my apartment for God's sake! He's taken everything, Abigail!"

"No. Not everything," I say as I jump to my feet and run to Asher's drum-kit, half wondering if the excitement I still harbor for him will be met with disdain.

"What are you doing," Danny questions as I flop down Indian-style and eagerly unscrew the lugs off the front bass head.

"Before I called you, before I did anything, I hid Asher's timeline underneath the foam padding in his kick drum. He said it was the most important thing he had ever done; he said it was his life's work. And, even though he's clearly out of his mind I intend to hold this sacred and keep it out of the hands of that filthy Aztec."

Danny wipes his eyes and says in a way that lets me know he still loves him, "I'll help you keep it safe, Abby. I'll keep you and Joshie safe too. I see now that I undermined you last night in front of Torrez and I don't really have an excuse. It's just that after all the shit that Asher has put me through, I guess I needed to believe that he could still be saved or that it was all for some divine purpose, you know? It just took me a second to see that he's done the same thing to you and I want you to know that you and Joshua are my family now; the only family that I have left. So, please forgive me, Abigail. I promise you that it will never happen again."

"Yeah, well I've seen how much water the Radezlav promise can hold," I say bitingly as I busily arrange the pages.

"Well, I'm not my brother and as long as I'm alive, whether it be a wandering derelict or that hedonist goliath who's actively devouring The Eighth Plague, no one will ever hurt you or Joshua again. Not even Asher."

That's sweet of Danny to say and even though I want to take his little speech hook, line, and sinker something still feels a little off to me; like he's hiding something. So, I squint my eyes and cock my head to the side in curiosity, I rake my tongue ring back and forth across the backside of my teeth and I say hastily, "Danny, I'm going to be honest with you right now. You were all up on that guy's nuts yesterday blabbing away the old family secrets, which is completely your right because it's your life, but I can't say that I understand the sudden shift in allegiance. So, what exactly happened after I left you two last night?"

Chapter Ten

Torrez stared in a wide-eyed gaze at the Bad Brains patch sewn across your ass as you and Josh stepped out in the rain and he chuckled and shook gleefully on my sofa like a giddy ogre shouting, "Horale buey, I like her! She is one feisty mama. And, what's up with that attitude problem? How sexy is that?"

"Well, she's basically my sister-in-law, so I guess I wouldn't know," I said with a scrunched up vinegar-face sneering out from under my hat.

I cracked a couple of Pabsts and threw a mess of blueprints on my coffee table as Torrez cleared his throat and composed himself asking, "So Daniel, what can you tell me about these storehouses?"

I took a long swig, reset my face, and we began the unpleasant task of finding my brother under the second worst set of circumstances that I could ever imagine.

"Well, most of them have been abandoned since the late nineties and they're all locked up tight. We have in-house security that patrols our property twenty-four hours a day and every inch of the exterior is monitored by video surveillance."

Agent Torrez smiled an unnerving smile and his face seemed to swell and turn a scary, deep-olive color. His voice dropped an octave and he said in a low baritone growl, "That's exactly what I wanted to hear, Daniel. Get me access to those cameras along with the keys to every one of these facilities."

About that time I turned tail and retreated to the kitchen feeling a little unsettled by his sudden transformation and I asked from behind my counter, "What is it exactly that you're looking for, Agent Torrez?"

"I'm not sure yet. Just get me those keys," he demanded as he rubbed his big greedy meat-hooks together. "I hear you all have a cowboy bar here. Why don't you show me to it and we'll discuss this more there? I'm parched," he yelled as he slurped down the rest of his Pabst and threw his crumpled can in the corner like a child.

I walked him to the bar where he immediately opened a tab and bragged about his plans to file all of his expenses with the FBI under the heading *Food and Drink*. Like a big shot Torrez shouted, "A round for the entire bar!" and the few out of work contractors and machinists in attendance all silently raised their nearly empty glasses in a depressing toast.

Torrez soon got his sloppy fill and evidently the line-dancing cowgirl waitresses got him all worked up because he just had to inquire about a few of the looser ladies in the house. I compliantly told him what doors to knock on and how to reply when they answered. Shortly thereafter he met with them upstairs to conduct an investigation. And, a very thorough and invasive investigation it was from what I hear.

After he was spent from that endeavor he called on me and inquired of Early's whereabouts, to continue his very necessary *investigations*. Well, we all know how good, old Early feels about willing participants. Now don't we, Cal? He helped Torrez conduct a series of experiments in the field of psychotropics. And, a very enlightening series of experiments it was. Wasn't it good buddy? Have I mentioned that I am not amused?

It was beginning to look as though Torrez had settled himself down into quite a nice little vacation disguised as detective work and we the citizens that he so diligently serves get the privilege of shouldering the expense, the blessed expense.

After the giant had filled his black-hole stomach and emptied his manhood, we toured the facilities at the profane hour of two AM with all the guarana-wired security goons in tow. Like a bloodhound hot on the trail, Agent Torrez raised his inebriated nose and sniffed at the night breeze. He signed in the air like a black-ops lead and all the security dorks scattered themselves around him like little ninjas, hiding and ducking from invisible assassins.

"This way," he whispered and motioned to me as if I were going to buy into that whole alpha-dog bit the same way his new found fan-boys had.

After we walked aimlessly for hours through storehouse after storehouse with Torrez stuffing one of his duffel bags full of evidence, slash, unclaimed and expired merchandise, we made our way back to the security office where he commandeered the video surveillance system with the boys falling all over his prowess and procedure. Like love struck teeny-boppers they gave him every bit of information he needed without question or discernment.

Agent Torrez holed us up in that filthy office with a few cases of Tecate and an entire pack of Early Cal's *special cigarettes* and we poured through what seemed like years of nearly unchanging industrial scenery. My vision clouded over and my chin hit my chest as the sun began to break the peak of the surrounding hillside and Torrez abruptly shouted, "Jackpot, baby!" violently jarring me awake.

Even through the eye fatigue, an overabundance of liquor, and the fearsome bitch slap of Cal's secret blend, Torrez had managed to catch a minute variance in the nearly unchanging screen. An interruption in the time-code alone had alerted him to a section of missing video. It was a catch the officers thought next to impossible, yet he caught it and could now smell the scent of fear that had out-gassed from their pores and filled the room like a heavy skunk spray.

He immediately started in on the officers who evidently had not been prepped for such an occasion. One of our heroes piped up informing him that section of video had contained footage of you kicking Asher in the face and dragging him into his alleyway, then another officer chimed in and said that Asher himself edited the video because it was embarrassing to him and he swore the entire department to secrecy for that reason and that reason alone.

When Torrez asked the officers why the time-code continues to skip for a period of a few hours they all clammed up and started to panic as if the wind were being sucked directly out of their lungs. Their secrecy it turned out was only skin-deep. After a few short minutes of pointed questioning followed by a series of feckless fumbles, one of our less constituted officers finally let loose with the crucial details. He confessed that the original video contained footage of Asher dragging a man across the street; footage that never shows the man exiting the building.

And, all but one of us sighed in remorse of the damning confession. The one who did not sigh again turned olive-green and was rocking back and forth and wringing his hands with a frightening evil grin under that disgusting, pencil-thin mustache.

It turns out that Asher had paid the officers a handsome sum of money to keep that little tidbit under their hats. Bad investment, little bro'.

Agent Torrez threw a couple of joints on the desk and made sure to thank the boys for all that they do, we left the security geniuses in their kennel, and I followed behind him as he marched straightway to the storehouse across from Asher's alley. He kicked in the side door and scanned his torch around the room until it landed on a discolored crate and I shuttered in fear for my brother as Torrez ominously whispered, "Bingo."

He grabbed a nearby crowbar and instantly pried the lid off as I turned and faced the wall with my eyes closed and he yelled out like a calloused pro, "Well, that wasn't so hard now was it?"

Out of respect for the dead I faced him and hesitantly opened my eyes. I looked down on the straggler's shriveled beef jerky body lying atop a huge pile of crusty dark-brown underwear with his neck flayed open and curling over all dried and flaky at the ends. All of a sudden I began to feel sick, my jaw tensed and my tongue poured saliva with the sensation of bile rising and burning my throat. All at once my dinner rushed up and out of my mouth in an embarrassing display of bodily function.

"I hear you have a four-star restaurant here. You feel like getting a bite?" Torrez asked me as I stared deep into the derelict's throat with a pile of memories attacking me from my youth. The mummy that Asher and I found as kids leapt at me in my mind and I yelped a short burst and clapped my hands over my mouth.

"Danny, look at me. Look at me! I asked you a question," the giant sympathetically attempted to redirect me as I grew woozy and faint, keeling over and landing first on my hip, then my elbow, then my head.

When I woke up the giant was gone and was replaced with a gang of policeman, photographers, forensics techs, and coroners, and they're all still over there. The chief of police who was once a friend of my mom and dad's asked me to come here and prepare you for what's about to happen next.

Abigail pulls herself together as much as she can and she replies through a waterfall of tears and slobber, "Okay. So, what *is* about to happen next?"

"A manhunt, Abigail. A full scale manhunt."

り

As I inhaled a balloon and held the nitrous in my lungs the exposed brick of my new found friends' flat began to push in and pop out interdependent of one another, each turning every color of the rainbow like a rotating bowl of crackling Fruity Pebbles and I began to feel a bit guilty for having such an awesome time while my family was no doubt worried sick about me. But, what options did

I have at that point? Hide in the hills in a cave or party like a rock star with an entire community of free wheeling, love devoted rejects who pulled me in from the streets like magnetics?

Various punks, artists, and street goombas oscillated around me in an uproarious party mode as a bad grind-core band speedily banged out a standard dirty four-four trash beat with lackadaisical moaning vocals floating lazily on the top like a meager layer of grease on the surface of a pool. So, we swayed predictably in and out of each other, thrashing our bodies about, attracting and repulsing to the rhythm with my oily mess of red and green mop hair standing on end in an electric buzz as I eagerly poured jungle juice cup after gelatin-shot down my always anticipating throat hole.

Suddenly my gaze snapped to the back of the flat where I spotted a frightfully familiar middle-aged greaser who was eyeballing me in an intense mad-dog stare, so I flipped him off and turned my attention to the live art being created on one of the walls behind me. I picked up a tagger's pen and joined in, scrawling and scribbling free form lines and flowing patterns in an open expression around the entire piece as an oblong frame. Just then I was spun around and pinned against the brick at the shoulders, adjusting my spine and smearing ink and paint all up the back of my jacket.

Evidently the aging greaser didn't care much for my offering and he aggressively pushed my forehead back with his combined middle and forefinger. He spat in my face, "Wake up!" just before he was violently pulled off me and ejected

from the party by an assembly of peace loving
freaks and hippies. As he was shoved out the front
door I looked down at the groove worn floor boards
and witnessed a trail of fresh budding zinnia
flowers and cloverleaf sprouting mystically out of
the wood everywhere he had stepped.

As the party swung back into action I couldn't
help but feel a kinship with the greaser and
somehow I just knew that he was meant to be in my
life. So, I ran through the crowd, out the front door,
down rotten staircase after termite-eaten staircase,
and out onto the vacant street where I stood alone.
He had vanished like an elusive banshee and I was
unexpectedly covered in a smothering wash of
confusion and emotional bruising. Somehow I felt
almost abandoned by him and all of a sudden I
didn't much care for the thought of celebration, so I
started to walk along alone again.

I strolled past hotdog stands and ogling drunks,
influential billboards lit in harsh lighting and
presented for your approval in stark, high contrast;
and hookers; scores and scads of heinous, decaying,
lonesome hookers who called out to me in
desperation as their pimp leered at them from the
shadows while impatiently batting the back of her
calloused hand against her masculine palm.

As I walked and witnessed the night the nitrous
wore off completely and the booze faded away
eventually. I was far too proud to beg and much too
scared to use my highly traceable fingerprint to
purchase anything, so I gradually grew sober and
became increasingly cold and ever despondent. I
longed for the warm embrace of my Red Queen, the
hilarious grunts and skin gripping squirms of my

little Joshie, and even the rough and judgmental touch of Cowboy Danny. Although it had only been a few weeks since I had inhaled their presence I found myself finding it impossible to stay out there in the ether-world.

It wasn't real anymore. It was vapid and hollow, devoid of any substance as it were white bread to the wholesome whole wheat that is my family. My need for them became a crushing, insatiable hunger and sharply I knew that I could no longer exist bereft of them. They had grown necessary. They had become sustenance. A haunting addiction they were, more powerful than any drug, more edifying than any high, and more infuriating than any detox. I knew that I had to go home and I belatedly realized that I finally had a home to go home to.

I checked into a Catholic shelter for the night and when the morning came I began the process of resurrecting Manny King from the deep, dark depths of my bowels. I told the resident nurse that I had a head full of lice which earned me a nice, clean shaven scalp and a shower. I lined the bathroom sink with my jacket, creating a receiving vessel for my gear. I roughly pulled my studs and rings out of my left ear and face, decommissioned my bracelets and necklace and chains, stripped down to my birthday suit and laid my knives atop the whole mess that I then folded and wrapped into a tight little present. That present was then shoved into a complimentary green plastic bag marked *Personal Belongings* and I gladly jumped in the most sanitary of the moldy communal shower stalls.

I showered in scalding city water that contained high levels of fluoride to keep the masses malleable and nostril burning chlorine to sterilize and agitate the bacterium that innocuously lives on us all. When I exited the shower a pile of tattered street clothes laid folded neatly on the sink with a simple razor, a small bottle of shave cream, a soft toothbrush and toothpaste, and a sweet little note that read, "I truly believe that you're going to do great at your new job, Manny. God be with you. —Sister Magdalena"

So, a few white-lies to Sister Magda' got me what I needed: clean, shaven, and most importantly clothed in a boring and unassuming Caspar Milquetoast disguise.

"If you don't know me well, you wouldn't know me at all," I remarked to myself as I slipped an IOU in the donation box and hit Telegraph Avenue in search of a fine clothier so I could steals me a tuxedo in commemoration of my triumphant return.

I flew past flyer plastered utility poles as I ran for both life and liberty from an absolute gorilla of a security guard, looking awesome as can be in my new suit with my high gloss, high stepping dress shoes *clicking* and *clacking* the disrepaired pavement as I went. When I finally stopped running I looked back behind me and saw the gorilla about a quarter mile away huffing and puffing with one hand on his knee and the other hand scrambling through his pockets for his rescue inhaler, making me realize that a modicum of sobriety and exercise had cut my pain and pops and creaks nearly in half. Then I turned and rolled my ankle again and fell to the sidewalk, covering the entire front of my tuxedo with a fine layer of city sediment.

When I looked up from the ground I was face-to-face with one of those leaflet littered utility poles from which a bright-pink, handwritten flyer was flapping its crisp corners at me, reaching out from beneath an industrial strength staple, playfully flirting with the idea of delightfully scraping across my eyeballs. I sat up in front of it and my vision slowly focused in on the message. In thick, bold, sloppy letters Daniel's handwriting read, "The Asher Radezlav Goes to Prison Extravaganza! Featuring the musical stylings of Jerrod Twig, the entire cast of Eighth Plague players, and a seemingly never ending line up of local bands, craft-brew stands, circus acts and freak shows, skateboarders and BMX riders, fire twirlers and belly dancers, and the finale... Asher Radezlav himself will actually be incarcerated! It all happens this Friday at sundown! You better fucking be there, Asher."

As I rose in shock I looked out down the street behind me, then in front of me, then across the way and I saw that every single pole had been hit up with the same flyer that was flapping in the breeze and reaching out for me like groping little couriers.

So, I snatched it off the pole and folded it into my breast pocket as I entered the nostalgic and dying post office across the street where I attempted to schmooze a terrific, young, pierced, pink-haired postal gal named Patty into believing that I had just been mugged on my way to a St. Jude Children's Hospital fund raiser, hence the tuxedo, and that I desperately needed to get my package to our office in Muddle.

She was a cool chick and the lies only made it worse. She leaned in close over the counter and out her window whispering, "St. Jude, huh? So, what you're telling me is when this package, the package that was not stolen from you when you were mugged, the package that is clearly marked *Personal Belongings* and reeks of the street, secretly makes its way to Muddle, along with you hidden in the back of the postal van under a fifty-pound bag of mail, you're going to get your ass to that party and just before you're put in handcuffs and hauled away for your crimes against humanity you're going to publicly announce a donation of no less than fifty-thousand dollars to the St. Jude Children's Research Hospital? Is that what you're telling me? Wow, that is really, really generous of you, Mr. Radezlav. I think we can make that happen."

I stood silent again, stuck on stupid as she slowly raised her thin, tattooed finger and pointed to the *Wanted* poster hanging on the wall directly behind me.

"How did you recognize me?" I asked.

"Are you serious? You're obviously the same dude, just without all the stuff. Oh, and your smile. You have a dimple when you smile."

"And, why would you help me?"

"Because, evidently you're not too good at editing video," then she leaned over the counter even further and kissed me lightly on the cheek. "That's for every little girl out there that still needs a hero.

"The real story was leaked and the footage is on the internet. The whole damn thing is up, including you getting knocked-the-fuck-out, which is absolutely epic by the way. And, don't think we forgot about your debut online appearance as *Naked Dad to Be*. I mean come on, that was a classic piece of viral-video right there. And then there's your art, and your toys, and of course your jaw dropping letter, which is so spot on and, ugh!"

"Wait, my letter? What letter?" I asked incredulously.

"The letter you sent to the president and all his little cronies? It's all up on your website."

"Website? What website?!" I asked again from behind squinted eyes, beginning to feel a little disoriented and completely uninformed.

"You don't know about your own website? Evidently it's encoded with some kind of crazy, persistent scripting or something and the web-czars can't figure out how to pull the plug on it. It's all over the news, didn't you know? Our generation found a voice in Valzedar Rehsa. You're a fucking media sensation, man!" she said as she shook her head back and forth with her mouth hanging open.

Suddenly she snapped into business mode, slapping the counter and asking, "But, the real question still remains. Do I send the package and you make the donation or should you just start running home in that tuxedo?"

"Yes, please. Um, send the package I mean. Shit, thank you Patty. Thank you," I humbly stuttered and slipped away as she broke eye contact with me and an elated smile spread terrifically across her face as she returned to her mail sorting while chuckling, evidently still replaying my finest moment in her head.

"Sir, large packages like yours need to be checked in with Emmanuel in the back," she giggled as my feet locked and I fell backward through the front door and out onto the street, filled with thanksgiving and appreciation for life's little serendipitous synchronicities.

As I crawled under the suffocating mail bags with Emmanuel's mariachi music blasting my ears, I couldn't help but meditate on what Postal Patty had said about me being a hero. Was I indeed a hero? Is there anything truly admirable about taking another's life under any circumstance? Not that there aren't instances in which it would become necessary. Such is the case with life decimating rape, retribution of premeditated homicide, or the preservation of self while under the bone chilling shadow of death. Necessary, yes, but is it admirable? No, destruction of life should never be celebrated. Released from boundaries of flesh with respect, yes, but never celebrated. I was no hero.

After Emmanuel finished his entire route we hit the freeway and a few hours later the postal van climbed up, up, up the great spiraling mount. He dropped me off in the crisp morning air as an anthill of workers scurried about propping up tents and booths, constructing stages and ramps, and sneaking cups and mugs of delicious local home-brews into their mischievous bellies.

I dusted myself off and employed my skills of a ghost-boy as I walked casually past officers and detectives. "Master of ceremonies," I said to one of them as I approached The Eighth Plague.

"Excuse me?" he asked while straightening up

and adjusting his gun.

I looked him right in the eye while tightening my bowtie and I summoned the broadcaster from my dreams, announcing in an overly deep and hammy voice while holding my left ear, "M.C. Tim Boston and Tim Boston Entertainment invite you to take an exciting ride this Friday evening! Be there or be square as alt-pop recording artist Jerrod Twig takes the stage!" Then I jumped back and posed like a celebrity asking, "Well, do you recognize me? Do you want a signed eight-by-ten glossy or what? You want a glossy. Let me get you a glossy."

I persisted like a self-serving salesman until the officer shouted, "Beat it, guy. We're looking for a psycho right now, not some poor excuse for a disc jockey."

"Well, what does he look like?" I asked.

"I said move it, fella'!" he snarled while kicking at me as if he were shooing away a stray dog.

So, I walked up staircase after psychedelic staircase, ultimately making my way to the defunct Twig residence. As I approached the front door I began to hear a soft, soul penetrating melody filling the halls; the song that Jerrod had played for us since I was six-years-old. His guitar was singing sweetly as I lightly rapped on the door.

He answered with long and shaggy, candy-blue Jesus hair, a jet-black goatee, and a shocked and surprised look became his face as he shouted, "Asher!" and burst into me in a much needed show of love and affection.

"Ssshh, no one knows I'm here," I whispered as Jerrod pulled me in by the silky lapels and slammed the door behind me.

I collapsed on Jerrod's mattress on the floor with the exact same mess around us that we made as kids and I felt as if we had never left. I pulled the extravaganza flyer out of my breast pocket, tacked it up with the rest of his flyer collection, and I made believe that there weren't an entire mob of authoritarians outside waiting to lay anxious hands of violence on me, I declined to believe that punk-rock Danny was now Cowboy Dan, and I pretended that Mom and Dad and Mr. Twig were at the factory toiling away at their passion as their hearts overflowed with love for us kids.

I began to drift off as Jerrod adeptly picked his guitar strings and hummed that age-old enchanting lullaby of safety and serenity which weaved in and out of my consciousness as a melodious spell that thoroughly plummeted me into a weighty, dreamless slumber.

When I woke it was pitch-black in his room and I was alone and covered in a pile of pungent blankets with a spiked, red leather bracelet affixed to my wrist. The spotlights outside intermittently lit the room as I heard Jerrod's voice calling out to me over the loud speakers, "Asher, we know you're in there. Come out with your hands up, Mr. Valzedar!" and the crowd that stretched from The Eighth Plague to BA Toys, Inc. roared like a capacity packed coliseum anticipating its very own lion slaying gladiator.

I flew through the labyrinth of halls and doorways in a guided clarity, down the sticky stairs as a single step, and slid out onto the seventh plague floor where California, Daniel, Joshua, and

Abigail were all waiting for me in the dark with tears in their eyes that were glistening and reflecting those same rotating Fruity Pebble colors of the carnival just outside.

"We knew if we threw you a party you would have to show up. You never could resist a good old party," said Danny in a shaky and betrayed voice.

"I missed you guys so much!" I cried as I ran to them and pulled Abigail and Joshua in like daddy bear, but daddy bear was not well received.

Joshua slapped at me and screeched in my ear, "Ma-ma-ma!" as Abigail pulled him closer and turned her face to the ground, slowly inching in toward Danny while remaining silent and inconsolable with her feet turned in pigeon-toed, looking like a freaking parody of herself. So, I stepped back a few heart broken paces to behold my beautiful family in all their radiant splendor and I inhaled the deepest breath that I had ever inhaled in my entire life, as if it were my last olfactory sense of them.

The courage to speak rallied itself from the recesses of my unconscious mind and I whimpered, "I am truly sorry for ruining this, you guys. I see now, right this very moment, that you four mean everything in the world to me. Absolutely everything," and then I turned my back on them and ran headlong through one of our bay windows, landing in a pile of glass shards out on the street.

They simultaneously yelled, "Asher!" as I bloodily rose from the pile and scrambled feverishly past cops and guards, up stage-left stairs, and out into the retina-scorching spotlight to greet the public and announce my charitable donation.

But, before I could get the words out a gigantic Cab Calloway looking mother-fucker with a totally gross John Waters mustache clotheslined me, wrenched my arms behind my back, coldly crashed handcuff hooks against my wrists, and took me into custody for the heinous crime of righteously protecting the love of my life.

Chapter Eleven

The Kenites and The Zadok

Whether voluntarily or mandatorily, when you first stop taking drugs you don't really know what to do with yourself. The apparatus for ingestion or injection is exposed as a prevailing enemy against you. The muscle memory of your hand autonomously lifts to action and ideation of terror confounds your mind and clouds your judgment, keeping you from the revelation that the crutch has lost its usefulness, that the break or sprain has healed.

You can run again, but you don't. Your breath becomes invisible as the smoke clears your lungs. You can run again, but you won't. Your skin binds back together as the toxins extrude through permeable layers of flesh. You can run again, but you're scared. The haze drains from off your eyes and in the face of change, poison himself slowly releases his dark grasp on you, the grasp that he had held so tight for so many years. You can run again and believe me, my son, you will. It just takes a while for you to see and to settle, that's all. It just takes a while.

When I was twenty-six-years-old I was made to live in a confine. The Judge told me I would be fifty-nine-years-young before I would again roam the earth as a free man; the exact age my dad was when I was born, which meant that he was just seven-years-old when he and his parents fled their place of origin for the land of the fee, home of the caged.

My trial was a beautiful affair and everyone I

loved, and some that I didn't, was there to support me or testify against me respectively. Also, the agreeable young gents down at the jail gave me a spiffy new grass-green and true-orange, vertically striped jumpsuit that I have to admit fit me like gangbusters. And, with good fortune such as this I was again forced to ask myself, what more could I need?

Postal Patty and an amassing hoard of destroying locust activists were protesting loudly on the steps of the courthouse just outside, chanting messages of freedom and individual justice, bolstering my burgeoning hypothesis that I would soon be an end-times apostle and a dreaming prophesier for the coming rebellion. But, I was currently being made controversy incarnate and I just couldn't help but feel the slightest bit used.

Evidently my website whose code was found to be authored by the fugitive hacker known as The Black Mushroom, or as I call him fucking Cal, had sparked a national debate on personal protections, the ever diminishing right to bear arms, police response as pertaining to the limitations of time, space, and the perception of urgency; and the nature of homicide itself while living daily under the oppressive weight of an increasingly evil society on the brink.

It seemed as though Cal had been framing me as the public figurehead of the modern discontent for sometime now and I'm not quite sure how that was supposed to help my case. Not to mention the fact that Mr. Early had apparently been operating a digital revolution from an undisclosed location within the walls of The Eighth Plague. And, with the obvious ties between Manny King and The Black Mushroom it was only a matter of time before that Torrez fucker became the wiser and hauled Cal's ass in too.

"By the way, Dan, I sure hope you've been enjoying your roommate," I snickered over my shoulder from the defendant's chair.

"Yeah, fuck you, asshole," said Danny so lovingly from amongst the seated murmuring crowd behind me.

"His Honor" repeatedly clacked his gavel on its base and a hush fell over the courtroom. With all the above in attendance I regrettably heard the words, "Asher Radezlav, also known as the vandal Manny King, also known as the political terrorist Valzedar Rehsa, I hereby sentence you to thirty-three-years imprisonment in the Arkansas Ozark Highlands Facility for the Criminally Insane. You have been found guilty of committing the transgression of voluntary manslaughter for which you shall dutifully pay your debt to society in full. Make sure you thank your lawyer, Mr. Radezlav. Without his persuasions I may not have come to such a good-natured judgment."

Although my lawyer, Harvey the Slick, had previously been marvelous at swaying and influencing the minds and verdicts of my little assault and battery foibles it looked as though I was going to have to take this one on the chin. In consolation for his lack of ability to wave a slippery palm and make it all go away he had arranged for the androgen to testify as to the fragility of my mental state, Baryshnikov the bartender provided accounts of my volatility and proclivity toward violence, and my family attested to the evolution of my continued mental erosion, all leading the judge to the conclusion that I was largely mentally unstable; a conclusion that was most likely not far from the truth, but I still resented the implications.

The last witness Slick Harv had arranged for was a seminal member of the AOHFCI, Dr. Eli Pesache. Doc Pesache was a tall, thin man with a tightly trimmed head of radiant silver hair and a razor sharp gentlemen's goatee. He wore your standard smarty pants uniform: thick black Buddy Holly glasses, a tweed jacket, tan corduroy pants, and a tie-dyed Grateful Dead shirt for good measure. With legs crossed and expressive hands expressing, he delivered an absolutely astounding dissertation on why he believed their facility, above all others in the country, was uniquely suited to my specific deficiencies and I naturally assumed it a cake walk; an arranged white-collar vacation of sorts.

So, my family and I entered an inner sanctum and I said a sorrowful goodbye to my beautiful Joshie who tugged at my ears and gnawed new teeth lightly on my cheek, spreading a terrific layer of slobber across my face that I did not wipe clean. Abigail hurried in and embraced us in what felt like a desperate plea to hold onto something that we both knew was in the process of decay. Not that her love for me was spent, but rather changing. And last but not least, Danny sidled up and silently and tearfully enveloped us all as Doc Pesache entered the room and peaceably whispered, "It's time, folks. Asher, you have to let go now."

That was but one in a handful of times in which I actually saw Danny cry and it meant the world to me that he had decided to plug the wires, one red, one yellow, and one blue; back in so he could properly assimilate the bittersweet sting of life, a necessary sensation for a patriarch.

As I relinquished Joshua to his mama's ever nurturing grasp and released our bond they both burst open in a unified wailing moan and naturally shifted into Danny's welcoming arms as a familiar guard respectfully reapplied handcuffs to my trembling wrists. The guard compassionately took me under his wing and ushered Doc Pesache and me out a back door and into an unmarked white van that had been retrofitted inside with a series of shoddy, odd angled, spot welded bars. As the sliding door secured, the dwindling cries of my ex-fiancé and son were finally squelched altogether and I was eerily reminded of being stuck inside the lattice of plumbing cube from my dreams; that leaky cage that held my family photos and saved me from the rapture.

The driver of the van, who looked a great deal like my dad, lit up a humorously large cigar and turned to me with his breath all steaming and rolling and winding through the shoddy bars. He asked me in a strange high pitched, raspy voice that did not suit his body type, "Are you ready for this, kid?" I redirected my focus to the floorboards and kept solemnly quiet to which he squeaked, "Have it your way, guy, but I'm warning you it's going to be a long ride."

He faced forward again and lightly shook his head back and forth, making the large glowing coal at the end of his cigar drift in and out of my view as we began our stealthy getaway, rolling slowly toward the swollen gates of the hallowed house of the law.

As we snuck into plain view we were instantly mobbed by a sea of news crews and activists who slammed against the vehicle like a school of angry trout, smashing wire-enforced windows with bricks and rocks and rocking it back and forth like a covered dinghy on discontented waters. But as always, machine beat muscle and we emerged victorious from the sea of mashed toes and insteps.

As we parted the crowd Postal Patty burst forth like a siren sounding out from a solitary island. With a look of satisfaction and grace she beamed bright rays of positive sunshine from a force-field of psychic energy as her long lustrous hair flitted in the wind like little pink scalpels. She pulled her well worn flannel open to reveal a homemade, red stenciled undershirt that held tightly to her stunning curves and braless breasts and she inaudibly read aloud, "Free Valzedar Rehsa."

She confidently blew me a series of airborne kisses while raising a cardboard sign over her head that read, "Remember St. Jude," and she watched me as I watched her become a simple dot on the horizon with our images fading to memory as the bountiful trees of Muddle grew distant and blurry through the battered back window.

A few somber minutes passed and I turned to my doctor who was seated next to me and asked, "Just how long a drive is it, doc?"

He took his glasses off and rubbed his eyes awful then squinted at me and replied ghoulishly,

"Three and a half days in the grave, Mr. Radezlav."

"Three and a half days in the grave," the driver parroted.

I assumed them trying to intimidate me, so I paid it no mind and inquired, "Why not just fly there?"

Doc Pesache put his glasses back on, blinked three times distinctly, and shifted his head toward the driver as if to warn me of mixed company.

"We're not exactly your normal mental health care providers," he said. "We like to get to know each and every individual on a personal basis, so we get the whole picture. I figure the drive will give us a good head-start."

"Well, you'll have to excuse me if I'm not exactly thrilled with your profession, doc. I'm just a bit sketchy when it comes to sorcerers, you know?"

"Are you talking about *pharmacia*, the use of drugs and psychology to control the weak minded?" he asked surprisingly hitting the nail on the head, making my Doubting-Thomas-face suddenly show a bit more respect.

As the driver leered at us through the rearview mirror, Doc Pesache undid my cuffs, pulled a joint from his right front pocket, and held it in front of my face saying, "While I certainly do not practice mind control, from time to time I do recommend pharmaceuticals. Please do not construe this as an invitation to misbehavior, Mr. Radezlav. I am a licensed physician and after much deliberation I've decided to medically recommend you marijuana as a means of psychological regulation while in a state of mental crisis; and I do believe you to be in a state of mental crisis."

He handed it to me along with a lighter, but just before I could grab them he retracted his offering. "As your physician and resident sorcerer as you so nimbly phrased it, I've taken the time to conduct a few interviews with your family and friends and they've all said that you tend to episode worst when sober for an extended period of time.

"Since you've apparently found what works best for you and it appears that you've been able to regiment your self-medication for the majority of your lifetime, in conjunction with the years that you've spent misdiagnosed and incorrectly medicated, I am willing to consent to this aspect of your personal plan of care." Then he handed it to me again and again withdrew it and continued.

"But, know this Mr. Radezlav; while you are under my care you will follow my instructions *without hesitation*. You will do as you are told and if you do not you will be summarily punished by way of solitary confinement and sensory deprivation. Is that completely understood?" he asked as he suggestively nodded in the affirmative and openly handed me the smoker.

I waited an impatient second or two then quickly snatched it from his providing hand like a thankful pup answering, "Yes, sir. You are understood."

"After all, you did kill a man," he said emotionless as he confidently sat back and threw the lighter in my lap.

I sat still for a moment and shot him a perplexed look then lit up and puff, puff, puffed away like an elated and eager adolescent, making the driver scoff in judgment as his smoke and mine indiscriminately intermingled in a thick dancing fog.

With a big hit in my lungs I garbled, "You know, I see what you're trying to do here, but the first thing you ought to know about me is I'm a talker. All I do is talk. Blah, blah, blah with no need for solicitation. Just ask me anything. Really, anything."

"Okay, since you put it that way. How does one behave like a hedonist and reconcile himself a Christian? How long has it been since you've read the word? How much have you healed since your parents died and why aren't you further along in that process? What's with the chemical-dependency issues? You're not thirteen-years-old anymore. You've shirked your duties as a father and for what, the life of a transient? Oh here's a good one, what in the holy name of sweet-Jesus would make you think it was a good idea to expose your genitals to the entire world? Why did you disgrace your family name by unnecessarily staining your hands with a man's blood? And, above all else, Mr. Radezlav, why in the hell would you willingly turn yourself over to the authorities? Do you even know who you are?"

I covered my mouth and choked my hit out through my fingers, my eyes locked open like Alex DeLarge, and I sucked my chin in and muttered, "What in the shit was all that about?"

The good doctor just shook his head in disapproval and from out of nowhere removed a syringe from his inner breast pocket. He snapped the cap off and said, "You've got a long way to go, son, and a whole lot left to learn. You'd better finish up that smoke. I have a feeling you're going to need it."

The driver cackled menacingly as Doc Pesache tapped the chamber of the syringe and carefully pushed the air bubbles out in that classic, cinematic way. I tensed in fear and scattered myself back in a panic response, but instead of closing in on me the doc silently reached through the front bars and all at once stabbed the driver in the neck and injected him with a healthy dose of knockout juice.

The driver shrieked a high-pitched, "Gah!" and his head toppled over as his neck gave out. His hands went limp and slid off the steering wheel as his face hit the horn and I puffed uncontrollably on my doob like a tranquilizing security blanket.

The yellow lane dividing Pac-Man dots pounded out a boisterous warning from under the tires going *thimp-thimp-thimp* as the doc calmly fastened his seatbelt, crossed his legs and pointed at my all but consumed joint saying, "See what I mean? Dependency issues."

"Why did you do that?!" I screamed at him as I held horrified to the front bars, watching a ditch swiftly approaching through the hotbox fog and out the shattered front window.

With one eyebrow raised he looked deep in me and earnestly replied, "Because I believe in you, Asher, and because they're not who you think they are, now put your seatbelt on."

"Who isn't, doc? Who isn't who I think they are?" I asked in desperate curiosity as the solid white sideline began to sprint dangerously beneath us, leading us into the gravel.

He answered pensively, "The Kenites, Asher.

The Kenites."

My seatbelt clicked just seconds before we crashed into the ditch going about seventy miles an hour. The driver's side headlamp impacted into the hillside crumpling the front end and making the van flip ass up and somersault over as the doc and I hung heavy against our belts. We violently met the unforgiving earth and burst into a barrel roll with the seats and glass and makeshift cage tumbling around us and busting down bit by bit; pummeling, scraping, and cutting every inch of us in a painfully even dispersal.

Time all but halted as a huge shard of glass flew by my head and decisively severed my shoulder strap. It slackened from off me and I hung weightless as the van pivoted around me like a gyroscope, positioning my right hip directly above the metal bar that ran across the top of my seat. As we impacted for the last time the moment exploded and the bar bluntly interjected itself into my side and perfectly snapped my hip screws.

The crash had unsecured the side sliding door and somewhere along the path claimed a chunk of Doc Pesache's head. He hemorrhaged appallingly as he pulled me from the wreckage with me screaming disturbingly like a pubescent, braying rooster. I guess the doc was a bit more of a man than I was, because he ripped his *Steal Your Face* shirt right off his body, tied it around his head, and ran up the mount toward the tree line.

When he reached the top of the ridge he turned to me and called down, "Your father was a great man, son. Remember every word that he said and look for new meaning. I'm sure he left you instructions. He must have. Oh, and one last thing, physician, heal thyself. You can run again!" Then he turned and bolted into the thick manzanita.

As I lay there in the ditch, sunken in the gravel and the gasoline-mud, I had the notion to follow the good doctor's orders, but when I tried to move my hip, fierce pain and dense agony pinned me to the ground. The shock shifted me out of my body about seven inches toward outer space and it was there in the waiting that I realized the world I knew and my perceptions of it were all illusory.

Pain was revealed to me as but a warning and a limitation that could be overcome with enough understanding, so I shifted into it and fell back in my body, fully experiencing every little nuance and realizing that I could control my vessel to a greater extent than I had ever thought possible.

I lunged into my hip and heard a loud crunch and a pop and the pain subsided a bit. I wrapped my talons around a root piercing the excavated, red-clay hillside and as I climbed to my feet I was pranked in the back of the head with a tire iron. Smack dab on the bull's-eye he laid it, right across the gift that Danny gave me those few years back.

The scar fibers speedily unzipped and my head reopened in a fabulous spray as the driver sleepily squeaked from behind me, "How holy are you now, God-boy? Last apostle my ass."

The world went triple-black as the tire iron dropped from his hand and plopped down in the mud next to me, then he crashed down with it and when he landed the ground broke away and we both fell down the tunnel of dreams, fighting and colliding and gouging at each other.

When we hit the basement floor of the dream world I snapped awake to find myself locked in solitary confinement with no light and no sound, just like the doc said would happen if I did not follow his instructions without hesitation.

I quickly learned what three and a half days in the grave *really* meant. It was their colloquialism for the solitary room or as they sometimes called it, Mr. Black. Over the next few days Mr. Black and I got to know each other very well and it was there that I reconvened with God and received my messages of the future. While under the confines of the dark and externally silent expanse he instructed me that I was to record these messages in a mound of letters addressed to a darker flock whom I referred to as the Eking Ants. But, more importantly God taught me how to protect them in the recesses of my mind, so that no man could displace them from me.

When I was finally released from my hole and made familiar with the AOHFCI, I found that it was actually quite a healing environment. Nestled in the Arkansas mountains, the structural design of the building appeared to be straight out of a seventies architect's vision of the future. Clean, sharp lines ran up to the heavens and swerved carefully into high, vaulted ceilings; everything that could be painted stark-white was painted stark-white, and inmate art collected with age in a massive collage that covered the majority of available wall space. There were art and music therapy rooms, a chapel with access to many works of interfaith literature, and a capable staff that genuinely seemed to care about us. It was indeed sanctuary.

My addiction specialist kept me sober and walked me through the steps of not only physical, but mental detoxification and I slowly became clearer and more focused on my goal of sanity and sobriety. My psychotherapist patiently and professionally helped me manage my pain and panic through non-narcotic medication and mental exercises, some of which I had shockingly never been taught before. With the help of my surgeon, my rehabilitation therapist worked with me on the daily to restore my deconstructed hip, which to their astonishment no longer required the screws I had acquired as a teen. And finally, my neurologist tackled my seizures and helped me to understand the physical progression and mechanics of my neuroses. And, with completely free, world-class services such as this I found myself considering taking my boots off and settling in for a spell.

During my stay the goon-squad and I enjoyed open access to the therapy rooms and of course I made a few superficial acquaintances while frequenting the common area, but I couldn't help but yearn for the desensitized serenity and communion that I found while seated in the bowels of Mr. Black, so in consequence I hermitted myself away and disobeyed the authority as often as possible.

The days that I did not send myself to the dark I attended group with a bunch of whackos who all seemed to share the same past. They had been raped, abused, psychologically beaten, raised in makeshift dungeons, and no matter how hard I tried to sympathize with them I just couldn't relate to those kinds of experiences.

I found it difficult to heal from my comparatively shallow wounds in that heavy atmosphere, but for the goons I would fake it to make it and I was more than comfortable with helping them navigate their torn emotions. I often led group and for the most part I was an open book. It was also quite an ego boost how smart and well adjusted they all thought I was and because of them I realized how truly blessed I had been. I was raised in a supportive family, had come from wealth and education, and having been supplied with the appropriate faculties to weigh life's moral equations and make consequent decisions, most of which would fall within acceptable societal bounds, I actually started to feel alright about myself.

Despite being mentally-deficient rapists and murderers, they actually weren't a bad bunch of guys. Sure most of them would have re-created the same set of atrocities that had been revoltingly thrust upon them, only this time with *me* locked in the basement and *them* with the whip, but we were all there making an honest effort to heal. Plus, the guards did an absolutely fantastic job of reigning in the fuck ups by way of verbal redirection, especially during the potentially volatile situations that would arise during group. I guess the Tasers and pepper-spray they wore probably helped a bit too.

That week's group leader was a particularly degenerated sewer dweller. His teeth were scraggled hard from poor genetics, his face was tattooed with tears and crosses and blotches from bad stick and poke prison tats, his mannerisms were crude and gross, but oh how he tried to rise above; oh how hard he tried. Like a childish sponge he had soaked in the establishment rhetoric and out of a sincere yet manufactured compassion he asked me in front of everyone in his unfortunately irreparable white-trash gangster voice, "Why does your arm say Christian?"

Seated in the circle I looked down my plain cream colored scrubs and stared at my standard-issue beige canvas shoes. I scratched at the simple black tattooed block letters that ran vertically down my left bicep and I replied in a whisper, "Because that's how I self identify, okay? I don't really want to talk about it right now. Just move on to someone else."

He snarled at first, then quickly composed himself and politely articulated, "Really? After all that we've shared with you, Asher? You do realize this is the purpose of group, to discuss the matters from which we hide, to make known the crooked paths and to set them straight? Perhaps, if I ask you in another way. Asher, *who* was Christian?"

That kind of feel good talk didn't mean much to me coming from Bucky the backwoods beaver who had previously confessed his visceral sins of brutal patricide and as such thirty more seconds passed and I just sat there silent and stoic.

"We'll wait," he said to the unsettling group of bastard people as he impatiently tapped his tattooed fingers that read *Kill* on his right hand and *God* on his left.

The guards sprang to action as I ruptured sudden and they pulled me back while I leapt and screamed at him, "Alright Bucky Beaver, since you asked me so nice and eloquent-like, Christian was supposed to be my first born, okay? But, my ex saw

fit to do away with mine, just like you saw fit to do
away with yours!"

At first he held himself from behind a fuming
dam of rage and violence, but the call became all
too much for his meager set of learning and of
course he tackled me and the guards and he hastily
bloodied my face as I giggled and hollered and
thrashed about like Cal in the gravel with my red,
red blood spurting all over them.

That night in my cage I dug at the remaining
pepper in my eyes and acted out a bit by inciting
the inmates to frenzy with parables of the end. I
told them of the slain lamb that spake as the
leviathan of the deep, the five stalwart virgins in
waiting who had saved up enough lamp oil for the
long stay ahead, the seven headed, ten horned
dragon that were the governments of the world and
the leaders there of; and how each sixth of the three
sacred sets of signs of the end foretold of the
antichrist and how he would steal the world away
and those who had not fortified themselves along
with it.

Well, you can just imagine how much the
inmates loved that manner of mentation. They all
went off like Gilliam's monkeys and again I took
company with Mr. Black.

When I next saw the light of day I was made to
meet with the resident chaplain who hotly
informed me that he did not appreciate my
"impromptu sermons" and that each time I decided
to spread my "venomous disinformation" I would
be relegated to Mr. Black.

I calmly responded, "That'll be just fine, my son.
Mr. Black is my portal to the voice of God and no

earthly man can silence that. If every riot that my sermons spurn lead me back to Mr. Black then every coming out of Mr. Black will lead to another riot, now won't it?" And, again I took company with Mr. Black.

Over the course of my first year at the AOHFCI, I had spent nearly three months in the hole and had become quite accustomed to receiving my meals in the noir. As I ate my daily bread I traveled wherever I pleased and strolled through my memories as a painstaking observer. I relived my life again and again, looking for patterns and listening closely to the words of my father as the incomparable Doc Pesache had instructed.

It took me a few passes, but I eventually found the pattern of my life and the sacred geometry that ran through it. There in the black my memory hiccupped painfully and the ancient identity of my family tree was again revealed to me. We are members of God's elect and the opposite side of the Kenite coin. We are descendants of the priest-line and I am Zadok.

My father had long spoken of the Kenites and the Zadok, but I always took it as a night story, because that's the way he told it. But, over the time I spent in the interfaith chapel I realized that every legend was born of a preexisting truth and that every truth is not exactly as it seems. For we are creatures so subject to perspective and conditioning that it is impossible to clearly see, well, anything really; much less the generational pass-down of a complicated allegory wrapped in the guise of a simplistic fairytale.

On at least the weekly my dad would tuck me

into bed and with the hall light magnifying big and small through his thick bifocal glasses he would outlandishly act out one of his narratives as if he were some kind of old-world Czech minstrel.

With his wine breath chuffing through his waning accent he began, "The common man asks himself, 'How did this evil come upon the earth, what is the meaning of life for the righteous, and above all else if there is a God why has he done this to us?'

"Are we so quick to forget, my cherub? The sides were drawn, our minds were made, and now we must all pass through this life that *we* have deemed hell. Every last one of us.

"That includes the good army that stood against the rebel leader in the heavenly realm, the downtrodden and common man whose steps were indecisive and destined for mediocrity, and last and yes least, the serpents."

As my father's words resonated, my memory broke and I found me standing in a lush garden of primordial flora. An asp snapped a defensive warning at my ankle as I rounded a bend and beheld a pair of naked humans, man and woman, standing petrified in the company of Wormwood in the thick of the Fertile Crescent.

My father continued, "The serpents however came into the world a bit sooner than the others did, for they were the offspring of the first child born unto this woman."

The image of an apple being bitten into and sexually exploding its juices flashed across my eyes as I approached.

"But, coincidentally the elect came from the

same womb when she continued in labor. So, how can it be that the good and the evil of this world came from the same woman? An intelligent man might say, 'If they had two fathers.'"

Suddenly, they became aware of my presence and the man and woman turned to me in shame as Wormwood burst into hysterical laughter and simply walked away into the encroaching darkness. The two scrambled at the ground and the trees around them, trying desperately to produce cover for their nakedness as they motioned for me to flee and their images and the garden died off and dissipated like a screen of gossamer web drifting into the lightless abyss.

And, just like that, another three and a half days in the grave concluded as the solitary door opened and the sun overfilled my gaping pupils. When I was escorted to my room I found that my writing utensils and papers, my canvases and paints, my sermons and drawings, and the New Oxford Dictionary that had been given to me as a gift upon arrival had all been displaced from their homes.

It had been determined by the head of the AOHFCI that those items in particular were aiding in my psychosis and as such had been confiscated. But, try as they might, they couldn't remove the master copies from my always circulating computer-head. In order to access my protected files all I had to do was pay a visit to Mr. Black, a process that I had since learned to recreate day or night, dark or light, whenever or wherever I saw fit.

That night I laid me down on my stripped down bed and crashed out hard due to the exhaustion of my interstellar mind travels. As I drifted off into a crushing slumber I heard the diminishing words of my father fall back into the recesses of my mind and echo, "So, where are the good, the bad, and the unlucky today? Well, son, they're out there... and we're in here. Aren't we, my boy?"

Chapter Twelve

The Coming Out of Zerubbabel

As I sat quaking in the dark and silent cube with my hands held out in front of me as a seismograph I heard explosions, a succession of explosions, and gunfire, a smattering of gunfire. I wondered if the noises I heard were imagined or factual and I worried not for self, but for others afar off; family members from which I had not heard in years. And, why hadn't I heard from them in years?

I solidified there in a discontented lotus seat of meditation for the three and a half days and contemplated why I had not been fed, watered, or medicated in the last two. Then another two days passed. Five and a half days in the grave? That doesn't even make sense.

It amazed me how quickly my body dehydrated and revolted from me in those days. My mouth became dry cotton after the first, by the third my temples bulged out and sucked in on a metronome heartbeat with the word *hydra* turning and growing in my brain, on the morning of the fifth my body cried out like a barren, splitting desert waiting to be quenched by its seasonal monsoon seen coming at a distance; and at midday I considered the terrifying odds that I may have been locked and abandoned in Waylon's great tomb that knows no sound.

The damming thirst that ravaged my tongue was awful, the clenching hunger fist that pounded my puckered stomach had become unadulterated pain of fire, but the lack of reference materials was by far the worst. That slithering reptilian *hydra*, that underdeveloped and nearly formless informatic, was boring through my mind and secreting hallucinatory trauma.

In my delirium I saw visions of the south rising again. A confederate flag excitedly fishtailed from the back of a military Jeep as heaps upon heaps of militiamen poured and spilled out over the hillsides like bad little stop motion puppets. They shouted lip-synced battle cries in unison as their black powder muskets and AK-47s exploded from their meaty shoulders in great pluming clouds of metallic slug death.

I laid me facedown on the cold, hard floor enacting one of the few senses they could not take from me and I put my ear to ground to see if I could hear anything through the thick concrete slab. Just then a massive detonation shook the room and sent shockwaves of concussive thunder straight through my ear bones and directly into my already beaten brain. I jolted back and pressed my palms firmly against my ringing ears as I unwittingly sucked in big, fat hits of lung stinging concrete dust. Sitting pained and panicked in the big black empty, I knew for sure that the last blast could not have been my overactive imagination.

A muffled electrical power-down sounded through my deep cell walls and I dared to daydream of a valiant and courageous rescue mission led by some random crackpot zealot who haphazardly mistook my image for a drunken messiah. I heard a series of breaker pops and the high-pitched ramping charge of generators firing and suddenly the security of my confine was compromised. The lockset tumblers tumbled and the thick, heavy door cracked open sending a sharp silver sliver of light shooting audaciously across the floor of my black hole detention, up the fractured wall, and back to its source.

Like a free-falling bottle of beer I sat in gut wrenching suspense and raw anticipation of who it was that would fling my door wide and release me from captivity. But, of course the door just lazily opened itself and traveled to its capacity to reveal no one at all, and I mean absolutely no one. Apparently I had been deserted in a panic and was miraculously spared by a designer's failsafe, may the Lord increase his or her prescience.

Lethargically I climbed to my feet as my pupils constricted to pinholes and I exited my capsule like a creature birthed into the strange. Immediately my eyes snapped to the catastrophe that had befallen the main entrance wall, the one that stretched to the heavens. It had been breached by what must have been a rocket launcher or some such comparable device and had been rent from top to bottom like a giant curtain pulled apart, exposing the main lobby to the glory and splendor of the autumn elements.

A mob of large crows dove hauntingly through the mammoth divide and opened their wings like parachutes just seconds before landing on the admissions desk where they happily strutted back and forth, calling out a brash message to me like cocky little paisans as great gusts of wind pushed in behind them, tasking a procession of happy, little dancing golden leaves to cartwheel and twirl up and over the piles of powdered concrete and mounds of pebbles and stacks of rocks and loads of hulking boulders that had been rudely blasted from the wall and cast about the room, creating a landscape fit for aliens.

Remnants of a troubled exodus lay strewn throughout my entire field of vision and I heard lingering shouting traveling away from me in the distance, so in consequence I began to dance lightly with the leaves and the crows, feeling neither danger nor fear.

Under sickness of hunger and madness of thirst I trudged along to the kitchen sink where the world's best water flowed free from a rusty pipe that jutted out from behind busted blue tile. It extinguished my thirst with fluid grace and I got my fill, but my body did not agree with my recommendation and the liquid uncontrollably expelled from my stomach. I let the unfiltered faucet pour out over my head, in through my long brown hair and bushy beard, I took little sips of it out the corners of my mouth and it begrudgingly settled into my intestines.

In a half charged lope I galloped to the first food I saw and my memories of Cal and me chomping yellow nibblets with heads full of acid projected from my mind onto the giant cans of corn that peeled enjoyably off the painted pantry shelves and turned in a graceful pirouette under a large food service can opener.

Then and there I submerged myself in hot water in the kitchen sink as I crudely masticated scoops of corn and crunched down hard on icy tater tots and gnawed on frozen chicken patties with the sun going down over the hillside, casting its orange inferno lighting in through the destructed entrance and up the mismatched mess-hall tiles. It filled my eyes with a fearsome and awe inspiring glow and I was truly a happy boy. A man and his chicken pucks, frosty tots, and monster can of corn sitting in a kitchen sink hot tub at sundown, now that is a beautiful thing.

With my belly distended and my emotional ties to humanity beginning to fray and unknot I wandered around the facility shivering and dripping wet as I observed the destruction and evident signs of distress. I began to feel a great sorrow let down upon me and although I had busied myself with the pursuit of God and the investigation of self I could no longer hide from the fact that the entirety of my stay at the AOHFCI had not yielded contact in any manner by any member of my crew. Not by my family nor by my friends, not by phone, not by fax, neither email nor snail-mail, not by text nor in person, not at all, not at all! So, I just fell inside myself and came to the completely unnatural sense that my family no longer loved me, that they were fully healed and wholly beyond me and again I reached a sobering decimation.

Through the exasperatingly high-def, crystal clear clarity of sobriety; coupled with the sharp shooting bind of cranial pressure that was now my head, I spied the med-room door that was swung open wide, wide, wide with a slew of colorful pills and pill bottles splayed across the floor. Like a cartoon mouse floating hypnotized on a beckoning aroma cloud of cheese odor I flew to their warm embrace and excitedly poured over my options, my cornucopia of deadly options. Every pharmaceutical known to man lay in my hands and in consolation of loss I freaking laid into them with a furious vengeance.

First I zonked myself on diazepam, then I dabbled in chlorpromazine, then I rounded the whole mess out with my bad old friend oxycodone. And, that was just an hors d'oeuvre.

As the moon sat high in its honorable sky seat I gladly donned my dripping sludge monster persona like a weighty royal robe pulled from the recesses. I lurched playfully around the facility, my facility, slamming into walls and breaking locks and rummaging through drawers, kicking in doors and chopping angrily at electrically fried computers with my misappropriated red and white fire axe, snooping through the doctors' scandalous closet secrets and searching like Scooby and the gang for scraps and craps and clues, all the while bonkering myself on fistfuls of doof-balls.

I sluggishly fumbled through backroom tub after storeroom crate until I happened upon a box marked *Property of Muddle* and my entire body went straight as a board with my face becoming a joyous birthday smile. I nervously pulled the cardboard lid back to reveal my Doc's and my bright-green and orange striped jumpsuit and we giddily merged in a warm embrace. I pulled my fire axe into the hug and sighed in relief, knowing that my days of fashionless standard-issue cream and beige colored attire were over and that AOH Asher's costume was no doubt surfacing from the depths.

A wash of confidence was instilled in me as I emerged green and orange from that storeroom and I knew I fucking owned that place. Every room, closet, hall, drawer, and staircase in that joint was mine and for a moment I thought I was having a blast, I really did, until I found myself melting reverently in front of Doc Pesache's office. I considered continuing my acts of inquisition and juvenile vandalism, but instead I just stood there and ate a few more pills.

Instinctively I dropped my axe and suddenly my body seized, my feet froze to the floor and the doc's door autonomously squeaked open about half an inch in a ghostly invitation, but I couldn't bring myself to enter, I just couldn't.

Through the open window blinds I could see hand-stretched and painted African drums, a collection of colorful aboriginal relics, mounted bones that appeared to be his own personal archeological finds, an ebony bust of the genius poet Poe, an ornate glass bong inconspicuously peaking out from behind his expertly crafted mahogany desk that was affectionately covered from coast to coast in picture frames; and a collection of degrees, awards, and certifications that proudly purported his intelligence and hung humbly in no specific manner of importance around the room.

My body gradually unlocked and I slowly moseyed away, wiping tears from my eyes and wondering why I was having such an emotional response to the belongings of a man that I had met only once before. For the first time in my life I grew tired of my emotions, so I buried them along with my suspicions and returned to my snooping.

Even though my heavy boot strikes crushed

locksets like big juicy bugs, even though my axe-head crashed glass panes and snapped welding joints like bad metal-shop projects, I just couldn't get into that damn common area. Ironically the only room in the facility that I could not gain entry into was the *common area*; the area that housed the only working computers and televisions, which thankfully I could see through the thick wire cage were on and fortuitously tuned to the late night news.

As I watched the screens with my fingertips poking through the network of stubborn wire bars and my face pressing against them and pudging out the other side in little diamond shaped pouches of fat I witnessed image after image of upheaval and discord. From what I could tell at that distance I had not hallucinated the rising of the South, but it wasn't just the South that was rising. Peoples of all diverse creeds, colors, demeanors, and walks, all around the world were rebelling in localized pockets and I just knew that it was the beginning of the end. So, in celebration I slid another fist full of pills down my gullet and swallowed hard.

To cheer myself up I consumed the art and music rooms as sporadic explosions popped off in the background like balloons at a sadist's party and I spewed drawing after painting after song after sonnet and literally rolled in the inmate art. I wrote sermon after psalm and made preparation of oration in a great booming voice for those who would be in the back as I drank down juice-box codeine cocktails and did as I damn well pleased, free from prying eyes and abusive preconceptions.

I listened to the entire recorded catalogue of jam

sessions that were collected from the years of madmen before me as I fashioned what I thought was a jacket from their art and photographs and I gallivanted around the place in an impenetrable stupor for what felt like months.

In my searches I came upon a cupboard filled with entire rainbows of inks and as I pulled at my overgrown hair with a pair of safety scissors in my hand I thought to myself, perhaps AOH Asher has a wild mop of chunky rainbow hair. So, I randomly hacked at it and dyed the hunks and curls and waves with every color available to me, every color that was available I dyed it. So inspired I was that I stuck and poked at my arms and legs and torso, tattooing me with the symbols and logos of my life, recreating my absent family inside my skin.

All that I needed was there for me, all that I needed *was* me, but all that I wanted was them, so I zonked myself again and again and I got weirder and weirder. I had met my version of opulence and I didn't see me coming away from it alive. Although the gunfire waxed and waned dangerously toward and comfortably away; although the drugs masked then revealed, then plummeted, then heightened; although I absolutely ached for human and alcoholic contact, I did not see me coming out. I saw me dying there.

I checked in time and time again with the broadcaster and each time I did the effects of the world had worsened, until one day I heard his words reverberate, "It has truly been an honor and this reporter's dream to be the voice of history, if even for a moment, but as the events of these past few dark and hallowed days have unfolded it became increasingly clear that we would soon stop meeting like this, America. So, it is with a heavy heart and great sadness that your humble servant bids you a final good evening and may God bless us all. May God bless America," and the television became a row of calibrated bars and a constant fine-tuned tone.

The impulse to wander off into the woods to face my destiny grew in me and as the tone pierced my ears with my mind swashing buoyantly in my skull I prepared my dulled emotions and decided to boldly enter the self-imposed forbidden lair of Doc Pesache. If I was going to wander off, surely I would have to meet whatever lay there in wait for me first.

The knob squeaked and the door creaked as I gingerly pushed it open and I timidly entered and ran my shaky fingers along the wall as I circled the room soaking in the experience. I patted drums lightly, made silly faces at Poe, blew a novice breath into a didgeridoo, and as I scanned the photographed faces that topped his desk I froze again like a chicken puck with a picture of the doc and my family at the opening of BA Toys staring right back at me.

There Danny and I stood as little boys behind a huge yellow ribbon with our parents holding our shoulders sweetly from above and my heart just couldn't take that. I guess somewhere in the back of my mind I knew my past was in there, a past that I was trying so desperately to disavow and to pharmacologically numb away. So, I grabbed the doc's bong from behind the masterpiece mahogany desk that was obviously a Grandpa Radezlav original and I started to lose it as I rummaged painfully through its lovingly crafted drawers. I found his rather large stash of potent, wreaking ganja sitting atop my dictionary that had a note affixed to it in Abigail's handwriting that read, "Please see that he gets this". I took the big glass piece up under my arm, grabbed Poe in my other, and exited the emotionally assaultive room with the doc's stash, now my stash, hanging heavily from my teeth in the grip of a dog and my dictionary in its right place at home with its master.

That night I decided that there was no destiny to be had for me out there and for months I wasted away at myself. I gobbled my drugs down to the point of fatality, I amassed my psychotic sermons in totality, I done smoked my bag up to the last fiber, I barely dented my supply of edibles and drinkables, and I thought, if I could just get into that damn common area I could be happy here for the rest of my life.

As I approached my daily meeting with the bars and tone I slammed my axe-head against the cage in futility. Again and again I threw massive blow after massive blow against that cage, until I just couldn't take it anymore. I began to howl and thrash myself against it. To the point of blood I thrashed my body against it. And, that's when it actually happened.

A special broadcast burst back in and I held fast to the gate as a witness to horror, the scene as a dream. It was Wormwood taking oath of office as the newly conjoined President of the United States of America and Secretary-General of the United Nations; in short, assuming the golden seat of antichrist de facto. Certainly, it would only be a matter of time before he would fulfill his last nefarious measure of standing himself where he ought not, in the resurrected temple at Jerusalem.

"And, I am out of here!" I shouted at the screens and punched the cage. Like a ravenous vulture I frantically circled the facility, gathering goods and supplies and foods stuffs and packing a pack in the manner I had visualized a thousand times before. I threw it on my back and headed for the gaping exploded entrance, covered in ink and poster paint and wearing my roughly stitched smock of thick layered inmate art over my vivid jumpsuit with my axe in my claw-hand and my mind rooted firmly in the soil beneath a rainbow avalanche of chopped mop hair.

The crows squawked a hearty farewell as I clung excitedly to a boulder at the entrance. I lifted my axe to the heavens and in completion AOH Asher shouted hard at the vaulted ceilings, "Good bye my beloved AOHFCI. Bonne chance my good friend Mr. Black. I bid you adieu my treasure trove of noxious pharmaceuticals, you lingering visions of death you. Wish me Godspeed my prison, for I am off to destroy the antichrist!"

Chapter Thirteen

Aughblood

Just as my foot crossed the threshold where the facility meets the forest a fat-headed, black and tan snake struck at my boot. He was just a tiny fellow and his fangs barely penetrated the leather, but still he delivered a minor dose of venom into my left ankle. Although it wasn't enough to do any real damage it did make me a bit nauseous and it certainly wasn't a good sign.

I shook the little guy off and he slithered away as I raised my eyes and beheld my surroundings. Tall, thin, white trees jutted into the sky and rained down twirling golden leaves to cover lush green and red foliage like leafy snow. Great sweeping valleys dipped down in the ground and swelled back up, mellowing into vast sprawling plains with streams and creeks flowing throughout like exposed veins of the earth. Burning bushes dug their toes into creek-side dirt and stretched long winding roots through cool, clear waters as inspiration infiltrated my lungs and stole away with my breath. So, I confidently ventured out to become one with the awe of nature, believing whole-heartedly that God would clear a path for me.

How quickly the awe of nature and the plenty of my pack did morph into a barren land of horror and primeval preservation. My greedy mouth sucked down all my liquids and in trepidation I drank from a brook that unfortunately made me sick, my famished stomach gobbled up all of my rations and I apprehensively ate scraps off the forest floor that made me sick, and at night I slept in actively freezing crevices and holes that housed pinching bugs and crawling grubs and biting ants that, you guessed it, made me sick.

Being a son of the city I was utterly astonished at how difficult it was to keep in good repair while in the wild. Not only does man require food and drink, but also heating, cooling, and shelter from the elements. Since cooling certainly didn't seem to be a concern I asked myself, how does one go about making a fire?

Attempting to conjure that basic human appliance that man had long since harnessed, I tried rubbing two sticks together, but that was of course futile. I had seen a bow-drill technique as a child, but I couldn't remember how it worked. I vigorously scraped a stick back and forth against a divot that I carved in a wooden trough with a small tuft of combustibles bunched up at the bottom, but that was next to impossible. So, instead I learned to lament sundown.

A few frozen nights later I lay tucked away in the hollow of a fallen black oak tree and I started to think that leaving the facility wasn't the best idea after all, so I rose in the moonlight and turned to head back, but the further I turned back the more lost and disoriented I became. Any sign of the path to the facility had apparently vanished, going the same route as social civility, both having recently sprouted wings and flown away into the vacant silhouette of the night.

After another early morning bout of stomach expulsion and with the murderous AM chill flowing freely through my art-jacket, my spirit began to wear down to an exhausted nub and as I gave in to the temptation of doubt I turned me to face the sky and was uncontrollably invigorated by the day-breaking sun blasting its glory through a canopy of shifting and blending color above. I lay still in the thick pillowy foliage as an inner peace befell me and I closed my eyes and tuned in with the earth. Sharply my instincts bit at me like the unpleasant sting of my chompy little ant friends and I sat up alarmed and gasping, searching my surroundings for intruders.

Out of the corner of my eye I saw the sleeve of a leather jacket disappear behind a massive oak. I made it to my feet as quickly as I could and all of a sudden the jacket alone sprang out from behind the tree and without thinking I threw my axe at it and was instantly filled with remorse that I had disarmed myself on instinct alone.

In my frailty I yipped like a frightened cub as a hulking, shadowy figure emerged from behind the tree. I turned to run, but as I made my scrambling one-eighty my inmate art jacket was divided in a great whooshing slice up my back and it fell off my shoulders, past my elbows and wrists, and off my hands in two separate molted pieces. About five strides into my escape my senses alarmed again and time seemed to slow as I looked to my right to see a glint of silver light pass by my face. The light had a thick black line attached to it and it traveled next to my head like a view of fresh asphalt speeding beneath me while seated safely in my best friend's ride. All of a sudden it stopped, time lurched forward, the glint whipped backward, and I was shockingly struck in the mouth by a large glistening hay baler's hook that expertly entered my gaping orifice and gauged out through my cheek with the precision of a surgeon's incise.

Like a fish I had been caught and was being reeled in by a thick braided rope that was strengthened and worked throughout with some kind of tar or pitch. My feet stumbled and I was jerked to the ground and dragged through the fresh golden leaves and crunchy desiccates below, trying desperately to hold onto the rope with one hand and pull the hook out of my cheek with the other.

As I came to a defeated halt at the feet of the figure, he vaulted over me and crashed down in a seated blow square in the middle of my chest. The figure slowly came into focus as he leaned into me furrowing his thick brawny brow and asked in a comforting southern dialect, "Now why would you want to go and throw an axe at your dear old dad?"

"Fuck you! You're not my dad! Let me go," I shrieked as I ineffectually wriggled beneath him, but I was too weak from lack of nutrition to fight and he pinned my head against the ground and roughly pulled his hook out of my mouth with blood spurting from my parted cheek.

I slapped crimson palms at him as he commanded, "Quit fooling around, Ash! I ain't letting you go this time, you understand? Now stop struggling, you'll only wear yourself out," then he braced my arms under his knees and painfully clamped my wound closed between his gnarled knuckles as he scanned out over the horizon like an extrasensory wolf searching for predators.

"How do you know my name?" I mumbled under his weighty grasp and in my peripheral I could see my bloody handprints stamped all up his crisp, white t-shirt with short sleeves rolled up like a greaser. "Wait a minute, *greaser*? You're the guy from that party, aren't you?"

He stood up off me with my blood running down his stomach onto his well worn, pegged Levi's and with the sun blaring directly behind his head he replied in offended disbelief, "Asher, it's me, Aughblood."

My mind reeled and sputtered as self-encrypted memories surfaced and fizzled like carbonation and he walked away while coiling his rope and hook into a loop that he attached at his belt. I took a second to look him up and down as he collected my axe and his leather jacket and though I could feel my thoughts forming around him I just couldn't pin them down.

He had a well groomed pompadour that he combed obsessively as he walked, sharply manicured side burns that started dark-brown at the top and cooled to gray and white at the tips, and an antique pack of Marlboro cigarettes rolled up in his left sleeve. With axe and jacket in one hand, he walked back to me while compulsively straightening his giant tractor belt buckle with the other saying, "Well, son, I'm waiting."

Nope, not for the life of me. I had absolutely no clue who this man was. His build was the same as mine, aside from the touches of gray his natural hair color was the same as mine, he wore highly polished Doc's the same as mine; his eye color, body language, and demeanor were all the same as mine. So, I squinted skeptically at him and took a stab in the dark asking, "Asher, is that you? Are you me from another time or a different dimension?"

He stutter stepped back a few dumfounded paces as if I had just burped in his face and he shook his head rapidly then shouted, "What?! What the hell is wrong with you, boy? No, I'm not you from another dimension, you freaking weirdo! And, thank God for it! What have you been smoking this time?"

He threw on his jacket that was impaled mercilessly with rusty fishing lures and was encrusted with salt around the neck, he threw his standard-issue US Army backpack over it, and as he turned his hip I spied a big old bowie knife attached to the other side of his belt that was tucked away in a hand painted leather sheath. The rusty gears in my head began to laboriously rotate, my body slowly filled with relief and joy, and I was rejuvenated as I sprang up and launched into him, feverishly shaking his hand and yelling, "Mr. Sutcher, oh wow, what a pleasure, sir! It is so great to finally meet you! I've heard so much about you."

He scrunched his nose up under his eyes as I excitedly jostled his gigantic hand about. He cocked his chin to the side and with speech growing he whispered, "You've got to be kidding me. You're joking, right? I shit you not; this is no less than the fifth time that we've met, Ash. Granted the first four times you had nearly the exact same reaction, but I thought you were just nervous or blacked out or maybe razzing me, but really? You don't remember me at all."

"Excuse me, sir, but I think I would remember meeting my own father-in-law, thank you very much," Then I corrected myself. "Well, the love of my life's father at any rate."

He replied matter of fact while counting on his fingers, "Meeting number one: the reopening of BA Toys where you embarrassed the hell out of us all, meeting number two: the dance at Zinnia where I gave you my blessing to marry my one and only child, meeting number three: my Grandson's first birthday where you couldn't stay awake if your life depended on it, meeting number four: at that lame-ass hippie party in the bay where I warned you to get your ducks in a row, and meeting number five: right this very moment; and yes, I would like to think you would remember meeting me as well." And, with that he reminiscently pivoted on his heels and turned to walk away.

As I skipped happily after him like a puppy with a new owner my blood began to evaporate and crust over on my jumpsuit. I laughed like a goof and slapped my forehead saying, "Duh, of course I remember you, sir. I mean, Mr. Sutcher. I mean... what do you want me to call you?"

"Call me Dad, boy, call me Dad. And, don't you dare patronize me. We got a lot of work to do on that broken memory of yours, you freaking burn out."

He hid his face from me and chuckled a bit as we began to walk along creek-side and I pondered why I had chosen to bury the memories of Aughblood. How could my mind have hid something from me so entirely? Just then it occurred to me that I may have been traveling with a deceiver, perhaps a Kenite even. So, I fell inside myself and met with mobile Mr. Black to confirm his allegations of presence and sure enough, there he was in every situation, uncloaking right next to me and congratulating me with slaps on the back, giving his only daughter unto me in all good faith, setting down a thoughtful gift so he could hoist his grandson upon high, rightly shoving me up against a painted brick wall, and lovingly pulling a hook out of his inherited son's mouth only to release me once again.

But, as I thought about calling him Dad my memories began to cloud and sink back down into my terrifying chasm of a subconscious and as I came to the conclusion that I was dead-set against anyone but my own accepting that title my mind divided and a space was cleared at the family table for Aughblood.

Whereas but one had worn that holy crown and but one alone had sat boldly on that sacred throne, now two stood together in solidarity of parenthood, one reaching back across the great divide and the other still with me in the field. I see now that I had obscured Aughblood from my mind as a means to preserve my father. And, because the pain of his death was greater than I could bear, I had sequestered him in a hermetically sealed coffin from which no emotion could escape nor penetrate. When I asked myself how I could have ostracized the memories of both of these terrific men I answered back, "From under the heavy weight of many manners of drowning anesthesia a selfish feat is none too difficult to achieve."

Aughblood snapped me out of my internal digression asking, "What did you say?" as we walked along and he scanned the hillsides.

"Oh, nothing. I was just talking to myself," I replied as the words of Doc Pesache began to ring in my head and I repeated one of his questions. "How much have you healed since your parents died and why aren't you further along in that process?"

It was because of this question that I decided Manny King would not be returning, that AOH Asher would be a better action figure than a person, and that it was Asher, just plain old Asher Radezlav, that would need to become sober enough to lead all of my separate incarnations into a singular, lasting state of sanity. Just as I became resolute in this, my psyche fractured from a fantastic narcotic detox and right then and there in front of my new friend I fell to my knees and embarrassingly submitted myself to madness.

I cackled and sobbed as he pulled me into the stream and poured cool water over my head. I retched out yellow foam on all fours and twitched in the current with the dye rehydrating and pouring beautifully from me, sending silky waves of inky rainbows downstream and restoring my dark-brown Lyle Lovett hairdo. He pulled me back and dragged me up a hill where he decisively began to set up camp and I blacked out knowing that I would be safe in the more than capable hands of Abigail's father, my second dad.

When I came to, the sun was coming up again and was filling my eyes with its standard awe inspiring glow as a camp fire's breath wafted over me with the aroma of coffee and the enticing scent of a mystery soup filling my nostrils. I jolted up and my face yelled out, "Aaahh!" from moving faster than my body should have allowed it to and when I looked at my wrists held out before me with my hands clenched and bent in pain I noticed that my bracelets were on and secured in proper fashion.

I felt my face and my rings were in, I grabbed at my lap and gathered up long lengths of chain, I flexed my shoulders forward and my spikes winked at me as my hands scanned down my real jacket and bumbled over patches and bottle caps and rings and lighter tops. I was home again.

Aughblood shrunk about as much as a gruff man could have and said, "Abigail sent your stuff out to me awhile back and you started to shiver from being in the creek, so I ditched your slave suit and got you looking how you ought to." Then he cutely turned down the corners of his mouth, lifted his hand in the air and finished in saying, "So, there's that."

He passed me a piping hot tin mug that was sealed forever in blue flecked enamel and proudly showcased inner rings from previous pots that graduated up the inside like tree-years. I creaked and popped and snapped into place as I sat up and gratefully accepted the cup asking, "How did you start that fire?"

He barely looked up from behind his coffee and curtly replied, "Fire plough." Then he silently shoved his nose back down in his steaming vessel.

I whispered nonchalantly, "Ah, fire plough. Of course," and then took a sip and mustered the courage to try it on for size. My mouth dropped open and the words, "What's for breakfast, Dad?" just fell right out and hung in the air like little animated zeppelins.

He looked up at me. We locked eyes. And, I started screaming. "Okay, I'm going to have to be honest with you, I can't call you that! I just can't do it!" and I spastically rapped my knuckles on my knee and rocked back and forth lightly, sloshing scalding hot drips of boiling black bean-water into my lap.

He didn't break eye contact with me and again he barely replied, "Squirrel stew," then a few seconds went by and he took another sip and added, "and you can call me Aughblood. It's really not that big of a deal either way, son. But, I'll tell you this much, you kids seriously need to learn to relax."

Chapter Fourteen

The Six Winged Butterfly

"Don't eat those, Ash! Those are destroying angels, not psychedelics!" yelled Aughblood, beginning the week long fight for my life.

But still, the all white bubbling fungi fell down my throat and with two more handfuls on deck I sassed back like an invincible child chewing with his mouth open, "Don't worry, I know what I'm doing."

Turns out I didn't know what I was doing and in fact I had just swallowed enough liver liquefying amatoxins to destroy a perfectly healthy rhinoceros. As far as my resolute resolve for sobriety goes, well, this time I guess I had simply forgotten.

We had just embarked on our nearly four day hike to Aughblood's farm and all through that morning's walk I had been sneaking insignificant amounts of naturally occurring cubensis into my stomach. Just a couple of hours in we took a break to meditate on an exceptionally beautiful sun drenched knoll that overlooked a breathtakingly verdant valley. As the cubensis began to touch me lightly a trio of jays swooped in overhead and chirped mathematically like tiny blue prog-rockers, so in faith of the moment I humbly requested that God reveal to me the nature of my addiction and the stumbling blocks that resided within me. I also asked that they be uncovered in a way that was neither frightening nor punishing, and so it was.

The words *holiday*, *alleviate*, and *stasis* were put in my mind as figures and maps and scrolls of old unfolded before me and when I lifted my eyes to look out over the emerald fields and background hills I momentarily understood my entire life, how the untimely deaths of my parents were actually quite timely and poetic and perfectly positioned in the great cosmic sequence, how my place in that sequence was as integral as any and every other, and how my addictions began as a protective reaction that slowly evolved into a habitual downward spiral. As I broke from this the understanding slowly dissipated and sank back down into the nether, becoming a trusted faith, rounding out, and losing its detail. It was at this time and due to the understanding that I realized the break or sprain had indeed fully healed and when I heard this in my mind God spoke to me as a command. "Never again."

It was in the wake of awakening that I promised him my days of hard drugging were over for good. But, when I saw those great big gurgling mushrooms arching curiously away from the sunlight and peeking out from under the rotting forest debris like filthy cowering sewer rats, I got so excited that my memory of revelation became next to nonexistent and I just scooped them up in two great grasps and excitedly gulped them down. Poisonous, magic, or otherwise that's not how you do it, but I was so damn excited about the prospect of full-blown smash-and-grab transcendence that I hastily put them inside me and those dirty birds were in there just long enough to begin the process of necrosis.

For right around twenty minutes Aughblood implored me to make myself spew and although my belly was indeed burning I kept replying petulantly, "No way, man, they're going to kick in any minute now."

As we walked along the trail with me nibbling more and more amanitas in staggeringly ignorant delight, Aughblood finally stepped in front of me and spat in my face in the voice of two fathers shouting, "You know, I saw you munching those cubensis a ways back and I didn't say a word, but now that you're openly snacking on one of the world's most deadly toxins it has become absolutely vital-idol that you comprehend what I am about to say next.

"What you are eating *is not* a magic mushroom and right now a positively massive dose of poison is absorbing into your liver tissues and will soon cause profuse vomiting, diarrhea, and eventual liver failure leading to your certain and horrifically painful death! Now are you going to get that shit out of you or am I going to have to go in after it?"

I threw the remainder of mushrooms in the bushes and again naively touted my expertise with my hand flippantly gesturing like I was shooing away a fly as I stepped around him and just kept on truckin'. I figured he hung back a few paces to mend his bruised ego, but when I turned to see what he was doing his hook was spinning high above his head like a ranch hand's lasso. Soon enough his rope was circling my feet, climbing my legs, and securing around my mid section in a tightening tensile embrace.

I yelled out, "Bull shit!" as I toppled over like Gulliver the average sized giant and again Aughblood crashed down on top of me and made me subject to his fatherly correction.

In record time I had been wrapped up like a sweet and tender rodeo calf with all of my appendages tied off in a series of loop knots and pretty bows and I flopped about under him with the leaves dancing excitedly above me like giddy little spectators. He cartoonishly reached deeper in his bag than it was tall and like an Acme brand black hole it manifested whatever he willed. In this case it would be a canteen in which he concocted an awful solution of activated charcoal, black as night, and a homebrewed milk thistle reduction that he attempted to pour down my stubborn, clenching throat hole.

Of course, I immediately choked and spat it back at him to which he shouted, "Wrong answer!" and quicker than I could possibly see I was sucker jacked in the chin button by an open-handed palm strike.

Again he uncannily reminded me of his beautifully dangerous daughter and my eyes fluttered shut as I fell down the tunnel, descending past my furiously undulating stomach, past my angrily vibrating liver, my equilibrium shifted and it felt as if I were falling upwards, and all of a sudden I hit a fleshy floor in a soft and decelerated goosh. Everything about the tunnel of dreams had changed, I hadn't fallen far enough, and as I rose to behold my enclosure I realized that this was a different tunnel altogether.

Through a dimming vignette, the kind that surround bad childhood portraits, I could see Aughblood untying and sitting me up only to have me fall over in his lap with my face smearing black soot throw-up juice all down his nice new shirt. He squinted his eyes and looked a bit confused as he lay my head back on a bed roll and all but peered inside my skull to see me hovering there. "Ash, if you can hear me, I'm sorry I hit you so hard, okay bud? But, you got to start listening to me, alright?"

I floated closer to the diminishing vignette as he tended to my health and the iris constricted completely closed, leaving me alone to continue down the ominous tunnel that had opened up wide in a collision of memory and cognition. And, just as my mind locked behind me I unfortunately figured out where I was. I was standing in that terrifying chasm of my unruly subconscious.

Just then a single point in the distance grew and expanded across my vision, splitting the horizon into two equal planes of turquoise and indigo. The center birthed a long approaching corridor and on fleet feet it marched in as a millipede whose back was a concept. It knelt subserviently in front of me and its feet fell away leaving behind a series of illuminating doors; each one an atrocity, a nightmare, and a terror. Every deep-seated and ill conceived premonition, every unfinished and buried horror was now a room unto itself waiting in lusty desperation to be discovered and concluded.

The corridor shifted and bent like a shaky drawbridge as the vignette of my flesh eyes tore and expanded open again and I could see Aughblood standing over me, slapping the shit out of my head and inaudibly shouting and signing instructions as he poured glassy pools of cool water in through my lashes, but I just couldn't shake it and again the vignette did fade, the hall became crystal clear, and this time I was there. I was actually there.

A seemingly physical manifestation inside my own mind I was, wondering if at any moment the place was going to turn on me and trap me there for good or was it mine to control and manipulate as I saw fit and if I chose to deny the portals and consciously wander out into the infinite unconscious would it be my final resting place that I would find or was this the punishment for breaking my vow and the discipline that I so desperately needed?

As if the illusion of choice had triggered a response, the walls and ceiling slammed shut on me like a gumdrop man in a finishing gingerbread house and the doors groaned in and droned on in anticipation.

Each one had a personality of its own. Some fearsome and enticing and splitting in wood, some strangely exciting and alarming and jiggling in jelly, all of them familial and ancient and glowing with splendor. But, one and only one called out to me for help. In no known language, in a blathering of unrecognizable words, it audibly called out to me for help. So, I approached, I took hold of the soul searing handle, and I entered.

჻

The Radezlav homestead never looked so good, my vintage Masters of the Universe pajamas fit snug on my overgrown body, and long strands of Mom's prized beige carpet worked up in between my toes and caressed the arches of my bare feet as I approached our TV set which had a silver haired pastor thumping his desk on its screen. The pastor's eyes shot straight through the divisive glass, right into my engorged heart, and he spoke earnestly to me in Aughblood's same dialect; not of the end to come, but of the present impending doom.

Sky-blue, crushed velvet curtains trembled in the background when he pronounced forth as a trumpet before the battle lions. His call rang throughout my home as Danny seamlessly materialized next to me and we less than calmly scurried about the house like a pair of chickens with their melons lopped off, throwing the meaningless accumulations aside and pawing at possessions which we had thought were paramount. But, in the end we gathered nothing.

Through the back door Jerrod ran to us with a quickness as Mother elegantly glided down our palatial staircase to grace us with her shining face. Bringing much needed comfort and asserting the might of the family twine she waved her hand lightly and crooned melodiously, "Good night my three princes. I will be with you always." Then she blew us each a kiss and ascended like a rightly revered queen.

The TV pastor suddenly boomed back in behind us and in his last few moments on air he broke free from state mandated censorship and shouted urgently, "Good night, my lambs. I too will be with you." Then the rebel king Wormwood smashed through his set like a wrecking ball, fully revealing his contorting soul to a predisposed world system that immediately embraced him in an unfathomable sea of marked masses.

Barred from the heavens he had claimed the golden seat and sent forth the enforcers of the law from each nation, province, and town to round up the dissidents and imprison them for the rest of their days. But, as he fancied himself a benevolent master he promised not a hair of their heads would be harmed.

We struck out on the street and hid in the bushes as helicopters flew overhead and beamed burning spotlights into the heartfelt homes of our orange lit cul-de-sacs, filling them with unnaturally blue lighting that judgmentally burst through the slats of their closed shutters in the name of transparency. In a carnal panic we ran back inside to wake mother from her inopportune slumber, but before we could climb the last stair and reach her death bed, the doorbell rang fierce and pierced our ears in an aural insertion.

Fear struck my heart like a fist wrapped tight, but still I approached the colossal wooden gate and I approached alone, buzzing boldly with sheer vengeful madness as Danny and Jerrod clung frightfully to the banister and faded backward up the obtuse, creaking wooden staircase.

The door breathed deep as I snuck to it with spy hole shining through me. I offered forth my quivering retina and through the eye of the mounted spectacle I could see that everything had changed. Disorienting clouds of ominous shifting green sulfur filled the air and was worming its way into the heartfelt homes that the light could not penetrate. It breached through leaky window gaps and unsealed door jambs with beautiful bruise tones painting across the sky above and an enormous ministry of long studied clergy folk distributed below. They spread out, down, and corkscrewed around the frightened streets of Muddle and I leapt for joy believing that the cavalry had arrived. But, when I opened the shrinking door there were none who could withstand the tribulation and they had come to ask for *my* help.

"Where is my comforting one? Where is my surrogate shepherd?" I inquired of the hushing masses. "Lord, send me an angel," I pleaded to the darkening violet firmament, fully expecting that at any time a rowdy hoard of chariot riders would violently part the sky and intercede, destroying our enemies from off the face of the earth right before our very eyes.

But, instead that old familiar voice replied, "It is as you have said. You *are* the angel."

Inside a wall of dense bone and a network of meaty brain lay the silver cord uplink to my God. There would be no surrogate for me and there would be no reprieve from here on out. Whole milk, a dense wheat-meal, pure butter, and thick honey; evidently they would flow through me, so I heartily pronounced to them, "Then it is as I have said. I am the angel and I am a conduit."

The masses sighed in relief and smiled. As one being they rose up and hastily led me to a woman's house that had been plagued by a demon, then quickly they left me to my work and nervously poured themselves from off the streets of Muddle, receding into the distant hills like a singular retreating tide.

I closed proximity on my neighbor's house whose yard had in the past held tiny scampering feet that were fearfully retrieving a lost soccer ball, playful young boys attempting to charm a cornered cat, or mischievous teenagers indulging their insatiable curiosities of what appalling secrets might lay inside.

Upon reaching the doorstep I spied a six winged prehistoric butterfly barely fluttering its oddly shaped iridescent wings atop a coarse, boot-scrubbing doormat with a single unreadable word printed on it. A young woman suddenly opened the door and just stood there staring deadpan at me, not speaking or moving at all.

Regarding the creature I bumbled forth, "What is it?" and she gave neither reply nor instruction, she just stood there. With her face falling limp she abruptly turned and entered the house like a controlled marionette, leaving the front door wide open. So, I took that as my invitation and I followed her inside.

With my hands in my pajama pockets and my senses on overdrive I uncomfortably soaked in the experience. The interior decor was non-threatening Americana that lent the home a smooth and loving hand. Their family photos hung in all the right places. But, when I approached their entertainment center in the alcove under the stairs the warmth and vibrancy of their living room soon grew cold and dark and gray.

The misses suddenly brandished a huge glistening kitchen knife and jarringly blurted out in a dull and monotone way, "We have heard that even the very hairs of your head have been changed by the Lord your God."

"Where is the demon?" I asked.

She didn't answer as she slowly stepped behind her kitchen counter and began sloppily chopping a slew of rotten veggies. Her mouth dropped open like she was actively having a stroke and suddenly she stopped and hauntingly cracked her head to one side as if her neck had been broken. She silently lifted her hand and awkwardly pointed with her wedding ring finger at the freezing corner, that modern marvel, that crude psychological infiltration of an entertainment center and grumbled, "Legion is there."

With slight fear, but needlepoint concentration I sealed the demons entry point by the authority vested in me and the woman's face instantly reanimated. The lights in the entire house brightened and she returned to her chopping as happy music chimed in and the kids ran down the stairs and clung to her legs while papa belatedly entered through the front door, sheepishly languishing another day's servitude.

I tried to instruct the family on how to protect themselves, but as soon as I had fulfilled my duty to them they thought me useless and preachy and disavowed their knowledge of my presence altogether, as if I had transfigured into a ghost-boy that resided in a dimension just askew their own. The term *blood angel* blew in through my mind in thick smoky bubbles and I said not a word as I slipped past papa undetected and drifted through their front door, out onto their porch. When I left them the evil came back seven-fold stronger and I mournfully regretted entering their home at all.

Before I left I placed my hand on their doormat and the six winged butterfly happily climbed atop my rising shoulder like a pirate's macaw. Just as my right foot materialized off the woman's drive a friendly, morphing creature that was a generic alternating conglomerate of every childhood friend and well thought of acquaintance ran up to me and hugged me way too hard in a celebratory squeeze. It ripped me back forcefully and shouted at me in an insanely frightening multi-voice, "I'm fucking energized, man! I'm ecstatic about what's happening around us; what's happening *to* us! Aren't you, brother-man? Aren't you, bro'?"

I pried it off of me and shouted, "No, I'm not excited! Haven't you noticed the world's distortion? It was beautiful once and now just look at it; just look at you. Look at what you've all become."

The Conglomerate began skipping and hopping around me in a merry little fool's dance, so I ran from it believing that I was alone and that I was the only one alive that was not blind to the fact that the antichrist was the pronounced king of the world.

With petty intent I dashed home to retrieve my symbolic spiritual shield of a jacket, believing that it would become my physical armor. I flung my door wide and ran inside to find an old cassette player lying in the direct middle of my kitchen counter, as if it had been set there specifically for me. I put the headphones on and pressed play to hear the silver haired pastor preach one last sermon in that soothing, weighty Arkansas way.

"Little children, my little children, hearken unto me. Our time has finally come. Stand up now and be not afraid for have we not practiced this moment again and again? In our minds and in our hearts, in our dreams and our visions, have we not practiced?

And, what is the rehearsal without its curtain call? And, what is the spar without the war? And, when war cometh to your door, my children, will you not take up arms? Are we not pre-girded? Verily I say unto you, yes we are!

"For our spearheads are honed my loves, my tempered steel, now grasp them. Our bows are drawn my archers, my sharp-shooting apprentices, now fire! Your onyx arrowheads will pierce the black hearts of the sons of disobedience. Your spears of amethyst will burst the eyeballs of the destroyer, the very eyes of destruction himself!

"Trust not the rising of bile in your throats nor the wavering weakness flowing from the trunks of your spines. Believe me now my battle lions, you-are-ready. Now go forth, my yearlings turned mighty steeds, go forth!"

Emboldened by the words of a true leader I ran up my fourteen stairs of stainless steel on all fours like I've done a thousand times before, into my room a thousand times, into my closet a thousand times, but this one time I was naked and my jacket was gone.

Suddenly, Danny and Jerrod produced from the darkness behind me and their unified voices broke the silence, again gripping my heart with fear as they uniformly closed in on me with their belts strangely interlaced at the hip. They spookily screamed at me as if from the next room, "Can you hear me, Ash? Asher, are you in there? We got to get going."

The entire world swayed and crashed to one side and with pictures and bookshelves flying off the wall I scrambled quickly to my curtains and drew them back exposing their solid-gold eyes to a procession of crimson tanks roving in over the crumbling valley hills.

I shoved the window open and the butterfly dug into my shoulder for balance as a blast of scorching umber wind filled the room and I screeched out nervously, "My brothers, the ones that I *need* during these times of heavy crisis and endless doubt, the braces of my infancy and the levies of my youthful indiscretion, from boyhood to manhood I have proclaimed to you the message of my heavenly father and I ask you now, will you fight with me? Will you be at my side?"

They closed in on me further and in their own separate voices they replied a simple, "No," and my heart sunk through the floor, through the foundation, and six feet into the underground.

The butterfly excited atop my shoulder as I shook and trembled naked before them demanding, "You will come with me and you will go where I go!"

And, again they replied a resolute, "No," and began to creak forward with grabby hands while drooling and changing into horrible monster fuckers drowned in heavy green and red lighting. "We like what has been promised to us and it is you who will obey," they snarled.

From behind them I heard a door creak and secure shut in the farthest off distance one could ever hear and in the crux of the moment I became lucid and remembered where I was. Like Dorothy clicking her heels I raised my chin to the cottage-cheese ceiling and uttered in all sincerity, "God, I am sorry. From now on I won't make promises that

I can't keep. I promise. The vow stands. Please forgive me."

Like a guard dog, the butterfly sprang from off me and attacked the two as a great vacuous blast sucked me out of my room, down the stairs, across the carpet, out the front door, and ejected me onto my face in a fleshy goosh on the slimy corridor floor. The vignette widened and revealed another strange space as the door sighed in satisfied conclusion. In its final thanksgiving it crumbled and blew away in ash and again I sucked down the tunnel, past my sleeping stomach, past my lazy liver, and I woke an emotionally devastated wreck, afraid to breathe, afraid to scream, and afraid to live.

Chapter Fifteen

An Army in My Living Room

I lay there awhile in the most comfortable busted
down bed that ever was and I wrestled under
fabulously heavy corduroy patchwork quilts that
still smelled heavily of my love even years later. As
I scanned the room I soaked in an amazingly hip
collection of gear, doodads, and memorabilia that
were all distinctly her. There wasn't a single article
in that room that wasn't her. And, as my mental
model formed even further I began to feel her
presence manifest beside me, but why was she
crying?

Her home looked homemade and was
constructed of pallets filled with hay that were
covered by random boards fastened with fistfuls of
rusted screws and bendy nails that left long black
inky trails to run down and absorb into the subpar
wood below. Although it was manufactured with a
fair amount of wonky craftsmanship and intuitive
artistry, it certainly wasn't up to code and certainly
was well deserving of the title, *unique*.

She hid nearly every inch of wall space under
her paintings and drawings and piles of magazine
clippings of random hilarious quotes and
amalgamations that fit oddly together, like a ring-
tailed lemur's head pasted on a seventies pimp
body with a blurb above it that proudly exclaimed,
"I thought it would add a plus to the festivities!"
Hundreds of secondhand store records and value
outlet six-pack labels filled in the gaps between
posters of Johnny Cash flipping me off, the late,
great Jack White and his mild mannered sister Meg

sitting down for supper; a mandatory copy of R. Crumb's Stoned Agin!; and a professionally framed, signed and numbered archival print of her heroine and a skeleton screaming at each other above a caption that read, "The Goonies 'R' Good Enough."

Suddenly, my sniffer went off and turned my attention to the bottom of her closed bedroom door which puffed a small gray cloud at first, then another small puff, and then the mother load came a rollin' in by way of a disturbingly thick gray river of smoke. I sprang from her bed to see what was the matter and as I approached her door which was flexing and puffing heavily on all four sides, making the full length mirror that it held tremble and dance, I was struck by the image that the mirror presented. It proudly reflected an awful and insulting picture of me all pale and gaunt and returned from the dead.

From behind my ears I heard Aughblood's authoritative voice call through the open window next to her bed, "You're not going to want to go out that way, boy. Hop on out here and let's get moving."

Vicious flames began to lick up under her door like a slew of peanut butter covered dog tongues and just as in my nightmare-epiphany I scurried around her room, pawing at that which I thought she would think was paramount. But, in the end I grabbed only her framed poster and fell out her bedroom window with my boot heels striking the thin glass panes above, causing buckets of jagged sharps and cups of fine glassy needles to rain down upon me mercilessly. I jumped to my feet all scuffed and dirty and bloodied and I gathered up

Miss Lauper who was no worse for the wear. Just as I rose to turn to view the exterior of the Sutcher homestead I was shockingly blasted back by a fire spike that punched straight out of Abigail's window at me.

The back of my hair and my entire back patch were singed as I hit the dirt and when I uncovered my face and rose again I stepped back to behold wave upon wave of flaming red destruction caving in the rooftop and pushing a synchronicity of fireballs from each window and door frame. With every little structural collapse stoking and impelling the fire one great big daddy ball peeled and inverted high into the sky, cooling into a huge sooty mushroom cloud and cuing the unsavories for miles and miles around to come scampering in to commence with the looting.

"Why is your house on fire? Are we under attack?" I yelled to Aughblood as I quickly scuttled up next to him all hunched over in a protected posture.

He just kept burdening down his beat up old Ford pickup with its stock red-orange paint all pocked and dinged and chewed by time and answered coldly, "No, we're not under attack. We're just not coming back here again, that's all. Got everything I need right here in the back of my truck."

When I looked in the truck bed all I could see were tools and ropes and guns and ammunition. There were no personal effects, no memory boxes, no furniture or clothing to speak of, and what was worse, he had gathered absolutely none of his daughter's belongings; not a one.

"What about Abigail's stuff?" I asked in confusion. "What about all her memories or her childhood pictures? What about any remnant left of her mother? It's all on fire and you're okay with that?"

He just leaned against his rig and sighed. Staring at me in agitation and convincingly stuffing down his emotions he said, "What's temporal is temporal. Now get in the truck."

I began to get all worked up and I started shaking and yelling at him with rolling heat waves assaulting my back in an offbeat rhythm, "This ain't my first cruise, Aughblood! I've been through this shit before. You have to trust me; you're making a huge mistake. You need to get your ass back in there and gather up your life!"

Instead he just threw another duffel of guns and rope and tools and ammo in the back and grumbled, "This ain't open for discussion, Ash," then he loaded up and crashed down on his torn and squeaky bench seat. He curiously cranked a lever that rolled his window down then lit up one of his cigarette rarities and slammed the heavy metal door shut. With one of his big meaty arms hanging out his window he finished in saying, "There are some things in this world and in this life that you do not yet understand, son. Now I'm going to ask you one last time to get in the truck."

"No, *you* don't understand!" I broke open. "You get your ass out of that Flintstone-mobile and back in our house and you save our shit, Danny! Save our house you fucking asshole!" And, with that I melodramatically dropped to my knees and clung to the picture frame with perfect drops of chubby eyeball rain falling like little bombs, plopping into tiny piles of pillowy dirt that puffed out upon impact.

Aughblood just rolled his eyes at me and blew out a gigantic cloud of nicotine claws then banged his truck door and spat, "I understand your loss, son, but we got to go," then he turned the grinding engine over and revved it twice, looking so ruggedly handsome and mired in scarification.

Well, I thought I would just cut right through that shit with a bit of the old insubordination, so I readied myself by making what I thought were imperceptible glances toward the house, but Aughblood was the wiser and he slowly narrowed his eyes and whispered very seriously, "Don't you do it," just a split second before I defiantly jumped up and did it.

As I bolted around the front of their crumbling home I was instantly halted by an absolutely gorgeous burning sunset diving drowsily behind a lush rolling hillside replete with a farmland cast of horses and donkeys and pigs who milled about free-range and nibbled at Mother Earth's plentiful bounty without a care in the world. This was the view that had no doubt shaped my love's childhood and by her father's calloused hand this was the view that she forsook.

Past clucking chickens I ran, in through their scorching door I went, and I scanned their incendiary home for anything that she may have needed, but it was too late. It was all coming down around me. Through their rustic living room, past their deconstructing hallway, out her bedroom window and into Aughblood's truck I could see him

seated comfortably, cruelly tapping his wristwatch
as he obnoxiously blew smoke ring after spongy
smoke ring in my direction while watching me
spring dangerously back into his daughter's room
as it warped and bent around me in life threatening
roils of heat.

"Where, where, where!" I yelled out as I spun in
ineffectual circles and as if she knew someday this
moment would come I spied it there waiting for
me. Illuminated in beautiful burning glints beneath
a twirling disco ball sat a modest wooden box atop
her secondhand dresser surrounded by scads of
preserved and burning funeral flowers with her
steady and deliberate hand driven across its lid in
bold, passionate brush strokes that read, "My
mother lives here."

I climbed into Aughblood's truck with the box at
my feet and her poster between my knees, reeking
like a campfire and feeling quite accomplished. I
glared hatefully at him as he silently and
unapologetically stared straight ahead, putting the
pedal to the metal with a hoard of filthy hollering
hill-folk pouring onto his property, shooting poorly
aimed potshots all around us.

With his inferno-farm billowing a message of
departure for the entire state to see, I laid it all out
saying directly into his right ear, "Now I see why
she left you. I could never get the full story out of
her, but now I've seen it for myself."

He didn't flinch, he didn't adjust at all, he just
kept his big, fat foot to the floor and took an extra
long drag of his death-stick then turned to me and
blew a harsh choking reply in my face. "You know,
you might just want to watch those words there,

fellow. You and me have a bit more in common in that respect than you know," he said.

And, I reeled horribly in a dastardly disorienting sense of supposed dismissal as the hill-folk militia threw their last lazy bullets from far too far back then turned and disappeared into the smoke to assess their plunder and I annoyingly snapped back at him, "What the hell is that supposed to mean, *Dad*? Is she going to leave me too? Is there something I should know about? Huh? Is there?"

"Well, let's just say that a lot's changed in your absence, shall we?"

"Oh yeah, like what exactly? How much could have changed in just a few years?" I sass mouthed him, secretly cringing and goading my heart's complete and utter incise.

Aughblood's face scrunched a bit and he straightened his hair and asked heatedly, "Excuse me? Last few years? Asher, how long do you think you've been gone?"

"Like I said, a few years, right? Like two, two and a half years tops," I answered in haste, but judging by the abrupt absence of Aughblood's calculated Cool Joe attitude I was off by a few and that is when I started to feel a bit uneasy.

He collected himself and steadied the wheel asking, "And, how long do you think you were knocked out this last time?"

"I don't know, a few days maybe? Look, I get it. Would you just get to the punch-line already?" I replied as he repeatedly thumped his tattered steering wheel and looked out into the hills with nightfall settling in all around us.

He bit into his fist in frustration and launched

into me, "Really, a few days? Seriously, Asher? You were asleep for almost two and a half weeks. I had to fashion a stretcher out of tree branches and rope then drag your vomiting and shitting carcass through the remainder of the highlands and back to the farm where I tended to you like my own flesh and blood. I wiped your ass and fed your slacked jaw like a swaddled youngin', I covered you and uncovered you and monitored your temperature like a fine fucking trussed brisket smothered in cabernet and dressed with fresh sprigs of rosemary and thyme and you think you were out for a few days? Dipshit, you have been gone for over six-fucking-years! Do you hear me? Six years you've been gone. Now do you get me when I say that a lot has changed in your absence? Do you understand me now?"

And-oh-snap, did I ever understand him. For the remainder of our ride I lamented the possibilities, the disgusting and heart wrenching possibilities. I kept as silent as he would let me and he not being any iteration of the Great Communicator I suppose there was a long silence to be had for the both of us. So, for the next three days we ate and traveled and slept and traveled and held our peace and traveled. We got no closer to each other and nothing further was revealed, but soon enough his anger would make all too much sense and soon enough my life would conclude again and again begin anew.

෴

The alarm sounds loud through the thin morning

air as my father's truck barrels toward the fiercely guarded gate at the end of our complex, but he's not alone. Who would be with him? Who *could* be with him? He said that he was just going for supplies and that he'd be back in less than a week, but it's been almost a month now and he's got a friend? That is so perfectly Pops; always late for dinner and consistently full of surprises.

An apparent problem comes over the guards' radios and everyone starts acting all frantic and begins running around like a bunch of frightened ants, so I pick up my toddling Ruby-girl and yell to big brother Yoshi to get the hell behind his dad. Danny readies his rifle and pulls Yosh into his waist with one arm then me and Rubes in with the other as Pops' truck is brought into us like Secretary-General Moodreaux himself, smothered in a mob of guards and Eighth Plague armament. Pops uncharacteristically rolls to a gentle stop in front of us and as the guards disperse to reveal Dad's mysterious guest my heart explodes inside my chest in disbelief and I hear myself scream, "It can't be you. It can't be. You're supposed to be dead!" and Yoshi looks up at me in complete terror.

Asher's ghost looks confused as he comes around the front of our truck and looks back at my dad saying, "You've got to be kidding me," to which my dad just shrugs.

He closes in on us holding my mother's ash box in one hand and my Cyndi in the other. He keeps on after us, keeps coming in to torment my family with guilt and doubt and unreality. He keeps coming into us with a massive ethereal grin pasted across his convincingly real flesh face and he opens his surprisingly well maintained zombie-mouth to say dry as a bone, "Well, my lover and my brother, I'm back. So, what's new?"

Danny breaks from us and lunges into his incorporeal brother in a spray of tears and screams and blows at his back and Asher pulls him in tight like he always has. He peers knowingly over Danny's shoulder with tears in his eyes. Right at me he stares with his seven-year-old son clinging to my thigh and brimming with excitement as Danny's daughter nestles into my chest in fear and confusion.

Danny kisses Asher over and over on his cheeks and his forehead and slips away from him in shame to rejoin me and the rest of his family in desperately mixed elation.

And, then it happens. Asher mandatorily lays into us in his classically never surprised sarcasm saying, "So, I'm dead now and you two are a thing, with child as I can see there and how lovely for the both of you. Judging by your daughter's age or lack thereof I also see that you'd waited for about what, three and a half years? And, I do appreciate that, yes I certainly do. How very modest of you.

"Oh, and what else happened while I was gone? Just about everything that I predicted came true exactly according to my timeline and it turns out that I'm not crazy, I'm back from the fucking grave, and I was just ushered at gunpoint onto my own property which now appears to be the hub of the Northern Californian chapter of the resistance. Is that all about right? I mean, I'm just trying to get up to speed here. Is it safe to say that's all fairly accurate?"

We just nod our heads in complete astonishment as our boy releases from us, he steps bravely forward to face his father, a father that he never believed he could know and says, "Hi, Dad. It's me, Yoshi."

My instincts attack me as Asher comes hotly into him and violently throws his little frame into the air. Yoshi's face lights as he heartbreakingly falls into the deepest hug that he may ever find and Asher smashes his prickly beard into his son's neck, blowing raspberries that make him giggle uncontrollably. Then he slowly sets him down and painfully peels him back, as if he never ever wants to let him go.

Asher removes his spiked collar and drapes it around Yosh's neck and says, "Let me get a look at you," as they lock eyes and immediately and inexplicably drop into their weird multigenerational feedback thingy. Simultaneously they reset and black out, falling backward into the gravel behind them, sending two little magical dust clouds into the air.

They both sit up at the same time and keeping their eyes from fixing together they jinx each other by saying, "It really is you."

Asher scoots cutely into him and asks in a whisper, "So, what's up with the whole Yoshi thing?"

Yosh leans in even closer and whispers back, "Mom told me there's no letter *J* in the Hebrew alphabet, so I changed my name from Joshie to Yoshi and that's what everyone calls me now. Or Yosh, my friends call me Yosh."

His Dad just squints his eyes, nods his head

lightly, and in my heartbreak he whispers back, "Well, then Yosh it is. That's actually really cool, son." And, as he pulls him in again through the wispy gravel smoke I can read his lips saying, "You know, I thought about you and your mom and your dad every single day I was gone. Every single day I thought about you and I need you to know that I love you all so very much, especially you my little Yeshua. Especially you."

He kisses his tear streaming face again and again, just like his big brother did his and from all the way down the block we hear three distinct wails let out and bounce down the alleyways as Patricia and California and Jerrod run to him like a trio of flailing Muppets. They all crash into their hero like meager pins attacking a mighty bowling ball, knocking him away from his son, and the four of them writhe around in the gravel working themselves into a gray wash of industrial dirt. They pick him up off the ground and haul him away like an injured team player as Danny grabs Yoshi and pulls him into us whispering, "Just let him go, son. That's what we do. We just let him go like we always have. But don't worry, he's not going anywhere. This time I can feel it."

"Daddy, why did he call me Yeshua?"

"He's calling you a savior, son. He's saying that you saved him."

I turn to my husband with our little Ruby-girl smashed happily and innocently between us with Yoshi scrambling at our belt loops in a flood of elated questioning and I kiss his dad passionately to put his mind at ease while my eternal love walks away from us arm in arm with his buddies, going off to drink his own beer in his own bar on his own barstool. And, by the looks of him he's going to need more than just a few.

⁓

"So, I'm dead am I? Does anyone mind telling me what I died from?" I asked as I stepped excitedly behind the bar to make myself a super tall whiskey-sour and cherry. The rumor of my death and resurrection spread throughout the complex and as Plague Seven filled in and spilled back out onto the streets with drinks being passed out the front and side doors, Postal Patty, fucking Cal, and my brother Jerrod all went belly up to the bar and silently pointed at my framed Certificate of Death hanging ceremoniously over the register behind me next to a picture of me laughing my ass off at a house party wearing only my SpongeBob underwear and gobs and gobs of silly string.

A stream of dread pulled me down as I read of my own demise. The document stated that my initial cause of death was "Blunt force trauma to rear of skull", the secondary cause was "Burning", and it was signed by none other than Dr. Elijah K. Pesache, MD.

"What? What the hell is that?!" I shouted like a buffoon pointing stupidly at the deed.

California interjected, "You know I knew you were coming home. I kept having dreams about you and they got stranger and stranger and more and more lucid and real and then BAM! There you are."

"I love you too, Cal, and right on topic as always. Now what the hell *is* this? Why is this signed by the doc?"

Jerrod took a chug of his Newcastle and piped up, "He brought it to us the very same day you left for the facility. He said the three of you had just been in a terrible accident and that you and the driver unfortunately didn't make it."

"Wait a minute, the driver? But, the driver was the one who hit me in the head."

"Well, even the news reported that the driver died. They said you guys had a blowout and hit a ditch going about seventy miles an hour and when the doc woke up, the van was on fire and he only had enough time and energy to pull himself out before it exploded.

"When we asked to see your body he said it had been so badly burned that you were unrecognizable, so instead he supplied us with your death certificate and what seemed like his very sincere condolences. We had a funeral for you at Zinnia Hall and everyone was there. Well, everyone's still here, but honestly, Ash-man, you should have seen it. It was quite a stunning service."

"Quite stunning," remarked Patty.

"It was beautiful," mumbled Cal.

Jerrod finished in saying, "Look I'm sorry, Ash, but when the doc gave us those papers we didn't think to question him, you know. I mean, he had this massive head wound that was still bleeding into his bandages and all these forms to fill out and everything. We just couldn't have known. How could we have?"

I started to say, "But, I thought that Doc Pesache was a..." and from out of the shadows that hulking, skulking Chicano, Torrez, emerged smothered in entire bolts of dated and starched khaki fabric.

"The word you are looking for is Kenite. Doctor Eli Pesache was and is a Kenite of the highest order. Your father, however, knew him as Rabbi Pesache. They grew up together outside of Detroit and he considered him a great friend and resource for his theological studies, but it turns out the feds aren't the only ones that have been following your family, Mr. Radezlav. Though I must say it's great to finally meet you on equal terms. I've been watching you for far longer than you know and I'm really looking forward to actually having a conversation with you. That is, when you settle in, of course.

"But, first things first: the most important question of all. Are you going to pour the mescal or shall I?" and that giant Cab Calloway slash John Waters slash Dwayne the Rock Johnson looking mother-fucker laughed for what must have been at least a solid minute.

I made good use of the time by crushing unrefined sugar cubes soaked in lemon bitters in the bottom of five retro orange tumblers that I then flooded with fine tequila over rocks garnished with freshly planed lime-zest chips and as I passed them out I asked, "Are you still following my family Agent Torrez? No offense, but why are you here? Isn't the government disbanded?"

"Salute!" we all shouted then shot them back and nibbled on the rinds.

Although the giant indeed did partake he looked a bit incensed and replied, "I live here. This is my home," and Cal vouched for him by climbing up his back like a ladder and putting him in a friendly choke hold to which Torrez stumbled to and fro like a father being attacked by his harmless baby.

"Cal's the only one who actually likes Torrez. Everyone else simply tolerates him," said Patty as she chomped on her ice.

"You know what, fuck you, Patricia! You worked for the feds too you know."

Patty jumped off her barstool as Cal quickly climbed down and got between them with her pressing into him repeatedly like a docked ship and yelling, "Oh yeah, like delivering parcels equates to destroying lives and busting up families, you war mongering pig! And, just to let you know, you aren't the only ones who are *watching*. I don't care how long you've been here. I got you all figured out, cousin."

"Okay wait a minute, just to summarize," I said diffusing the two, "The guy that I thought was my mentor was my father's childhood friend, slash, enemy..."

"Frenemy," Cal interrupted again while still pressed between them.

"Don't say that," I replied.

"Don't say what?"

"Frenemy, don't say frenemy, you're better than that. And, the guy that I thought was against me and a stooge of the government is now supposedly with us and on top of that my brother and my ex are all shacked up with my ass left out in the cold trying to pick up the pieces fast enough to understand what the hell is going on around here."

"You're never going to be left out in the cold as long as I'm around, sugar," said Patty who winked at me and broke away, swiftly reaching over the bar and obnoxiously and skillfully clamping down on my left nipple.

She smiled sultrily as I screamed and California jumped away from Torrez shouting, "Well, I think your legend just got a lot more legendary. This is all going to make great additions to your website and I just can't wait any longer," and he ran off up the stairs to geek out in the solitary before I could express my disapproval of his martyr making practices.

As Patty tore back into Torrez, Jerrod leaned into me and said, "Cal knows that only about five percent of internet users still have access, but we don't mention that to him anymore.

"When the governments of the world all started merging and splitting and splintering off the internet corporations couldn't keep up with the increasingly absurd regulations, so big-brother took over and you know just how much they love free speech. They shut the whole thing down in the name of defense and only a few of us like Cal know how to hack back into the wires and satellites. Mr. Early is actually quite brilliant."

"Well, I've known that since day one, but why the hell is he hanging out with Torrez?"

"Cal told me when Torrez first got here they dosed and smoked and got to know each other so well that Torrez had an apparent change of heart. He said when Torrez was in the depths of his high he planted a message in his brain that went something like, 'If you're honestly going to serve the people first you must shed the sheep's clothing and be the wolf that you are.' He said he really took to that statement and they've been friends ever since."

"So, Torrez isn't an agent anymore?"

"Oh no, he still is through and through. He files paperwork and has monthly audits and everything. He's been writing reports detailing his embedment for years and he's been able to articulate his need to be here in such a way that they just keep letting him do his thing."

"So, is the government collapsed or not?"

"Well, yes and no. There are collapsed sectors. Like, we're in a collapsed sector because the militias are so strong here that this area has been deemed seceded, but if the UN decided to re-seize it we probably wouldn't be able to last too long. But again, since we're such a calculated threat based on Torrez's reports they really don't screw with us too much. It's like I told you when we were kids, man. All it took was enough people waking from the dream to change things and when we did the entire monetary system collapsed. And, I mean altogether.

"Society just started to break down little by little. Don't get me wrong, big government is still in control. It's just that the illusion of the people's control has finally been stripped away from us and they're beginning to realize just how powerful we are when we stand together."

I sat dumfounded with my stupid mouth hanging open and my brows low and I asked, "What about water, electricity, sewage? How is that all still running?"

"Well, it wasn't for a long time, but when you take money and regulation out of the equation people end up following their compulsions. Like you're compelled to draw and to create, so you do and that's your contribution. Well, it turns out some people are absolutely fascinated by plumbing or electricity or you name it. Whether it be for love or even a sense of duty, we all work. If you don't work, you don't eat. It's just that simple. We don't really need money. We never really did.

"Oh that reminds me, if you didn't already know this, all the money you had, all the money your folks left you and Danny, the entire fortune that I built on the road? Gone. It's all gone. Money doesn't work like that anymore."

"Well, how does it work then?" I asked incredulously.

Unfortunately that comment peaked Torrez's interest and he gladly stepped around Patty and spoke up like Herman Munster saying, "Well, to be quite honest money never really did exist. It was just a construct to pacify the idiots and hold society in a little box set on a little track in a little world smaller than the tip of your pinky finger."

As Torrez held his oversized pinky aloft, Postal Patty came around him and sat back down at the bar saying, "Yeah, thanks for that, Torrez. Why don't you just cram it with walnuts and pour us some more shots, okay tough-guy?"

Suddenly, Torrez sprang into the air and twirled over the bar like a pirouetting top and everyone shouted, "Whoa!" and laughed their asses off at how unnecessarily awesome of a move it was. He threw bottles up and over and around like Tom Cruise and then slammed five glasses out in one fluid motion with one hand and half-filled the glasses with the other while shouting at me, "In the language of your people Mr. Radezlav, Nostrovia!"

Suddenly Early rematerialized next to me and we five shouted, "Nostrovia!" and shot them back. I have to admit, Torrez was actually kind of a charming and entertaining guy, in a rough around the edges, total fucking prick kind of way.

For the rest of the day people rotated in and out of the building to say hello and welcome me back. They danced and jived and imbibed all around us in a terrific celebration of life and just as I began to feel like I was home again Danny and Abigail each came down independent of one another to tell me how happy they were that I was back and how sorry they were about the way things had turned out. And, oh how thankful I was for that.

Like a master thespian I acted as if I weren't utterly destroyed as both of them assured me it was the right thing to do at the time and under the circumstances and that neither of them had any intention of dissolving their relationship. Then each silently slipped out the same side door like burnt acquaintances, the kind you would've ducked into odd aisles at the supermarket to avoid.

So, I latched onto my crew of Jerrod, California, and Torrez sort of, but I had special plans for that absolutely gorgeous Postal Patty.

All drunkards up I was from my long awaited reconvening with my never ending booze oasis and all torn to shreds was I as I disturbingly thought of Abigail riding Cowboy Dan into the sunset, so in response I launched heavily into Patty, swiftly pulling her back into the swaying crowd and announcing, "Red Queen step aside, the Pink

Queen has arrived!"

"What does that mean?" she asked just before we crashed together and made out like drunken teenagers in front of the rotating bar crowd who cheered and hooted around us like high school football.

Next thing I knew Cal lit up a joint and then every other guy in the place lit up a joint and we were back in action just like the old days. But, one thing was different. When Cal shimmied out and offered me a liquid dose from his antique blue apothecary dropper I politely declined and stated, "I'm already there, man. I'm done with that stuff."

After about thirteen hours of taking shots and downing pints and talking shit it had gotten around the room that while I was in asylum I had written a monumental pile of sermons and some of the drunks started to get a bit rowdy with me while asking for a taste, so like a comedian requested to perform at a dinner party I answered, "No, no, no. I simply mustn't. Alright, let's do it."

Soon enough we all literally spilled into Plague Six and filled it to capacity with our cups sloshing and the audience waiting in curious expectation of the psalms of a ghost-boy. Indeed I was a drunken prophet, but I never intended to actually be intoxicated while prophesying. But, when the moment calls you must answer, for are we not pre-girded? "Verily I say, yes we are," I randomly shouted.

Jerrod and a few other tech-nerds hilariously manned an overly aggressive show of lights and fog as a hush fell over the crowd and I approached the mic-stand with my voice ominously booming in over them. Through tasteful amounts of reverb and sublimely dialed tone I nervously began to perform my first ever letter to a darker flock.

The microphone squealed as I cleared my throat and announced, "I call this piece, Excerpt Number One.

"The night was putrid and sweaty. The oil from the rain rose to the surface to slicken our already blood stained streets. The sin of the city dripped from every pore and every crack, until it seeped down to its rotten, decaying grave. These are the nights our forefathers died for, in a place like nowhere you've seen or they expected. This is a place you should pray to your God you never see. This is a place where I close my eyes every night only to arise one-minute later and find the muck still there. These are the muddled towns.

"Deep within the tangible walls I call home lives my salvation, the key to end all this misery. The light penetrates my soul, a new day arises, and the crooked synagogues drunken of their eight plagues fall to their scabby knees.

"Then I wake up.

"The filth still oozes and I still live. The sons of disobedience rule the night, yet there is no day. The sun is dead, rotting beneath the earth, dripping, slipping between the stars like an elusive whore or a quivering jewel. Souls are sold and eaten, traded like damaged goods. Yet there is no good, no right, no justice, only tyranny, until they come and make peace as they destroy, setting aside the righteous and doing away with the chain of the unworthy.

"But until that particular moment comes for you and you alone, you're expected to be the master of your own destiny, your own provider, and your very own vested protector.

"So, I say unto you my Eking Ants, welcome to Hades. Now rise up and claw your way to heaven."

And, man did I ever create a dense silence in that place. There were a few sparse and polite claps here and there, but the amplified silence came by the hundreds. People didn't quite know what to make of it and I even heard a guy down in front whisper to his girlfriend, "What the hell was that? Is he done? Was that supposed to be a poem or something?" then from behind me, ever so lightly at first, I heard a strumming guitar.

Jerrod slowly and dramatically waltzed onto the stage to greet his stirring and truly captive audience and they roared as the house lights came up, fog poured down from the ceiling, and to my complete surprise the lights flashed in a choreographed dance over head as California Early joined with the drums and waved to the crowd like a seasoned veteran and Postal Patty took to the bass with strong and rigid claw-hands that rhythmically plucked and slapped her thick metal strings like a knowledgeable jackhammer.

Jerrod stepped to me and shouted in my ear over the music, "Remember when we used to jam together as kids and you would do that stream of consciousness shit? Well, it's just like riding a bike, only this time do your sermon over the top and watch me for the changes, alright?"

Jerrod nodded at Cal and Patty who abruptly snapped to a different time signature like old pros laying down a psychotic driving back beat as he leaned into his classic Shure box-mic and echoed in its natural tone, "Thanks for coming out tonight, Muddle. We'd like to welcome back our special guest, our very special guest, straight from the nether regions of time and space, Ladies and Gentleman, your shepherd and mine, Mr. Valzedar Rehsa!" and the crowd cheered embarrassingly as Jerrod added, "We're Grave Burns Green and this song is called Asher's Excerpt Number One."

With Patty and Cal snapping the best beat like a pair of taut double-dutch ropes I began to hum with my eyes closed and when I gathered the courage to jump in I jumped in it with all my might.

In that same familiar cosmic clockwork we fell and coincided, anticipating every little turn, every little stop and curve and drop and swerve. Like Autobahn racers we sped faster and faster, dropping in and out of each other and intertwining in terrific sonic ear bliss and when we stopped together on a freaking dime that is when the people really roared and let us know that we had laid down something special, something they could sink their teeth into like a colony of ravenous rock badgers.

For the rest of the night and on into the early morning the beer flowed like wine and impromptu band after poorly executed bad idea took to the stage and goofed around on a few hundred thousand dollars worth of rock gear.

With an absolutely frightening symphony groaning and crashing like whales in labor, Patty and I climbed the psychedelic staircase and she became my girl, the most accepting and supportive girl I would ever know. But, we didn't sleep together that night, because there was someone else on my mind, someone else whose image I just couldn't shake; the image of my one true love.

So, when Patty fell asleep in my arms and the party died down I snuck away from her and roamed my streets again in search of my haunting love. Past armed guards I strolled, next to bruisers and lonely carousing night owls I sauntered and I finally made my way to the entrance of my old home, now their home, my estranged BA Toys.

From behind the building I could hear a repeating grind and clack and as I walked around the back I saw that a miniature skate park had been built there and little Yoshi was tooling around at about one o'clock in the morning under the cool-blue streetlight.

So, I took a deep cleansing breath and straightened my posture then closed in on my one true love while proclaiming, "Your neon splatter painted Bones Brigade hoody hangs too big on your little body while your homemade Vision Street Wear shirt clings to you too tight and hangs too low over your mom's old punker pants. Your jet-black hair with random streaks of red and white falls completely over one eye in a perfectly sleek sheet that cleverly and protectively hides half of you away from me as your feet swash buoyantly in your boots unlaced. Your funny little braces happily glint inside your heart deluging smile and how did you get those braces, boy? Does an orthodontist live here or something?"

Yosh just smiled huge and laughed as he covered his mouth with both hands then brushed his hair out of his face and buckled his spiked collar while I walked up to him under the inorganic, but highly efficient and non-buzzing streetlight saying,

"There you are. Now I can see my son."

"My mom says you have trouble sleeping too," he commented with his back turned to me as he rolled away contemptuously and attempted a kick flip which he didn't even come close to landing, but I was still impressed and overfilling with pride.

That night we stayed up until dawn talking about the adventures that I had and how he ought not to follow in my footsteps. He talked of the short life he had experienced and how I ought not to have missed a moment of it. Every lump that he gave me I accepted and in return I gave him love, love, love. Enough love to fill the missing years I gave him.

As we began to fall asleep on his vert-ramp with him enveloped and swimming in my toasty sleeveless jacket and his parents silhouetted and watching over us from their bedroom window, the morning chill penetrated my recuperating skeleton and I whispered, "Yosh, is Danny a good dad to you?"

"Yes," he whispered back with his sleepy little eyes closed on his perfect and scarless face.

"Dad," Yosh asked, "are you going to try to get back together with my Mom?"

"No, son" I replied. "No, I'm not."

"Well, that's good because she said you look like s-h-i-t," he chuckled through a huge shimmering grin.

I pulled him into a spoon as an actually restful sleep became us both and with the sun rising up high in its honorable sky seat I thought to myself, pretty good for a freaking seven-year-old. But, that attitude is far too familiar for my liking. So, before we both fell down the tunnel and met with our overly active dream worlds I whispered to him in all earnestness, "You are not to follow in my foot steps, boy. Is that understood? You deserve so much more than that. You deserve so much more."

Chapter Sixteen

The Witnesses Revealed

"Postal Patty? Are you freaking serious? She's gay you know," said Abigail. "Well, now that I think about it that actually kind of makes sense for you."

"What? Come on, don't do that. We're friends, right? Everything's cool. Relax," I answered as Danny and family gave me a tour of the complex in all its staggeringly morphed re-appropriation.

"I'm just saying you're a woman, that's all," she added.

"Yeah, I gathered that much. Thanks, Abby. Are you done yet?"

She pointed her right foot in cutely and made a stupid face while nodding lightly as I turned three-sixty to view the storehouses opened as extended living facilities with the surrounding hillsides populated with tents and makeshift shacks that stippled down into the plains as peoples of all manners and orientations milled about and congregated throughout like a colony of civilized fire ants on the great spiraling mount.

Various mechanics, doctors, artisans, and trade workers filled the streets where they peddled their long studied services and soul bearing goods, while baker's baked reclaimed-brick oven quiches, while masseuses dug down deep in a hurt so good, while beat-kids banged buckets with hobos who struck poorly tuned guitar strings on every alley corner. But, their cases weren't open for the collection of change and their vaults were not filled with treasures of gold or sparkly spangles. They already had what they needed and they were momentarily free just to be and to do.

How quickly the high of microcosmic utopia was stripped from me as the tour of our daily bazaar concluded and Danny and Yosh and I split off from the girls and they took me down to a darker place. We walked in through Plague Seven, descended into a new cellar that had been dug out in the back, and we entered a machine bored shaft that led into an underground maze of booby-trapped tunnels, false endings, and deadly bamboo spike filled drops. With glow sticks cracked we navigated the claustrophobic tunnels for about fifteen minutes until we came to the mouth of a great thorny cave that Yosh jumped into and yelled like a mad little professor, "Behold my glorious army!"

The reinforced echoing cavern was alive and buzzing with electronics and war-room personnel who methodically inventoried their stockpiled artillery and scanned over maps and diagrams which included an awe inspiring interpretation of my timeline as a mural that Abigail had painted on the foreboding sienna expanse of the west wall. The mural was accompanied by numerous wheatpasted prints of Dig Dug who was busily pumping up his enemies, Pooka and Fygar. Those were obviously California's doing and they were pasted everywhere; on walls and crates, on boxes and grates, in various poses and at an array of angles.

We were smack dab in the middle of a real life secret lair and unbeknownst to me I was set to meet with the omnipotent leader of the Eighth Plague Army himself, none other than the great and powerful Oz, no doubt.

"No way, I had no idea this was out here. There's

just no way," I said in stark surprise and wonderment as my eyes scanned over the stalactite riddled ceiling.

"No one did, until Early found it with his homemade sonar. He sure doesn't look it, but that twisted little space-cadet is seriously a fucking genius," Danny begrudgingly admitted.

"Bad words, Dad," shouted Yosh who held his tiny hand out and was swiftly supplied with a defunct dollar bill.

"So, is there a general to this operation or is it more of a fly by the seat of your pants kind of thing? I mean, who the hell's in charge around here, who's in charge damn it? Manifest your fearless leader, I say! Manifest him forthwith!" I bellowed like Jerry Seinfeld as I stomped around and pounded my fists in the air like a stupid little monkey and suddenly everyone hushed and stopped dead in their tracks.

Danny rotated his hands in the air like a turbine and yelled, "He's kidding, folks. Just a bad joke, everybody. Please continue," and suddenly from behind us we heard a familiar, no nonsense southern dialect.

"A fly by the seat of your pants kind of thing? Is that right? Just fly on by, la-de-da," he said as we both naturally fixed upright and rigid with Yosh running around us in delighted circles, punching us in our butts while giggling spastically.

"Oh, great. Please don't tell me," I whispered to Dan out of the side of my mouth.

"I'm afraid too," he whispered back.

"Pleased to meet you, private!" yelled Aughblood who spun me around as Yosh latched onto his leg and he ran a comb through his beautifully pomaded pompadour.

"You may refer to me as Sgt. Sutcher and just in case you were wondering, your first detail will be to report to Environmental Services, now get hot, soldier."

"Environmental Services? What's that?" I asked Danny.

"He means crapper duty, Asher."

"That's right, Ash. Booty duty!" yelled Aughblood with everyone in earshot cracking up and hollering with their hands held around their mouths in a C-shape to amplify the humiliation of their apey-calls.

So, I scrubbed a few toilets, big deal. I wasn't going to give that A-hole the satisfaction of me actually giving a shit and even though these people were my guests I had little problem with ascending their supposed ranks.

I was made to wake too early each morning and scrub like Cinderella as I dreamed through mine open eyes and rehearsed my sermons aloud with great fervor, then at night the ever increasing cast of Eighth Plague players would gather and we would destroy the ranks as one in a wash of liquid and musical abandon.

Little by little I gained my audience and bit by bit Aughblood's control waned into my hand causing two different schools of thought to emerge from us. His school was structured and formulaic, whereas mine was free and intuitive. His was militaristic and all "Yes, sir! How high, sir?" Whereas mine was spiritualistic and driven in faith and liberty and in my opinion both were equally necessary and married together like citrus and fish, two very different things from two very different places that mingle and dance together in one harmonious sense.

During one of my increasingly regular question and answer sessions that would usually start out with just a few stragglers pulling me aside next to a pristine and dazzling toilet or at the bazaar or the bar or the cave and would slowly grow by the tens and then the hundreds, I was asked why I let Aughblood push me around in my own house to which I graciously replied, "He saved my life and became a father to me, so if he wants me to learn some respect and humility through general labor then so be it. I trust him."

When word of this got back to Aughblood I was released from my less than hygienic detail and was requested to scrub up and meet with the sarge at The Discerning Pallet over a few plates of insalata caprese lamb sliders accompanied by an extra large gin and tonic for myself and just a tonic for him.

"Why didn't you tell me about my brother and your daughter before we got here?" I asked him as I deconstructed my sandwich and ate it one component at a time with a fork and knife.

"It was none of my business, Ash. I try to stay out of matters that aren't my own and I figured you'd find out soon enough," he replied curtly as he crudely and indiscriminately crammed his slider into his pie-hole.

"Then why did you collect me from the Highlands at all? Why didn't you just let me die out there? Everyone already thought I was dead anyway," I coarsely shouted, throwing my flatware down on my traditional Tuscan dinner plate, making the patrons from all walks, most of whom had never enjoyed fine dining, cringe and disavow my emanating field of negativity.

Like always, Cool Joe just kept his cool and pushed his plate forward while leaning back, wiping the corners of his mouth with his hand. "Because, just like you and just like my daughter, I receive messages from above, but unlike you two I've distinguished my rank in this world and I follow my orders."

"Well, that's all well and good, but you could at least act like you care. I'm the father of your cherished grandson, your daughter's first love and dare I say it, your friend, and all you have to say to me is that you follow orders? Even if you don't care about me could you at least act like you do?"

He blew his nose sharply into his fine linen napkin and threw it down in the middle of the table answering, "Asher, If I didn't care I wouldn't be here watching over your flock and I certainly wouldn't continue doing so while you're out on the road spreading your, quote-unquote, sermons to the various other sects."

"One, where am I going; two, what's with the quotes, I worked really hard on those sermons; and three, what's that supposed to mean, my flock? No one around here takes me seriously."

"It means your message is catching, son. While your delivery may be a bit stilted and your speeches convoluted, people are talking about you and not just people around here. I received word from a higher authority that you and Abigail are being named the official chaplains of the New Rebel

Army and a tour has been arranged for the both of you. It looks like you're taking this little freak show of yours on the road and Yoshi and the band are going with."

"What about Cowboy Dan?"

"Daniel will stay here with me and tend to Ruby-girl and his other duties, but that's not for you to worry about. Just concentrate on the task at hand."

"You got big, bad, Cowboy Dan playing wet-nurse?" I shouted.

"Asher, I'm warning you. You're on thin ice with me," he said from behind an uncontrollably budding half-smile.

"So, me and Abigail, huh?" I asked beginning to fill with inappropriate elation.

"Yes, you and Abigail. Some folks in this movement, folks that matter, believe that you two are the witnesses foretold of in the book of Revelation. Do you know who the two witnesses are?" he asked as a foggy charcoal vignette faded in and I was made to meet with Mr. Black.

Once again I fell inside my mind and sat down next to a young Danny who was already seated at our father's feet as he lounged in his favorite burgundy velvet club chair while swirling his glass of fermented Sonoma red and pronouncing, "In the final days of this penultimate dispensation, my cherubs, the two eternal witnesses will emerge on the world stage, calling forth churning torrents of fire from their bowels and hoards of starving locusts to abound at their feet. Evil will flee from their presence in a futile escape, but none shall transcend their earthly authority, not a one that trespass against them, for they are the blessed reiteration of the two of old, they who did live and had not died, but rather were extraordinary of the Lord and were transfigured unto him.

"But, beware of your adoration, my children, for their story is written to end with their deaths in the streets of dogs and at the hands of our oppressors. The world's vast array of mortal underlings will rejoice for three and one half days as they lie struck down in the field where they continued their work in the face of antichrist. Three and one half days will they lay struck down before they rise again with the consuming wrath of the Lord waiting furiously in their recomposing hands."

Suddenly I snapped back to Aughblood and our dinner table and I blurted out, "I'll do it, but why Abigail?"

"Yeah, I freaking know you'll do it and we think it's Abigail because she's a warrior and a mother and a damn fine representation of what a human should be, that's why we think it's Abigail! She was an integral part of forming the local movement that just so happens to see her as a giver and taker of life. Some have even reverently referred to her as the womb and the sword. Did you know that? No you didn't. Yet you have the gall to sit there and act as if you're not surprised that they think it's you, but you can't believe it could be her?"

I took another chug of my drink and said quickly through my ice, "I just think it's a little suspicious that's all."

"Yes, well, we all know that you have a little problem keeping on the straight and narrow and indeed she will be right next to you keeping you in line, but it's not all about you."

I threw back the rest of my oversized drink and leaned into him saying in a way that I knew was really going to roast him, as if I hadn't heard a thing that he'd said, "I respect the shit out of you, Dad, but I can take care of myself thank you very much. I don't need her looking after me. She can stay here and take care of the kiddos. I'll be fine."

At that he trembled with rage and leaned right back into me with his eyelids fixed wide and us nearly touching noses. He grumbled, "Again, Asher, I'm going to remind you that there are some things in this world and in this life that you still do not understand and some of those things are vastly more important than your fragile little ego, so when I say she is going with you, guess what that means?"

"It means she's going with me," I said as I recoiled from him and bowed irreverently to which he stormed off up our four-star stairs.

Just before he disappeared through the ornately carved cellar doors and out into the gravel and the weeds and the dust and the dirt he called back down to me, "Since this will be the last time that we see each other, son, just know that I do care about you and that I would have come for you no matter what. But, if not for my dreams I simply wouldn't have seen you out there, waiting for me in the woods, dressed like a clown, and freezing your ass off in a ditch." Then he saluted me with a queer smirk on his face and finished by shouting, "I'll see you on the other side, boy!" And, with that he ascended and slammed the basement doors shut.

Again I yelled after him, "What's that supposed to mean, Dad?" but this time there was no reply.

The very next day Abigail, Yosh, the band and I mounted up. We took to the road in a caravan of hilariously war-girded, spot welded attack-mobiles hauling large black trailers full of rock gear and artillery. We made our way from sect to unruly sect while spreading the message of modern discontent in that convoluted and totally effectual Grave Burns Green kind of way.

On our way back home from our first trip out we settled in just a few hours north of Muddle at Mt. Shasta where we met and jammed with Lemurians and descended Ex-Oregonians who swapped horror stories and tall tales with us around a huge bonfire on which they roasted wild turkey and feral hog.

With Patty nuzzling into me on one side and Yosh pressed in on the other, Abigail spoke up saying, "You know, I forgave you the moment that you left that courthouse."

"Yeah, I know," I replied as I repeatedly squeezed my girl and my little man.

"Well, I just had to say it, that's all. I never thought I was going to get the chance and even though things didn't turn out how they were supposed to between me and you, I still love you and I always will. As the best friend I've ever known and the father of my child, I mean."

"I get it, Abby, I get it. But, let me tell you how I feel about the unfinished business I had with my parents after they died. It's exactly the same way I feel about you in fact. See, I know how they felt about me and they knew me just the same, so there really never was any unfinished business, was there? There is only love of which we always require more. There's only family and finality and absolutely no in between."

Even with Patty attached to me, Abigail launched into us and gave in to a nondiscriminatory embrace. Of course Yoshi came into it too, but I was honestly surprised at how receptive Patty was to the whole thing and she leaned in and accepted her sister in all her flawed and totally selfish and unjustifiable envy.

"What happened to your cheek?" Abigail asked me as she retracted from our dysfunctional family hug.

"Your father happened to my cheek, that's what happened," I replied as she resumed her seat and nodded knowingly while pulling her hoody back at the left shoulder to reveal the very same circular scar that he had given her as a defiant teen.

"Ooohh, now that makes sense why you would never tell me where that came from," I remarked.

We headed home for a few quick days of rest and recuperation, but I personally couldn't wait to get on the road again. My brother, however, was none too pleased with the brevity of our respite.

Over the next few months of travel and reconciliation and the booming forth of our messages like trumpets before the battle lions, Cowboy Dan got increasingly upset and envious. He sent me hand couriered letters of undue suspicion and to Abby he sent enraged ranting texts over Cal's personal and protected hacked network. He said that Ruby needed her mom to be home for more than just a few days every couple of months, and of course she must have. So, Danny came out to meet us on the road and to give me hell for encroaching on his woman; next to the only woman that he had ever known intimately and for sure the only one that he trusts.

"You had your chance, Ash, and you fucked it up," he said as we danced in concentric, dust summoning circles with our dukes up behind the caravan as a growing slew of foreign onlookers gawked and gabbed around us.

Danny got a lucky shot or two in just before I tolchocked him in the ribs and Yoshi shouted, "Don't hurt him, Dad!"

"Who me?" we both shouted back at the same time, which enraged Danny all the more. So, he tackled me and repeatedly bashed the back of my head into the ground, trying desperately to reopen the scar that he had initially supplied me. We did that shit for about fifteen minutes until we both collapsed in on each other like the couple of spent suburban wussies that we were. And, of course everything was cool from then on.

So, he and Abby and Ruby parted our company after a few more days and because I begged her to leave me with my son, she did, and my boy and I grew closer and closer like the painfully divided single celled organism that we are. He brimmed with pride as I took to my podium day after day and belted it forth.

I thumped his great-granddad's stately mahogany podium heartily and yelled out over the band's melodious grinding in a detonation of prophetic phonetics, "Have you ever been sitting alone in the dark, pondering what all this means? I mean everything, every part of the whole. And, just as you rise it strikes you. Like lightning on your brain it shocks you to your core, like a feeling of something from before. Not like yesterday, but before. Like a past life only not so trendy, like one special experience that either sways you to insanity or keeps you from it and when it comes you wonder how real all of us are. From your brother to your mother you wonder how real we are.

"Out of exhaustion and curiosity you let your guard down and suddenly, violently, the sense of old seizes you as an intoxicant. It enacts its ancestral will upon you like déjà vu and your eyes illuminate, your third-eye trepans, and all of a sudden you see life in a completely new light; as if the universe was all yours and someone took it away for your own damn good; you having been a chastised child who simply refused to play nice; you a naïve teenager that was too ignorant to know how to say no; and you a reckless and incorrigible young punk off on your own too soon and seeing more than you ever should have.

"As the sense of old becomes you fully and as those encrypted memories unlock, the swelling concepts pack your flesh mind tight and your body cries aloud for narcotic anesthesia, but it's too late for that. It has you now and you accept the fact that no drink or drug or psychological crutch is going to get you through this. You just woke yourself up a bit and from here on out nothing can lull you back to sleep.

"But, that's all right we scientists say, because we understand them now, these our infantile perceptions, these misfirings of the mind, this series of synaptic errors. We elite, we upper echelon, we arbiters of understanding know now that to believe as your heart has led you would be nothing short of folly and we see that now, we psychoanalysts say.

"But, personally and just speaking for myself, I can only see so much and I can only hear so clearly, for how limited am I in all my inadequate observations, how fixed am I in this moment and this temporal space, and just how blind have I become to the crushing inundation of preconditioning that has regrettably kept humanity at bay for so many subservient generations?

"If you're like me you've been asking yourself these questions for quite some time now and you're probably beginning to grow a bit weary and low on patience for malarkey, aren't you? And, the collar is beginning to fit a little bit too tight as of late, isn't it? For our oppressors preach society as a puzzle whose pieces fit together so flawlessly that if one piece were missing the whole plan would crumble and wither away, so fall in line and fit in tight, right? But, what's that got to do with me, where does that leave me? I'll tell you where it leaves you, right here on the fringe trudging along with one foot in front of the other and opening to the realization that the pieces of the puzzle do indeed fit, but the pictures atop them are all different. Now ask yourself, is this what I was born to do or is this what I was *made* to do?

"And, so back we go again; back to the day that we first parted the matrix to test the hearts of men. Back to the very same in which our memories were cloaked in preparation for the condition known as the hand of man. But, forget not the sea of dark angels that fled behind you. Forget not they that went astray to live their diminishing days on the frigid outskirts of Heaven. Forget not the choice that you made that day, my kin, and remember now so you will never find yourself begging the Lord for a second chance. Take heed, dear friends, for this is it.

"Now, look around you and behold our glorious state. Listen to the cries of the innocents throughout the ages and ask yourself, how proud am I of what we murderers and malefactors have accomplished here in this our allowance? How proud am I of this the current state of man?

"And, to those of you who are not impressed by your brothers, to those of you who have been less than inspired by our so-called leadership, our dark and nefarious guidance counselors, our smoke and mirror operators; to those of you who have decided to stand here in formation this day I promise you, we will prevail.

"In whatever derivation of the Lord you have allowed, you have chosen to prevail. For every great theology of this world, every sacred book of utterance, every single path that can be taken, leads to one single point perspective that unites us all, my Ants, and that single point has commissioned me to deliver this message unto you, a message not of division and denomination, but of true and unpolluted love.

"A message of pure inclusion for each and every one of God's many blessed and beloved children I bring unto you. A message of love I bring and how the power thereof is yours to wield as a potent sword; a power that is stronger than the entirety of evil; a power capable of uprooting nations; and a power that will soon heal the world.

"And, so here we stand, male and female. Here we stand white and black and yellow and red. Though we be Christian and Agnostic, Muslim and Buddhist, Hindu and Jew, together we are amassed in rank and file and we are ready to die for that which we believe. In unison we would die for it.

"But, before we go out amongst the devouring hoard, before we lay our intestines on the line, a blessing and an anointing I give unto you, for our gatherings are enumerated in sevens. We are the offspring of this world's lengthy lamentations. We are the sons of strife and the daughters of victory. We are arrived with the end and shall be of the new beginning. For we are justice incarnate, we are the sun which has risen, and-they-our-enemy-shall-fall!"

As the music drove on and I finally clapped my pious maw shut the gathered crowd roared heavily in flattering and humbling waves of serotonin and epinephrine. And, as I climbed down from my supposed pulpit I spied in the distance, Extra-Special Agent Benjamin Torrez, slipping between the members of the elated and buzzing audience with his pistola drawn and his eyes all lowered and bloodshot and full of purpose.

Chapter Seventeen

I Get Shot Through the Heart

"Do you think he can see us right now? Do you? Does anyone else feel him here?" I asked his multiplying congregation as I uncomfortably stepped up to the microphone in front of his Plague Seven Bar that was always more popular than any of *my* venues. I shamefully removed my pitch-black Stetson to let the bright morning sun cast down its radiant judgment upon my hideously burnt and bald head with our streets littered with every kind of flower you could imagine, all of which had just been freshly plucked from the surrounding hillsides and valleys in their final sacrifice of beauty in repose.

"Even though this is the second time I've had to do this, little bro', I don't think I was prepared to lose you again and I miss you now more than I ever did before. Tell Mom and Dad that I love them, okay?"

"I'm really happy that I got to meet my Dad before he left again. I hope I grow up to be just like him. He was really cool and I miss him a lot," I said while trying my best not to cry. I mean, if I'm supposed to be some kind of great leader or something I'm not supposed to cry. Right? Jesus, what do these people expect from me? I'm just a little kid. I can't even land a freaking kick-flip for God's sake.

༃

"This was my brother, no offense Daniel, but as much my brother as yours in my approximation and I'm going to miss the hell out of you, Ash-man. Even though you were the youngest of the three of us, in a weird kind of way I looked up to you and I got to tell you, if you can hear me right now, I still expect great things from you. And, by the way I want my bracelets back," I screeched through an inordinate amount of feedback, feedback like none I've ever heard before. Maybe he *is* still here. That's Asher for you. Always one last trick up his sleeve. Always stealing the show.

༃

"I don't always remember much, Asher, but I do remember the times we spent on that shitty, rusted trampoline you bought from that random kid downtown. I remember us hauling it all the way back here on foot and drinking the most ridiculously gigantic sodas underneath it and that time we laid out under the stars on it and we saw those orange triangle spaceships racing each other and that one time we dosed and you kept telling me to keep it down when I was freaking out next to those Berkeley horse cops and how that just made it worse and how you said that I was your best friend and that you could read my mind from time to time and... oh, shit... this isn't going to be easy for me, Asher. I just got you back," I sniveled as my sister Patricia rescued me from my public humiliation and pulled me away from the mic.

I didn't know I could still feel humiliation and I

sure as hell didn't know that I could feel rage, so I ran back up to the mic and pushed and pulled my kinky afro out of my face while screaming, "I'll tell you this much, there are about to be a shit-ton of satellites crashing into the sea and a fist full of electrical grids frying in your honor. All I got to do is press *enter*. You best believe that!"

ↄ

"So, you're really gone this time. Like, for reals gone this time? Asher, are you out there? Asher, can you hear me, my love? You always told me that if you were the first one to die you would visit me in my dreams. Just like the time you woke me up screaming that you'd just received a message and that you had related a secret word to me in the dream world and that I was supposed to know what you were talking about when you woke me up, but I didn't did I? I didn't know what it was and you were so disappointed in me. God, were you ever disappointed.

"I couldn't take that, sweetie. That was the one thing that I couldn't take from you. All your psychological abuse and your drinking and drugging and God only knows where you would go when you would get too mad, but the one thing I could never take from you was your disappointment. So, just to make sure you and I are straight with each other, Asher, I promise you here and now in front of all these your Ants, we're going to get the bastards.

"Those mother-fuckers will not be able to hide, nor will they have the courage enough to run. And

Torrez, you bottom feeding double turncoat; I got something special for you. I'm going to mount your fucking skull on a pike or die trying. To Dr. Elijah Pesache, or so you call yourself, we're going to nail your ass to a tree and let the high mountain wolves pick at you for a few days and when that's all said and done were going to grind the two of y'alls sun bleached bones into the dust.

"We meet back here at the same time tomorrow my Ants. Be always mobile, ever down with the system, and death to the machine!" I shouted and kicked over the mic-stand as our civilian army roared. Suddenly, I felt faint and almost blacked out, but I rallied myself and grabbed up my Ruby-girl in one arm and with the other hand I wished them peace and then flipped them off with my amazingly brave Yoshi standing like a badass at attention at my right side and my astoundingly well adjusted husband holding his rifle aloft at my back. I turned my Bad Brains patched ass to them and with my thin platinum chains furiously thrashing at my hips the main crew and I departed into Plague Six, down the musty corridors, and into Dig Dug's Cavern to finalize Asher's Project Six Six Five.

Over the next three-and-a-half-days the authorities left Asher's body right where it fell, so they could prove to us in all their feigned political correctness that he would not be standing back up to breathe fire upon them and to cause them to turn to blood. And, when he didn't some lost faith and others became zealots. Besides, the New Rebel Army had gotten that little tidbit wrong. I know this to be true, because it was my father who could conjure fire and it was I who could call upon the locusts; my sweet babies. But, only Pops and I knew that and we had been reserving our freaky little secret for our entire lives.

After many meetings with the heads of the New Rebel Army and after much debate we realized that the tribulation hadn't even begun and that Louis Moodreaux was not the antichrist, but rather a pawn to further set up the system for his father Wormwood and that destroying him would only prolong the inevitable. Moodreaux himself had no real power of his own, but the unilateral omnipotence of the United Nations sure did. They re-seized our sector in a holy war they labeled The American Reclamation Act of 2033.

Calling it American was supposed to make us feel like empowered free citizens who had just been waiting for big-daddy to come home and fix it all, but we knew it was far too late for that, so when they came knocking on our doors we were suddenly no where to be found. What they did find, however, were packs upon packs of California's homespun Willie Pete duct taped to every load bearing beam inside the Eighth Plague building.

Our militia sprang out of the ground around the perimeter and funneled them into The Eighth Plague in a maelstrom of artillery and we pinned them inside with the Radezlav crest dislodging from the entrance and splitting in two on the cobblestone threshold of the bar. We ran for our lives and manned the perimeter from the high ground, firing down upon the remainder of International Army and US National Guard as Pops sprang from behind the bar and opened his overly salivating mouth, flicked his vintage Zippo lighter, and he spat liquid fire at them in a wondrous blast that ignited the phosphorus as he disappeared into the tunnels with a huge steel door dropping behind him.

With The Eighth Plague imploding behind us, we pushed the soldiers back into the surrounding hillsides and I called my little ones to swarm upon them and climb into their eyeballs and into their mouths; any available orifice would do really. They all ran screaming into the valleys with an inundation of grasshoppers rubbing a deafening call of victory as their brothers attacked after them in wave after heaping and crashing wave of buggy goodness.

Of course it was only a matter of time before the UN drones collapsed our entire complex, but by that time we had long since entered the caves and fanned out through a janky system of underground rails that joined with our nearest neighbor sects and lo, we lived to fight another day.

So, we said goodbye to our exploded home that was pluming thick white smoke screens into the stratosphere. We said au revoir to our youth and to the last shreds of our innocence. We bid farewell to our eight plagues and we blew goodnight kisses to our beloved Bad Attitude Toys Incorporated, but it all seemed so senseless to me and I couldn't help but feel a little guilty.

Did I do right by you, Asher? I sure hope you're not still disappointed in me, but I get the distinct impression that you're going to let me know one way or another, aren't you? And, to be quite honest with you, I just can't wait to hear your voice again, my sweet.

This, my entire account, has been dictated to you from a moment my Ants, a moment that always was and always is and always will be, the moment my life flashed before my eyes, the moment that I died.

In all my thirty-three years I had never felt such pain. Not in my brain, not in my muscles or my joints, not in my liver or my hip, but in my heart. At first I wondered if that classically cliché ending would hold true for me: the officer's badge that saved him from the slug or the drunkard's flask that kept him from the shot, but alas the pocket dictionary that resided above my chest for over two-thirds of my life was no match for a speeding bullet and as such there was shock and anguish and copious amounts of blood.

As the exploding pages of my dictionary hang in mid air like friendly little moths my spirit unfolds and resonates throughout the ages and as the silver cord parts, the one that connected my heavenly soul to my earthbound animal-vessel, I begin to recall where I came from and the primary goal of my bodily possession.

As I stick here in the ageless ether and review my linear timeline as tragic theater, I look around me and see that we've always been here, waiting and floating together in the charcoal-gray expanse of limbo. My entire family floats next to me, interfacing with the world through a fettered medium of flesh. The less I knew you the further away you are and so on throughout humanity, but we all connect here with each other in sects and satellites like atomic structures and I see now that any manner of segregation was simply a lie.

I step to my neighbor, my apparent closest kin, and I lightly touch her shoulder and she jostles as if waking in my world and nearly fainting and falling to the ground in hers, so I retreat a pace and whisper words of affirmation into Abigail's right ear.

As the momentarily dead and currently waking call to each other and wander off into the great deconstructing expanse, déjà vu suddenly makes perfect sense to me and why it sometimes felt layered as if I had done the very same things under the very same circumstances, time after time, again and again. Every time I revisited a moment, whether with the help of Mr. Black or from my silver cord uplink, I experienced it as if it were the first. In multiple overlapping cells I experienced it and because I had re-inhabited that moment somehow the present me could sense the future me joining with him and each time we did it spawned a new layer, leading me to the conclusion that somewhere in time and space our world and our entire existence has already concluded to whatever end mine architect saw fit.

His voice calls out to me from the center of the hollow-gray and he instructs me that time is like a helix, which viewed from a plane above will appear as a circle with no beginning and no end, but when experienced and observed by the living it will take on a different dimension and appear as a series of linear instances, each of which must happen at least one time. "That time is now," he says.

Although my dreams of dying had been intensifying over the preceding days and weeks, I have to admit that period of my life was the happiest I had ever known. I was reconciled in all ways, I had achieved inner peace, and of course the healing touch of my young son had made me complete. For he will carry on as I fall down in defeat and as my body continues to the ground mine architect instructs me to pay close attention to the last remaining seconds of my life, so I lock back into my animal-vessel and look to my right to view an unfortunate scene.

The first thing I see is my beautiful little Yoshi running to me in slow motion with a look on his face that seems to say, "I can save you, Dad." But, what can you do for me now, my boy? How much more can you save me than you already have? How much more my child?

To my left comes Postal Patty, my final heart, and Jerrod Twig, my spike laden image to emulate, and California Early, my inane Shaman and truest acceptor. They four embrace me as I rerelease from my body in finality and submerge into the infinite fathoms of death, but I do not descend, nor do I rise. I simply was and I simply am, for I have been transformed and I am now become the blood angel, Valzedar Rehsa, the man who is neither here nor there.

When Torrez's bullet penetrated my chest it first penetrated my dictionary. Oh, my literary acetaminophen, how you served me well my written reliever. Forever you will hang in undue shreds in that moment and although you've been destroyed into many thousands of pieces, three distinct words float from you and display perfectly before me as I slip away. Word one: sin, word two: slay, and word three: self.

Perhaps I should have tried harder for you all while I was with you, but my best was only as good as I could let it be at the time and I belatedly see now that the purpose of life was not for the gratification of self, but for the service of the family of man. So, in consequence I hold fast between our two worlds, walking parallel with you all in what appears to be the dream manifested and I believe that I may still be able to reach you.

It's just too bad that my last dying words to my family were, "Torrez gives love a bad name." Sorry about that, guys. I meant to say something more profound, but I couldn't help myself.